RESERVATION UNDER MY NAME

CHERIL N. CLARKE

For the women brave enough to rewrite their stories when the first draft no longer fits their truth. Your second chapters are often the most beautiful.

LEARN MORE about this series (photos, videos, music, maps and more) on *keyholechronicles.com.*

CONTENT WARNING

This story contains depictions of psychological manipulation and controlling relationship dynamics that may be distressing for readers who have experienced similar situations.

1

CURATED EDGES

5:15 am
"Three years of turning this place into Miami's most exclusive boutique hotel, and the sunrise still gets me every time. Pure potential," I sighed wistfully while pulling into my reserved spot. The hazy shimmer rising off the pavement told me that it would be a hot day despite being early Spring.

Buzz. Buzz. My phone went off just as I gave my frohawk a final check in the rearview mirror. "Show time!" I hyped myself up. Arriving always felt like stepping into a new character when got I to work—becoming the unflappable GM my guests needed me to be.

"Mm hm! Perfect." Finally, I glanced down to view the caller ID: *Simone Chen*. My pulse hastened. Simone was the manager of our top partner hotel. She never called this early unless something big was brewing.

"Nyla, please tell me you can handle a miracle," Simone began without a preamble.

"Well, good morning to you too!" I giggled, smoothing my blouse as I stepped out of the car. Marco, my Front Office Manager, was already at his post. Chubby and cheerful, his usual grin was like an espresso shot without the bitterness—always brightening the pre-dawn lobby. I gave him a quick wave before returning to my call. "What's up, Simone?"

"Hey, girl! Sorry. Legacy's team just called. They need a full buyout. Today through Friday."

I kept walking while processing the news, my flats are silent against the polished floor. Legacy was the hottest name in R&B right now. "How many rooms?"

"Eighteen crew, plus the inner circle. The Thimble had a major HVAC failure in their VIP wing, so they're scrambling to relocate," she told me. "They're willing to pay a premium and cover all reloca-tion costs for current guests. And...their team already has arrange-ments with The Vestige for anyone we need to move."

This was the kind of situation where my theatrical training paid off - staying perfectly composed while orchestrating chaos behind the scenes. "Send me the details. We'll need to arrange VIP transfers and compensation packages for relocated guests." I responded while walking across the marble lobby, stopping at the front desk.

Marco's orange-striped socks peeked out as he bounced on his toes, clearly sensing the energy shift.

"¡Buenos días, jefa!" He beamed, sliding a steaming cup of coffee my way. Like many Miami immigrants, Marco's family was originally from Cuba, and he was bilingual.

"Buenos días, Marco. Y gracias." I took a grateful sip, my mind racing through occupancy numbers. My Spanish wasn't perfect, but it worked. I refocused to my phone.

"Simone, we're at eighty-seven percent. We already have a couple in the Azalea Suite for their twentieth anniversary." I drummed my fingers on the polished desk. "They specifically chose us for the private terrace—I can't ask them to move."

"Legacy's people said they'll provide full compensation packages for *all* guests." Simone's voice was streaked with desperation.

Marco leaned in. Curiosity riddled his features. "Do you need help?"

I held up one finger, my mind working. "We can move everyone except the anniversary couple in the Azalea Suite." I switched back to Simone. "Give me thirty minutes."

My fingers flew across a tablet, pulling up guest profiles. "What's the earliest they need access?"

"Advance team at noon. Legacy arrives at two."

I smiled. It was the kind of smile that made my boss say I was born for this work. "Tell them we'll be ready. But I want their security team here by ten to coordinate entrance protocols. And Simone? We need a rider about noise limitations after eleven. The condo board is already on my case."

"You're a lifesaver, Nyla. Contracts in fifteen."

Marco was already extending a stack of guest files. "I can start making calls."

"Perfect. Focus on floors three and four first." I paused, noting his efficient organization. "And make sure housekeeping knows about the timeline."

"On it," Marco nodded, then hesitated. "Oh, and Alex called while you were driving in. He seemed eager about tonight's plans?"

I felt a familiar flutter at the mention of tonight's plans but pushed the thought of Alex aside. Crisis first, butterflies later. Right now, I had a hotel to rearrange and exactly four hours to make it all look effortless.

Just another sunrise at the Jeffrey.

By six, the lobby bustled with focused energy. I'd seized the private dining room, turning it into a command center. Marco had arranged coffee service and breakfast pastries—Cuban pastelitos, still warm. A thoughtful touch that made me smile, even as I noticed him document every decision I made in his meticulously organized notes.

"Nyla?" Ana from housekeeping stood in the doorway, clipboard in hand. "We've cleared floors three and four, but we got another call about noise."

"How many rooms left?"

"Six." Her efficiency matched her pressed uniform. "But 512 isn't answering."

I glanced at Marco. "Can you handle the noise complaint? I'll take 512." Then to Ana, "Please get your team started on the cleared rooms. Legacy's particular about air quality."

"Already on it," Ana nodded.

"Marco, after that, coordinate with the kitchen staff. Legacy's team will also want to inspect everything."

"Claro que si, jefa!"

"Gracias."

Within an hour, I'd personally spoken with each remaining guest. Luxury car service and champagne on arrival at their new hotels— sometimes a crisis budget came in handy. Our honeymooners had the terrace view they'd dreamed of, and the rest of our guests would have stories about the time they got bumped for Legacy. My, my, my... what a morning! In the command center, I leaned back in a chair and breathed in a moment of satisfaction as the last confirmation email arrived.

The Jeffrey Hotel's reputation was built on these moments—not just handling crises, but turning them into experiences. *Ding.* My tablet chimed with updates: housekeeping had cleared twenty-eight rooms, security protocols were in place, and the kitchen had adjusted their inventory for Legacy's specific requests.

"Water with precisely three cucumber slices," I muttered, scanning the rider. "At exactly forty-one degrees Fahrenheit. God damn celebrities..."

"That's nothing," Marco chuckled. "Remember that venture capitalist last month who needed his suite's entire minibar replaced with liquid chlorophyll and something called 'raw water'?"

"And don't forget the 'activated' part...because regular water isn't 'biohacked' enough," I commented while rising to head to my office. "I'm gonna head out. Thanks for rising to the occasion."

"Always," he beamed, and began clearing the room.

By noon, I was surviving on adrenaline and too much coffee. The tension in my shoulders eased as I reached for the sandwich I'd forgotten hours ago. The plans for Alex's second hotel loomed large. If things went well, I'd be looking at a Regional Director position by next year. Just then, Marco burst in grinning from ear to ear and holding a small, elegantly wrapped package.

"What's this?" I asked, eyebrow raised.

"From one of our VIP guests," Marco said, smile wide. "Just came via courier. She insisted it be delivered to you personally." His socks flashed as he placed it on my desk with a flourish, then quickly zipping back out.

Hmph. I perked up and took the package. A small card was tucked under the ribbon. My heart skipped a beat when I opened it and saw the name—Mikko Washington. She was an A-list actress, known for her blockbuster roles and a face you couldn't escape in Hollywood. The woman was breathtakingly gorgeous! Just the thought of her made me blush, and I barely thought of women in that way!

The note read: *Nyla, thank you for making my stay seamless and enjoyable. Your professionalism and warmth are unmatched. You're a true gem. Please take some time for yourself—you deserve it. Best, Mikko Washington.*

I remembered her stay vividly. Mikko had constant requests, and her entourage seemed to double every day. I had spent hours coordinating everything from last-minute spa treatments to obscure dietary needs, ensuring every detail was flawless.

I found myself smiling, remembering how she'd insisted on personally thanking each staff member.

Carefully, I unwrapped it to find a voucher for a luxury spa day at one of Miami's most exclusive retreats. A spa day sounded like a lovely break, especially one with no strings attached. But I didn't have another moment to ponder on the gift. The familiar click of approaching loafers soon announced Alex's arrival. He filled the doorway. His crisp linen shirt and pressed chinos a concession to Miami's heat.

"Surprise!" There was an edge to his smile that didn't reach his eyes. "Thought I'd check on my star General Manager. The initial negotiations wrapped early," he expressed. I thought he'd be in North Carolina until that evening.

I slipped the spa voucher into my desk drawer. "Everything's under control here. How did it go?"

"It's looking good," he beamed, moving around my desk. "The investors are impressed. We might get that second hotel sooner than planned!" Alex paused by my chair, his 5'10" frame casting a shadow over my workspace. His eyes caught on the blue ribbon I'd dropped. "What's this?"

"Just a thank-you gift from Mikko Washington. A spa voucher." I kept my tone professional and matter-of-fact. After a year-and-half of dating the owner, I'd learned to navigate these moments carefully.

Alex's fingers brushed my temple, lingering near my eye. The touch made me close my eyes and exhale—a caress from his fingertips typically made me melt. "You know, maybe you should consider Botox," he suggested, as if commenting on the weather. "And about the girl thing—"

"The spa."

"Timing's not great with the deal, is it?" His next words were all business. "Our investors are impressed. We might get that second hotel sooner than planned."

"Really?'

"Yes, indeed! That's why I need you to hold down the fort, babe. I mean, Nyla, if this goes well, you'll really be running this entire hotel! So, maybe hold off on the spa thing for now? Delayed gratification is always good discipline anyway." He took a beat. "Oh, and I have plans for us tonight," His blue eyes striking against his bronze skin as he continued. Alex was mixed—Ethiopian and White. "Opal & Vine at eight. Wear that white dress I bought you," he finished eagerly.

Brrring. His phone chirped, and his expression darkened as he read the message. "Oh, come on, what the fuck!"

I snapped to attention. "What's the matter?"

"The environmental survey results just came in for the Charlotte property." He paced. "There's an issue with the wetlands assessment that could kill the whole deal. Damn it! The investors want an emergency meeting first thing tomorrow." Alex stopped and ran a hand through his hair. "I—I gotta go back, Nyla. If we don't get ahead of this..."

I started to respond, but he was already heading for the door. "Rain check on dinner, babe. I need to hustle to the airport. We'll do Opal & Vine this weekend instead – same time. Don't be late. Got some beautiful plans for us," he turned back around to smile and blow me a kiss. "I'll text you when I land."

The whole thing felt like a familiar script. Alex's sureness that I'd be free, that I'd wear what he chose – it was so Alex.

I watched him leave, the energy of his touch still lingering on my shoulder. The way he spoke sent a flutter through my stomach – part excitement, part uncertainty. *Ding!* My tablet chimed. It was a video call from my parents. Dad's face filled the screen first, Mom leaning in beside him. How they always knew when I needed them...

"There's my baby girl" My father's bald head and big grin filled my screen. My mother's silver braids swayed as she jostled for view. "Though you look—"

"Mama, if you say tired..." I chuckled, sinking into the familiar rhythm of their concern.

"A mother notices these things." She tapped the screen. "When's the last time you took a real break?" This – from the same woman who always encouraged me to work hard but remember *a smart woman knows how to shine without outshining.*

"We sure haven't seen you!" My pop chimed in.

"Actually..." I pulled out Mikko's voucher. "A guest sent me a free spa package today. I thought maybe you'd—"

"Young lady, don't you dare try to give that away. Your empire will still be there after a massage." My father cut me off.

Not even being middle-aged could stop him from calling me 'young lady.'

My mom's "mhmm" punctuated his words and carried years of knowing me too well.

"I hear you." I assured them. "And I promise I'll visit soon. Love you both...gotta run," I said, ending the call.

During a mini break later, my phone lit up with a text from Alex: *Can't wait to see you this weekend! You've made everything possible, and I miss you already.* 🩶

I touched the spa voucher, then pulled up their booking page. Friday, 10am. Available. My finger hovered over the screen for just a moment before I tapped 'Book Now.'

2

THE WEIGHT OF PERFECT THINGS

My keys jingled in the lock as I pushed open my home's front door. *Gotta change the batteries in the biometric lock,* I noted. Work never ended. Wearily, I stepped into the house Alex and I bought together two years before. It was supposed to be our sanctuary but honestly felt like a showroom. The living room was sleek faultlessness: slate leather, steel accents, magazine-perfect. Beautiful, sure, but without much personality. I'd wanted cozier items with soft fabrics, you could sink into after a long day, but Alex's vision had won out. My only win was the knitted throw I'd draped over an armrest.

I stepped out of my shoes and hung my keys on a hook before heading to the kitchen. Dropping my purse on the counter, I moseyed to the fridge for a small carton of coconut water—loved those.

Ding. My smartwatch vibrated with a text form Alex. *Landed safely. Meeting prep tonight, but hitting the gym now for a quick pump...staying strong for my babe, too.* 💪

I grinned, typing back: *Good luck with the investors! The house feels too quiet without you.* It wasn't entirely untrue—I'd grown used to our routine, the way he'd pour wine while I told him about my day, how he'd handle dinner on nights like this when work had drained me.

Another text came as I ordered takeout: *Investors seem optimistic. Everything's falling into place. Yes, yes!*

Alex's confidence was contagious. It was part of what had drawn me to him in the first place. He had a way of making the impossible seem inevitable. Of turning doubt into something thrilling and unstoppable. I curled up on the sofa with a jar of candied pecans in my lap and pulled up my calendar. Between the Legacy event and the usual hotel demands, I hadn't had a moment to breathe. The quiet house was a gift, and tomorrow's spa appointment was perfect timing —a chance to recharge before Alex got back.

The next day blurred into a chain of emails, meetings, and management. Same old, same old. Soon enough, however, it was Friday. *My* day.

THE OCEAN BREEZE SPA lived up to its name. As the glass doors whispered shut behind me, the Miami heat dissolved into cool serenity. Mist curled around my ankles, and the scent of jasmine wrapped around me like cocoon.

"Welcome, to the Ocean Breeze Health & Wellness Club, Ms. Baines," a warm and understated voice greeted me. I blinked, surprised that she welcomed me so swiftly by name. Dressed in elegant black with a subtle gold pin at her collar, the hostess extended a hand. "My name is Bristol."

"Thank you," I countered, glancing at the décor. I loved the gold fixtures and exotic plants, and unique candles placed about the lobby.

"There's no need to check in," Bristol told me. "Everything has been prepared for you."

"Really?" No clipboard shoved in my face for a signature? This was a wonderfully seamless process.

"Absolutely. You're a new VIP client."

I could get used to this. Glancing around, I noticed everything breathed privacy and discretion. *So, this is how celebrities and rich people do it.* I thought back to Mikko Washington, who gifted me this experience in the first place. The vision of her in my mind's eye made my heart smile. I felt like the only one there, and the attention was amazing. I followed Bristol through corridors where water trickled down copper-veined stone.

As we turned a corner, she paused in front of a discreet desk. Waterfall sounds and bird chirps gradually became noticeable. Quickly, she requested I answer three questions about my health. *Aha*, I thought. They weren't letting anything slip, but still managed to make it feel like an afterthought rather than a formality.

"This is your private suite for the afternoon," She declared when we later stopped at a textured wooden door. "And this is Akira. She'll finish coordinating all your services," Bristol finished with a slight bow before excusing herself.

Akira greeted me with a smile and choice between bottled water and champagne. I opted for the latter, taking advantage of the rare moment to indulge and not worry about having to be on. The room was a sanctuary. A plush chaise sat near the window, overlooking a small garden where sunlight filtered through bamboo. A massage table draped in white linens stood in the center of the room. Off to the side, I noticed a hydro pool and a heated stone bed.

"This is heaven," I whispered, unable to contain my gratitude.

Akira she showed me the en suite bathroom where I could freshen up and shed my workday. The attentiveness made my shoulders drop a further in relief. For once, my ever-present to-do list stopped scrolling through my mind. I was just... breathing.

We began with a manicure and pedicure. Akira washed my hands and feet in warm rosewater, soothing my skin. Her fingers moved with practiced ease, turning the simplest touches into small acts of care that I desperately needed. It's funny how getting your nails done could remind you that you matter—something I slowly realized I'd forgotten due to overwhelm. Akira transformed my work-worn fingers into gleaming masterpieces. The facial that followed was pure indulgence. I couldn't remember the last time I'd been tended to like this. That I was anyone's guest or priority. The esthetician who took over offered gentle strokes to ease the exhaustion lines from my face. *Botox.* Suddenly, Alex's unwanted suggestion filled my mind. I fought it out. I didn't want to hear about what I could do to be more perfect. Not now.

I was starved for this kind of attention, and it felt amazing to sink into a feminine space. To be nurtured without the expectation for reciprocation. By the time the body massage began, I had fully surrendered. Each muscle unwound like a tightly coiled spring finally set free. Even my jaw relaxed.

"Your shoulders," the therapist murmured in accented English, "they carry much weight." Her name was Carmen.

"Mmm," I managed, too relaxed to form words. Her hands worked with practiced expertise, finding and releasing old knots. Her accent was different from what I was used to hearing in Miami – softer, with different cadences. "Where are you from?" I asked quietly, not wanting to break the peaceful atmosphere.

"Guatemala," she replied. "Near Lake Atitlán."

I'd never heard of it, but something in the way she said it made my eyes flutter open. There was reverence there, like she was speaking of an old friend.

"The lake," she continued, her voice barely above a whisper as she worked a particularly stubborn knot, "it has power. Maya people say it heals the soul." Carmen's hands moved with gentle precision. "I saved money from spa work and built small cabin there. Now, when life is too heavy..." She pressed into another knot. "I go home and find peace."

I let her words float through me like the soft music, making a note to research the location. A heavy exhale escaped me by the time it was over. The few hours had felt like a day and every part of me was grateful. "Thank you so much," I told everyone before tipping and heading out.

The sun's fierce embrace waited outside the spa doors, but it didn't bother me. My body felt lighter and my mind was clearer than it had been in months. Back home, I curled up in the bed with my laptop. My fingers hovered over the keyboard before typing "Lake Atitlán." I was still curious.

Images filled my screen: volcanic peaks rising from crystal waters, colorful markets, peaceful gardens overlooking the lake. "Whoa!" It looked magical and something tugged in my chest. I scrolled through photos of women on chairs near the shore, journaling in garden nooks, gathering in simple lakeside spaces – so different from everything I knew. I clicked through travel sites to learn more about vacation packages there. I knew the idea was absurd—not only wasn't it the time to take a vacation, but I had never even taken a solo trip! I didn't even know if my passport was up to date. Still, the images screamed rest and possibility. Raw beauty without pretense. The pull was soft but impossible to ignore. *Hmm.*

My phone whined with Alex's flight details for tomorrow. I closed the laptop, but the images lingered in my mind like the last notes of a song.

By Saturday, Alex insisted he get changed at the hotel while I groom at home. "Just meet me at the restaurant," he told me. "I booked a car for you so we can ride back together."

He was so energized about the night that he eclipsed the alone time I was starting to enjoy. "Okay, I will," I assured him. When I pulled up at home, the house opened like a jewelry box as I climbed the stairs. Everything sparkled of promise.

When I entered our charcoal and white bedroom, I clicked on upbeat music. Rays from the sunset ushered warmth onto the tight-tucked bedding. Hyperaware of the time again, I hustled into a shower and let steam fill our bathroom, turning the rectangle mirror into a cloud bank.

My mind drifted to the stack of contracts waiting for review as each hot droplet slid down my skin. I couldn't enjoy the fusion of honey and amber suds the way I wanted to. Soon, I wrapped myself in one of

Alex's favorite Turkish towels and wiped a circle in the foggy mirror. And for a moment, I stood naked, studying the woman looking back: strong shoulders, petit but with curves, a small scar on my hip that my mom still brought up whenever she talked about "that rusty old bike." Slender hands that were starting to show more veins and crinkles than before, and…breasts that hung a little lower than I'd liked, but still not too bad. At forty-four, my body was a map of my life experiences.

I slipped into the white dress and quickly applied my makeup—I didn't need much time to go from day job drab to date night dazzling. "Let's go, let's go," I told myself while glancing at one of the few personal photos of Alex and me. I smiled and sighed. The image was from a Porsche driving experience I'd gotten him during a trip to Atlanta. He was over the moon! The only thing Alex loved more than architecture and real estate was cars.

"Time to get going," I whispered before pressing my lips together, leaving a kiss mark on a coconut water bottle just because I could. *Wink.* I clicked off my playlist and gathered my essentials into a small clutch. Something happened with the vehicle Alex booked, and a replacement would be 30 minutes late. Couldn't do that. Alex didn't do well with late. So, I drove myself. One last glance in the hallway mirror: the white dress hugged in all the right places but were it not for him, I might have gone with red for our date. My coils were nicely defined and that deep burgundy lip added just the right amount of drama. Yes, girl!

"Good evening," a valet greeted me the moment I pulled up to the restaurant.

I grinned and made my way inside. Alex waited by the entrance. *Ooh! Good Lord.* He looked astoundingly handsome in a tailored suit that looked like it was painted on. Without a thought, I bit my bottom lip. *Mmph.* This man was a 12 tonight!

"Hey, babe!" His face lit up when he saw me, those piercing blue eyes sparking like a match struck in the dark.

The maître d' led us to what was unmistakably Opal & Vine's best table – centered beneath a crystal chandelier and visible from every angle of the dining room. I tightened my fingers around my clutch, sharply conscious of the subtle shift in other diners' attention. All of it was on us. A solo violinist played near the bar. His melody wove through conversations like silk.

Alex pulled out my chair and brushed a strand of hair from my face. With his jacket off, his sleeves were slightly rolled to showcase strong forearms. His skin glowed and his movie-star smile was framed by a perfectly groomed beard. *Just beautiful.*

"Good evening," The sommelier materialized beside us, presenting a bottle that made my eyebrows rise. Alex and I had barely gotten a chance to speak. "The '82 Bordeaux you requested, sir," he intoned. I recognized the bottle from our wine training sessions – impossibly rare, with a waiting list longer than most engagement periods. My heart fluttered as I took it all in.

"Excellent timing, Thomas," Alex grinned.

"Shall I?" Thomas lifted the bottle with reverence.

"Not yet." Alex's voice carried a warmth I rarely heard these days. "Let's order first."

The menu offered escargot, but Alex had already arranged every-thing. Each course appeared like magic. Butter-poached lobster. Wagyu that melted on the tongue. And meanwhile, the violin's tempo quickened, or maybe that was my pulse. I couldn't tell.

"Remember our first dinner here?" Alex reached across the table, his fingers gently finding mine.

"The night you convinced me to join the Jeffrey Hotel." I smiled at the memory, thinking of how proud he'd been. "Your middle name, I later learned. A little self-flattery in the naming?" I teased. "Wait a minute. That night...you ordered this exact lobster!"

"Yes! And yes. Now look at you. Running the place better than I ever could."

Thomas reappeared. At Alex's nod, he carefully twisted the cork free, releasing a soft sigh. Crystal glasses appeared before us as the violin music swelled. It's at this moment my mind went wild. *Is he about to...*

Alex reached inside his jacket pocket, and something fluttered to the marble floor – a folded paper that looked like blueprints. Quickly he recovered it and tucked it away. His chair scraped softly against the door and the room seemed to come to a halt as he stood to take my hand. Even the ice in water glasses stopped clinking. *Oh my God.* My heart galloped in my chest.

Then the ring emerged from his other pocket, catching the chandelier's light. *Twinkle, twinkle. twinkle.* It reflected everywhere. A collective gasp rippled through the room. The violinist drew his bow across strings that sang like stars. *This is really happening. Oh my God!* The choreography of the entire evening snapped into focus.

"Nyla," he paused to clear his throat and huffed, pushing himself. "From the moment you walked into the Jeffrey, I knew you were extraordinary."

My hands trembled as I listened to him.

"Your drive, your attention to detail, your ability to handle any crisis – your beauty and grace under pressure – you're exactly what I need. Together, we've built something amazing. And now, with the Charlotte deal, this is just the beginning. We could be unstoppable." He sank to one knee, presenting a ring. "Let's build an empire together?"

Wait a minute. My mind came to a screeching halt while the room kept going. The ring glinted – platinum and diamonds arranged in an architectural pattern—his favorite. Not a moment of this was actually about me.

Wait.

A.

Fucking.

Minute... My mind went completely blank.

"Nyla?"

I "came to" and realized Alex's hopeful eyes on me. The entire restaurant's, too. *Shit.* Everyone waited for the perfect ending to this perfectly orchestrated moment. My mouth went dry as the weight of their expectations pressed against me from all sides. It was hard to breathe, and a tear began budding in one of my eyes.

"Well?" He asked. "Will you marry me, Nyla?"

The violin's note held, suspended in the air like a question mark.

"Alex, I..." My lips quivered and my voice caught in my throat. I looked again at the ring: big, bold, beautiful—flawless.

"Yes," I finally said.

My world went white with the lie, but I had to go along with it. I didn't want to embarrass him, or worse, explain myself in front of all these strangers who already rose from their seats to clap. Thomas was already pouring champagne as Alex slid the ring on my finger. The violin had shifted to something celebratory. My smile felt as artificial as the tiny topiary trees dotting the dining room.

"Yes!" Alex announced, beaming. "I've already arranged our honeymoon. Ten days in the Maldives. The most exclusive resort on the island!"

Even through the champagne haze, something in me wilted. The Maldives. Not the Guatemala highlands I'd been quietly researching, where I might actually find some peace. Shit. Alex slowly rose off one knee. The ring was heavy. I stared at it, and in that moment, *every-thing* clicked into place. This wasn't just about marriage. The ring was a contract—a beautiful, sparkling commitment to his vision: the expansion plans, the Regional Director role, our entire future laid out with the same precision as this proposal.

This wasn't supposed to be how my engagement went. No. I'm not sure what I expected or wanted, but it wasn't this. Tears fell from my eyes and he pulled me in for a kiss. The room erupted with joy again. I felt like I was spinning.

The special dessert turned out to be a chocolate dome that melted away under warm caramel to reveal a "Mrs. Jones" inscription —as in Mrs. Alex Jeffrey Jones. Identity gone. Already. More champagne appeared. More congratulations. More smiles that made my cheeks ache. By the time we finished, the ring felt like it weighed a thousand pounds.

My phone jingled. I checked it under the table and felt a surge of guilt-tinged relief. "It's the hotel," I said, looking up at Alex. "Marco says there's a major issue with a VIP guest." A complete lie – I'm not sure what possessed me to ask Marco to text me with an "emergency" if dinner ran late, but I did. After so many years in hospitality, I knew exactly how to manufacture a graceful exit.

"Tonight? Really?" Alex frowned, but his business instincts kicked in. "Well, you better handle it. We can celebrate properly at home later. I'll head back and chill the champagne for when you're done." He signaled for the check.

Outside, the valet brought our cars around simultaneously. Alex kissed me goodnight, still caught up in his triumph. He clearly expected me to join him after dealing with work. Instead, once his car disappeared, I turned mine east...

I needed space. Needed air. Needed to think. The familiar curve of Dania Beach opened before me like a wound in the night. I took the exit toward the water.

My heels dangled from two fingers, swaying with each step as I made my way across the near-empty parking lot. The perfect white dress Alex had chosen got caught the sea breeze and billowed around my legs. God, the fresh air felt good.

I turned my phone to silent and ignored the three texts already in from Alex. *Made it home. Where are you? / The champagne's getting warm. / Call me when you're done at the hotel.* I wanted to hear the ocean, knowing the waves wouldn't judge my thoughts.

The sand was still warm from the day's heat, tiny grains working their way between my toes. I walked toward the water. How many summer evenings had I spent here as a kid? Back when my biggest worry was whether Mom would let me and my sister stay in the water five more minutes, back before spreadsheets and occupancy rates and curated images became my whole world.

My smart watch lit up on my wrist. This time it was Mom's photo filling the screen. *Fuck.* I hadn't planned on calling them yet, but—

"Nyla!" Mom's voice burst through before I could even say hello. "Alex just sent us the most beautiful picture! Oh *Lord*, that ring! When were you going to tell us?"

"I—" My voice cracked. A wave rushed in, erasing my footprints behind me.

"Baby girl?" Dad's voice cut in, deeper, steadier. "You there?"

"Yes, Daddy, I'm here." The ring caught the moonlight as I gestured. "I'm just... processing." The weight of it reminded me of my sister, Kendra's words at her law firm partnership celebration last month. It was the last time I'd seen her. *A woman should build her own legacy, not just manage someone else's,* she'd said, eyes flickering to Alex and me—at least I thought so at the time. She could have been talking about rising through the ranks and not us at all. Either way, I had dismissed it as her being too caught up in her own recent success to understand what Alex and I were building together. Now, her words rang differently. I really needed to text her back...I wasn't proud of it, but Kendra's last message sat unanswered in my phone: "Lunch soon? Miss you, sis." That was two weeks ago.

"Processing?" My mother's excitement dimmed, bringing me back to the moment. "Baby, this is everything you've worked for! The hotel expansion, your career trajectory – and my grandbabies aren't going to make themselves, you know!"

"Mom!"

"Regina," Dad's voice carried a warning note. "Let her breathe." A pause, then: "Where are you, Nyla? It sounds like waves."

In an undertow, I wanted to say. "Dania Beach." I didn't bother lying. Not to him.

"Mm." That single sound carried decades of understanding. "And does Alex know you're at the beach in that fancy dress instead of celebrating?"

Before I could answer, movement caught my eye. A woman walked along the waterline with a golden retriever padding beside her. The dog's fur glowed silver in the moon's glint, its tail wagging in slow, sleepy sweeps. Something about their easy companionship made my throat tight.

"I told him there was an emergency at the hotel," I admitted.

"Child." My mom's voice was aghast. "What is going on, Nyla? Are you okay?"

The dog noticed me, trotting over with gentle eyes and sandy paws. Its owner called out. "Sorry! He loves making new friends!"

I waved it was okay, watching as the retriever circled me with innate joy. The kind of mess Alex would never allow in our pristine house...the kind of spontaneous love that didn't come with conditions or carefully planned futures. How did I not see this proposal coming this way? How could I miss all the signs that my future would be planned for me?

"I don't know," I finally answered my mother, my free hand finding the dog's soft ears. "Everything's great on paper. The ring, the timing, the whole future he's mapped out...it's all so impeccable I can barely breathe."

The silence on the other end stretched like a Goodyear blimp.

"Your mother and I," Dad finally said, "we didn't have a perfect start. No fancy proposal, no big plans. Just two people who chose each other every day." He cleared his throat. "Perfect things, baby girl... they don't leave room for growth. I'm concerned that you don't sound happy about this. Did you say yes?"

The dog's owner whistled, and the pup gave my hand one last nuzzle before bounding away. I watched them disappear down the beach, a carefree union moving in easy synchronization against the silver-black sea.

"I did. But I have to go," I said, noting the time. Another wave rushed in, the sound like a clock ticking. "Alex will be wondering."

"Nyla," Mom's voice was gentle now. "Just... be sure. That's all we want."

"I know. I love you both, and I'll update you soon."

The call ended, but I remained a moment longer, letting the waves wash around my ankles. Each one felt like a countdown. I reached for my phone to text Alex back. Another message awaited from him: *Everything okay at the hotel?*

I typed back: *Handled it. Be home soon.* Then I walked a few more steps down the beach, my white dress a ghost in the darkness.

3

STAGED EXITS

"What the hell am I even doing?" The thought slammed into me as I pulled into our driveway. My left leg trembled against the floorboard—doing double duty to rid my feet of sand remnants as I looked at the house glowing from within. Every window lit up like a stage waiting for its actors. Alex's BMW sat in its usual spot.

"There's my fiancée!" He opened the door before I could put my finger on the lock. "Come in." He'd changed into dark loungewear and wore a triumphant smile. Definitely a few drinks in.

"The hotel situation..." I began, but he pulled me inside with a hand on my waist.

"Can wait until tomorrow." Alex pressed a flute of champagne into my hand. "Tonight is about us." He dimmed the kitchen lights, his fingers delicately traced my shoulder. "You looked so beautiful tonight, babe."

I took a long sip to buy time while my mind replayed all the times I let him choose, thinking he was doing his job as the man in our relationship by leading. The house. The furniture. My job. My car. What I wore. How often I changed my hair and even if I should get cosmetic work done. My stomach clenched as I realize how far I'd let it go. That I'd relinquished my voice.

Part of me wanted to ask about the folded papers that he'd dropped at dinner. But his lips found my neck. Kiss. Soft bite. Fuck, I did not want this.

"Dance with me?" he whispered, pulling me closer. No music played, but Alex swayed us gently in the half-light. His warm hands rested on my waist.

I also didn't want to fight. So, I played along, leaning into him. The alcohol blurred the edges of my doubt.

"I've been thinking about this moment all week."

I felt like I was choking. My heart palpitated as his arms closed me in.

"You're quiet," Alex observed. He turned me to face him.

"Just overwhelmed."

"I know, babe. It's a lot to take in." He misread my hesitation as emotion. "Let me take care of you tonight." Alex was thrilled and eager to tend to me.

Eventually upstairs, my mind rocked with "what ifs" about my future. I barely noticed him on top of me. Muscle memory guide my responses – a soft sigh here, an encouraging movement there. Nails in his back – just a little pressure. Reciprocal thrusts. *Sigh.* What would usually be a spectacular sex session felt more like a quiet surrender.

"I love you," Alex breathed against my skin.

I moaned in response, laying in the dark with his arm heavy across my torso. When I closed my eyes, a memory of the woman and the golden retriever flashed into my mind. The sound of the Guatemalan masseuse's accent rang in my ears. And in that moment, I'd never felt more alone. The woman who had just been so excited to dream about possibilities was just as crumpled as the white dress that lay in disarray on the floor.

~

MONDAY HIT LIKE A HANGOVER. Everything felt off-kilter. I'd been engaged for forty-eight hours and every breath felt like a lie.

My phone trembled with a photo from Alex in Charlotte—he'd returned. It was him making a goofy face in front of a colorful food truck. "Remember that Cuban food truck you loved? Found one here. Which dishes should I try? I miss your expert taste."

I caught myself smiling. This was the Alex who'd sit for hours in Little Havana with me, sampling everything, letting me teach him about my favorite foods. The one who used to spend an entire Sunday helping Marco's son practice for a hotel management course.

But as I reached for my laptop to check flight prices to Guatemala, my smile faded. These glimpses of the man I'd fallen for just made everything harder because now I really wanted to go. And I knew he wouldn't understand. I needed a break.

The morning room service inspection would give me an excuse to move. But every staff member I passed had the same congratulatory grin, the same eager questions about the proposal. "¡Felicidades!" "Such a romantic!" "You're so lucky!" By the time I reached the service elevator, my cheeks ached from forced smiles.

As a pleasant greeting, however, I heard a familiar reggae melody. Clive, one of our veteran bellhops, was expertly maneuvering a cart of designer luggage while humming "Three Little Birds." His salt-and-pepper beard was neatly trimmed above his crisp uniform. Beneath his name tag a corner of a red silk pocket square peeked out. His one subtle rebellion against the hotel's strict dress code.

"Morning, Ms. Baines," he said, pausing his tune. His warm Jamaican accent was a balm after all the shrill congratulations. Then his dark eyes studied me for a moment longer than usual. "You seem like someting is off today."

I hesitated. In three years, Clive had never been wrong about reading a guest's mood – or mine. "Just wedding excitement," I fibbed with a tight grin.

He nodded slowly, clearly unconvinced. "Well, if you need anyting, jus mek mi know."

"Thanks, Clive." I watched him guide the cart into the elevator, his soft humming resuming as the doors closed. Something about Clive's quiet perception made me feel both seen and unsettled.

Back in my office during a lull, my fingers hovered over the keyboard before pulling up the employee vacation policy. Three weeks accumulated. Never used. I drafted a quick email about taking two weeks to recharge and thoughtfully chose dates when occupancy would be lowest. Before I could hit send, Marco popped his head in.

"Got a minute?"

"Sure. Everything okay?"

"Oh, for sure. Going smoothly! Actually..." He settled into the chair across from me with unusual energy. "I wanted to run something by you. Remember when you mentioned that executive training program? I've been thinking..."

As he talked about growth opportunities, something warm and familiar tugged at me. Here was someone else who understood ambition, who wanted more. Without thinking, I heard myself continue the conversation we were winding down with, "I could actually use your advice on something too. I'm thinking about taking some time off. Maybe somewhere...different."

"¡Qué emocionante! My wife and I just got back from Costa Rica. Here—" He pulled out his phone to pull up stunning images. I explained what I already had in mind, and for twenty minutes, we scrolled through possibilities. His enthusiasm was off the charts.

"Nyla, we've got a situation in the ballroom," Ana's voice crackled over my walkie-talkie.

"What is it?" I inquired.

"The wedding party is here early, half the rooms aren't clean, and catering is short-staffed. It's a mess."

A loud crash echoed in the distance, followed by a string of curses. I flinched. My nerves lit up like a curtain catching flame.

"What was that?" I asked, pressing the walkie-talkie button to speak to all staff on the relay.

Trevor, our head of security, responded urgently. "That was the loading dock, Nyla. Some idiot just backed into the delivery truck.

We've got broken glass and wine all over the place. The driver's threatening to leave if it's not cleaned up ASAP."

Marco left without a word, knowing the drill. Tension crawled up my spine. "Perfect," I muttered, pressing a hand against my forehead. "Alright, I'm coming."

As I strode through the lobby, unease boiled in my gut. Rumbling. Relentless. A hail of stares soon pelted my back, dragging my attention toward guests at concierge. Trevor's voice still droned in my ears as I passed a cluster of them. Then, my phone chirped with a text from an unknown number: "Your boyfriend is watching you." I froze, staring at the screen. The message disappeared before I could screenshot it. *What the hell?*

"Nyla?" Ana's voice crackled through the walkie-talkie. "The mother of the bride is asking for you specifically."

I pressed the talk button. "On my way." So much going on. *Fuck, fuck, fuck!*

I thought back to the text as I hustled. It was probably sent to the wrong phone. Either way, I didn't have time for anything but the moment in front of my face.

The day dissolved into a haze of demands and solutions. I even rolled up my sleeves and helped clean, moving from room to room, changing sheets, vacuuming, scrubbing surfaces, all while my mind raced.

Between aesthetic maintenance, soothing the wine distributor and settling the wedding party, I barely had time to take a break. By evening, the chaos had settled. I sat in my office, staring at the draft email about vacation time. The cursor blinked, challenging me to choose me. *Do it, Nyla....* Before I could overthink it, I added dates, mentioned professional development opportunities in Central America, and hit send.

4

INVISIBLE WIRES

The next morning, my inbox dinged with a single notification: *Meeting request from Alex Jones – Priority: Urgent – Time: 10:00 AM EST - Location: Video Conference.*

I stared at my screen, the cursor hovering over "Accept." No call. No text. Just this sterile calendar invite – the kind he usually reserved for everyone but me. My gut screamed loudly at me. Everything in writing. Everything documented. I stretched my jaw, feeling it pop with tension release. I wasn't used to this, but felt guided to act differently.

The shift from our usually casual communication was a stinging jab. Where were his usual good morning texts with the stupid heart emojis? His statue-posing selfies from the gym? My chest constricted at his tactical move. *Noted.*

A soft knock drew my attention.

"Yes?"

Clive stood in the doorway, his red cap bent at the brim and slightly raised above his hairline. "These came back with the morning mail, Ms. Baines." He placed a stack of opened envelopes on my desk with unusual care. "Guest correspondence," he added meaningfully, sliding one envelope closer. "*This* one was already open when it arrived."

The return address caught my eye – Ocean Breeze Spa. *Hmph.* Instantly, I recalled the peace I felt during my day there. Felt the drop in my shoulders. And remembered the taste of the fresh fruit plated just for me, especially the frozen grapes. *Heaven.* Inside the spa envelope was a comment card from my visit, along with some promotional materials about their sister properties. Including one in Guatemala City. The coincidence made my fingers tingle.

I barely had time to tuck the brochure into my desk drawer before my laptop chimed. It was ten o'clock and Alex's face filled my screen.

"Morning, Nyla." His camera-ready smile had all the warmth of a boardroom handshake. "I got your vacation request."

I leveled into my corporate posture. "Yes. I think some time off would help me come back stronger. More focused on the expansion."

He leaned closer to the camera. "Nyla, baby, your timing concerns me. We're at a crucial point with our deal," he paused. "And Guatemala? What the hell is in Guatemala?"

"Professional development opportunities." The lie slid off my tongue with surprising ease. "There's a boutique hotel movement happening there that could benefit the Jeffrey." I twisted the ring on my finger. "Plus, I need to decompress before diving into wedding planning."

"I already started planning the wedding so you can take it easy, babe! And I've been working on our honeymoon itinerary. Five-star everything. You'll love it. Zero stress for you, I promise."

"You'll love it?" My voice rose sharply. Mockingly. "God, Alex. Can I just have this one thing? Just... just *one* decision that's mine?"

His expression hardened. "Nyla, you're being irrational. You *should* love this! Look, we can discuss this when I—"

"No." The word surprised us both. A shadow passed my door, but I couldn't stop now. "I'm going to on vacation. I need a break!"

"Damn it, Nyla! We'll talk about this when I get back," he said icily.

The screen went black. My hands trembled as the frost of what I'd just done sent a chill through my veins. Flickers of quickly dispersing staff flashed through my office window. *Shit. Shit. Shit.* I never raised my voice, especially not to Alex. Especially not at work!

THAT EVENING, I searched for my passport to ensure it wasn't expired. It had been years since Alex and I went out of the country. My nerves wobbled like a like a ceiling fan with a missing blade. Hustling to a corner of his closet, I crouched and opened the safe at the bottom. My legs shook, and my breath hastened. The metal storage felt cold, and my fingers trembled as I punched the code. *Click.* The top popped up, revealing both of our personal items–from birth certificates to crypto wallets—but I had no idea where the passwords to unlock the funds were. It didn't matter right now. My passport sat on top. I picked it up and checked the expiration date—still good. A knot in my chest loosened as I pulled the textured blue book close.

Beep-bzzt-click. The whirr of our front door lock prowled through the silence. My eyes bulged—Alex wasn't supposed to be back until tomorrow. *Fuck, fuck, fuck!* I hurried to replace everything. My movements were jerky with anxious energy.

"Nyla?" His voice carried up the stairs, followed by the clunk of his overnight bag hitting the floor.

I closed the safe and slipped out of his closet, pulse roaring in my ears. Quick steps took me to our en-suite bathroom where I flicked on the faucet. "Up here!" I called back, making it sound casual. "Just washing up!" The cold water felt great on my skin—instinct made me run a hand under it.

Stairs groaned under his steps as I dried my palms, trying to slow my breathing. His cologne reached me before he did.

"You're home early," I managed, hanging the towel with deliberate care.

His eyes narrowed slightly. "Surprise." The word was flat. Abrupt. Salty. And patronizing. Alex looked at me and then around the bathroom. He peeled off his jacket and moved toward his closet.

My heart jackhammered in my chest. *Did I put everything back properly?* I thought so.

"Were you in here?"

A swarm of electric hornets buzzed beneath my skin, both terrifying and oddly exhilarating. I walked past him toward the bed. "Yes."

Alex followed. "Why?"

"I was just..." Submission died in my throat. "Looking for my passport."

"This late?"

"I couldn't sleep." It was a half-truth. "The trip I want to take... I need to make sure everything's in order."

He puffed out a heavy sigh. "Nyla, come on now. We talked about this. The timing isn't right."

"*You* talked about it. And the timing isn't right for *you*. I...need a break"

Alex's jaw tightened. He moved closer. "What's really going on here, sweetheart? This isn't like you."

That's the problem, I thought. *I'm always like* you *want me to be*. But it hid in the depths of my throat. Not confident enough. Instead, I said, "I just need some time. To think."

"Think about what?" His voice dropped dangerously low. "About throwing away everything we've been working on? About running off to some—"

"It's just a trip, Alex."

"Is it?" He studied me like a contract with fine print. "Because it feels like more than that. I mean, who runs off to some random third world country by themselves? This is *not* 'just a trip.' I don't buy that."

Silence stretched between us like a rubber band ready to snap. Finally, he exhaled and ran a hand through his curly hair. "Look, it's late. We're both tired. Why don't I run you a bath? We can talk about this when we're both thinking clearly."

"Thank you but...I—I think I'll sleep in the guest room tonight." Something had changed. The hornets under my skin wouldn't settle.

His expression flickered – surprise, then something darker. His brows furrowed, and I could see him grinding his teeth. But he restrained himself. "Fine. If that's what you need....go."

I grabbed my robe and phone, avoiding his eyes. Eager to get away and call someone, anyone, to make sure I wasn't overreacting or making a mistake. Truthfully, I didn't recognize myself either.

Sleep came in restless waves. My dreams were full of airport terminals with exits I couldn't quite reach.

DEEP SLUMBER WOULDN'T COME AT ALL in the guest room. At 10 PM, I finally gave up and video called my parents, knowing they'd be up watching the news.

"Nyla, you're awake late?" Dad asked, his voice encouraging and familiar through the speaker. He knew I was usually in bed by 8:45 because my days started so early.

"I know." I curled deeper into the unfamiliar mattress. "It's Alex." My eyes lowered instinctively.

"What about him?"

"He's starting to be...too much," I confessed, fidgeting with my phone. "Everything is too much, so I told him I wanted a little vacation. Alone." My voice cracked on the last word.

"Nyla." My mom's voice butted in from the background. Jesus, those two were attached at the hip! "That man is trying to give you a dream life. Do you know how many women would kill for that?"

"Let her speak, honey," My Dad protected me.

She ignored him, speaking louder. "What? I'm just saying—"

"Well, let me say something. I don't want to get too in you guy's business unless you invite me in," My father rubbed the back of his neck. "Baby girl, I know you've spent your whole life making sure everyone else is taken care of. The hotel, Alex, even us. But at some point..." He paused and removed his glasses. "At some point, you have to ask yourself who's taking care of you."

"That's what Alex is trying to do!" Mom interjected. "He's planning everything, making sure she's set for life," she added. If I didn't know better, I'd think there was a tinge of jealousy in her voice, but I was unsure.

"He is starting to feel suffocating," I said quietly. I surprised myself with the transparency.

Quiet gulfed between us, broken only by the faint jingle from their television.

"A woman traveling alone..." Mom started again.

"Is something Nyla needs to decide for herself," Dad finished. His voice softened. I told him more details about where I wanted to go, why, and what inspired it. He was caught off guard, but said, "I admit, Guatemala makes me nervous. But you're smart and capable. Just... promise me you'll be careful? Research everything?"

"I will, Daddy."

"And call us. Every day – if you go."

"Of course."

Mom sighed heavily. "I still think—"

"I know, Mama. I know you want what's best for me. But right now, I need to figure out what exactly that is," I offered. "I should let you both sleep," I added, hearing the weight in my own voice. The television chatter had faded and in that quiet, I felt the distance between the daughter they knew and the woman I was trying to figure out the identity of.

Morning arrived like a head being dunked underwater. My mind flooded with anger and uncertainty. The guest room felt foreign. The bed was cold, and the dawn light slicing through unfamiliar curtains made everything look like a badly edited Instagram photo.

Still thinking about getting away, I waited until the shower started running before tip-toing back into our bedroom. Alex's morning routine was predictable. Fifteen minutes to shave and shower, then thirty minutes of calls in his office before heading to the hotel. I had a narrow window to get ahead of him. One step. Two steps. Three...I moved like a mist threading between mangroves.

My hands trembled less this time as I entered the password. Inside, documents lay scattered like fallen leaves, but the familiar blue booklet was conspicuously absent. *No, no...* The passport was gone.

"No!" My fingers scrabbled through papers, desperate to prove my suspicion wrong. But I wasn't. Alex had hidden it while I slept. The room tilted sideways as reality sank in.

The shower stopped.

"Looking for something?" Alex's voice filled the space behind me. Water droplets still clung to his shoulders, the towel riding low on his hips.

"Where is it?"

"Where's what?"

"Alex. Where. Is. It?!"

He walked away with lazy, controlled movements.

"God damn it, Alex! Where is my passport?"

"Ohhh, that. I put it somewhere safe," he stretched his neck. "Just until you're thinking clearly again."

Heat rose in my chest. "You mean thinking like you want me to think."

"Babe..." Alex stepped closer, reaching for my waist. "You're stressed. Let me—"

I jerked back. "Don't." The word cracked like a whip. "Don't touch me. Don't you try to manage me."

"Manage you? I'm trying to protect you! You're acting crazy—"

"If discussing what *I* want to do for myself is crazy then I don't know what to tell you." My voice stayed low but carried ice. "Because from where I'm standing, your kind of 'protection' looks a lot like control. Taking my passport isn't protection, it's imprisonment."

"Whoa, whoa, whoa, Nyla! Now, you're being dramatic—"

"I'm being clear."

"Don't get hysterical!"

The more he spoke, the less I cared about his feelings—for once. I met his gaze, refusing to shrink. "Protection doesn't mean take my choice away. It doesn't require submission. And it sure as hell doesn't involve stealing someone's documents while they sleep."

"You're not thinking about the bigger picture!"

"I'm thinking about the billboard display of your control and wondering how on Earth I never noticed it!" I announced before turning to walk out, leaving him mid-sentence. My body quaked as I grabbed whatever clothes were nearest in the guest room—a wrinkled silk blouse, yesterday's pencil skirt. No time for makeup beyond a swipe of lipstick. No perfectly styled coif today. Just me, stripped down to essentials. My reflection was strange and unfamiliar in the mirror.

How naïve, I thought while barely registering the glide into my parking spot, the same one where just a week ago I'd felt so much pride to have. That felt like forever ago now. I felt so stupid.

Marco chatted with Clive outside. His eyes widened at my appearance.

"Ms. Baines?" Clive's voice came through first though, giving me pause. His dark eyes took in my appearance, before then turning completely away from Marco. "The new luggage carts arrived. Perhaps you'd like to inspect them? In the storage room?"

Something about his tone told me there were no new luggage carts in today. I exhaled. "Sure." I followed him. I was grateful for the excuse. The storage room smelled of leather polish and cleaning supplies. Clive closed the door and adjusted his pocket square.

"I've worked here two years, Ms. Baines," he said carefully. "Never seen you miss a morning inspection."

Shit. There really was new luggage. I'd completely forgotten. Clive's gentle observation hit harder than any accusation. I straightened my clothes, professional mask slipping back into place. "Everything's fine. I just need to—" My voice caught as I realized I had no idea how to finish that sentence.

Clive waited, his silence offering more kindness than questions.

"Honestly, I need some time off."

"Exhausted, eh?"

I smiled. Relieved. "Yeah...I'm tired," I finally said, the words barely above a whisper. "But I can't find my passport. So...I guess no vacation for me, huh?" I gave a pitiful giggle, trying to make light of the situation.

Older. Wiser. And not buying it, but polite enough to let the lie stand, Clive took a slow breath. Something shifted in his expression, recognition, maybe. "The passport agency downtown re-issues them for emergencies. Within 24 hours, if you have the right documentation. My niece had someting happen to hers once..." I couldn't tell if he was testing the waters with that story or if it were my paranoia that I was more readable than I thought. "Police report, birth certificate, proof of travel..." Clive continued. "I think you would need all of those tings," he paused. "Just... information that might be useful. To anyone."

Hmph. I considered his words, brows furrowed as I never even considered all of this. "Thanks, Clive," I whispered, my throat tight. A way out. A real way out.

"Anytime, boss. Relax yuself, alright?" He smiled, his Jamaican accent coming out more pronounced as he got more comfortable with me.

LATER THAT MORNING, the Miami-Dade police station's fluorescent lights turned everything sickly pale. A row of posters lined the beige walls. "See Something, Say Something." "If You Feel Unsafe..." My gaze caught on one showing a hand gripping a passport: "Financial Control is Abuse." The word scratched against something raw inside me. I tried to focus: *I just needed a new passport.* That was all. It was easier to think about it that way than to admit what I'd screamed at Alex this morning was true. That this was exactly what those posters were warning about. And that wasn't me.

"When did you last see it?" Officer Jackson's voice was tired but kind.

My mouth went dry. The truth pressed against my teeth: *Alex took it. He's gone overboard trying to do things for me. Help.* But years of smoothing things over, making excuses, or keeping the peace kicked in instantly.

"I—I had it last week," I heard myself say. "I was organizing documents and now I can't find it." Each word felt like betrayal—but of Alex or myself, I wasn't sure.

"Were you planning a trip, or was there another reason you were organizing your documents?"

Behind me, a woman's voice cracked through the station's hushed atmosphere: "My husband burned mine."

The words hit like a physical blow. *Did she just...* My heart thundered in my chest. Cold prickles spreading up my spine as her statement dug in. I couldn't turn around. Couldn't look at her. Couldn't acknowledge how her words had shattered the faultless story I was building. I wanted to run away, but my feet were glued to the ground.

Officer Jackson's pen paused. For a moment, our eyes met, and I saw that she knew. We both knew. But she just nodded and continued writing. My skin started crawling as my eyes averted, noticing the posters again. This wasn't me. I wasn't one of those women. I just... needed my passport.

The rest happened in a blur: birth certificate from my bank's safe deposit box, a refundable ticket to Guatemala purchased in cash, the emergency passport application filled out in scatter-brained handwriting. By mid-afternoon, I had an appointment for 8 AM the next morning at the downtown passport agency.

I drove back to the Jeffrey in a daze. My body operated on autopilot while my mind replayed that woman's words. *My husband burned mine.* The familiar corridors that had once felt like my kingdom now seemed like elegant prison hallways. I smiled mechanically at guests, signed what needed signing, and somehow got through the rest of my shift without screaming.

But I knew I needed to steal some time for myself, and I wouldn't get it in my office. Compulsively, I decided to retreat to the back stairwell because it was always quiet this late in the day. But as I pushed through the door, Marco's voice drifted up from the landing below. He spoke hurriedly.

"...sí, mi amor, Assistant Manager! I'll be running the whole front office! Alex says with Nyla wanting time off, it's my chance to prove myself...No, no. She thinks I'm helping her plan... Guatemala, can you believe it? Such a random place to pick. Alex says to keep him posted on her research, just in case—"

My heel scraped against concrete. The conversation cut off like a slashed throat.

"Mar—" The word caught behind my lips. *Don't say anything.* My survival instinct barricaded tongue and the soft click of the second-floor door echoed in the stairwell.

I stood frozen. Bottom lip quivering as the bottom of my stomach descended like a broken rollercoaster. The concrete walls pressed closer. Had they always been this gray? This cold? This narrow. My fingers traced the handrail, finding an anchor in its solid reality while my mind spun through every conversation I'd had with Marco. I searched for the signs I'd missed. The enthusiastic travel planning – had his phone been on? Recording? Sending? *Betrayal.* The word unspooled through my veins. Damn it, Marco! My nails dug half-moons into my palms as bile rose in my throat. *How could you?*

A door slammed somewhere above, jolting me back to the outside world. The staff. The guests. My office. Shit! The fucking performance of it all. My mind screeched and my body quaked. Marco's words hit my consciousness like darts tipped with toxin. I had to get the fuck out of there.

"How did I get here?" I interrogated myself while hurrying to my office. I wanted to run out and to my car, but I didn't want to cause a scene. Didn't want to let on that I knew something was deeply, deeply wrong. Suppressed tears burned my eyes like tear gas. My soul...my soul hurt so badly. "What did I do wrong?" I wondered, but there was no one to answer. There was nothing. I was alone with unanswered questions on one hand and a devastating revelation on the other.

I couldn't sleep that night. Watching the hours tick by, I wondered if I was brave enough to actually do this or if I really was overreacting. But every time I closed my eyes, I heard Marco's voice. And I saw that poster: *Financial Control is Abuse.* The words echoed in my head until dawn, mixing with the memory of that woman's voice.

Maybe I wasn't so alone after all.

5

ALTITUDE ADJUSTMENTS

Alex was livid. I was afraid. And we were struggling. Three days after filing the police report, I walked out of the passport agency with new documents, forcing myself to breathe normally until I reached my car. But the air was jagged coming from my lungs. By the fourth day, I'd called the airline to confirm my ticket. By the fifth, I was counting the hours until departure: 72 were left.

The week felt like a negotiation between old comfort and new courage. Push. Pull. Three steps forward. Two stumbles back. Try again. Each moment brought fresh waves of guilt and anticipation. *What was happening with my life?* I kept wondering. *How did I get here? Where did I go wrong—and right?* I had so many questions and not enough answers.

"It's just a week," I'd promised Alex. We'd argued and given each other the silent treatment. And argued again. Eventually, surprisingly, he relented.

It was Marco who'd inadvertently given me the leverage I needed. *Or had it been intentional?* During a staff meeting, Marco had elaborately praised several luxury chains' cultural immersion programs – how hoteliers returned with fresh perspectives that elevated their service standards. "The Westin Camino Real does this brilliantly."

His eyes had flickered to me just briefly, then to Alex, then back to his ever-present notebook. Alex's expression had shifted, his business-man's mind already spinning possibilities. Suddenly my "reckless" solo trip transformed into research for the Jeffrey's future.

"Think about it," Marco had continued, his pen tapping rhythmically against his notebook. "These emerging markets are redefining luxury. More authentic experiences, unique perspectives..." His red socks flashed as he got up to speak more expressively.

Was he serious? Was this for me? Was I being overly suspicious? I didn't know what to believe or who to trust.

I watched Alex's fingers grip his mug tighter as he watched Marco's presentation. Thinking. Alex mulled over the possible opportunity versus everything else he had going on in Charlotte—I just watched. Marco might have been playing both sides, but he'd given me an opening to do what I wanted. The next morning, Alex cornered me in my office.

"I've been thinking about your vacation request," he announced, perching on the edge of my desk. "Maybe Marco has a point. We could use some fresh perspectives for the expansion."

"Really?" I kept my voice neutral, though my heart pounded like a thousand hooves.

"Yes. But...we'd need to structure it properly." His hand found mine, fingers brushing over the engagement ring. "Daily check-ins. Detailed reports. You'll focus on exotic luxury market research and stay in the safe areas." Each word was a satin-wrapped constraint. "No point exploring the less developed regions. I can manage here while you're gone."

I nodded, not trusting myself to speak.

"I'll arrange a driver to meet you at the airport. Those Guatemalan taxis are probably completely unreliable. They're probably shit," he vocalized with rolled eyes. "Start at Puerto Quetzal. They've got that luxury port complex. It's a perfect example of how they're elevating their hospitality standards," Alex rambled. "Besides," he added with a fake smile, "what kind of fiancé would I be if I didn't support your professional growth? And...you can relax a little in the evenings." Then, his grin widened. He was proud of himself.

The word 'fiancé' caught in my chest like a fish hook. But I was getting what I wanted – sort of. *One battle at a time.* Plus, Alex's need to control every detail had the unexpected benefit that he'd have to handle the Jeffrey himself while I was gone. There would be no time to follow me to the airport when there was a morning manager's meeting to run. Good.

MY LEGS FELT soft and shaky as Alex watched me pack...like newborn calves. His presence filled our bedroom like smoke. Heat rose in the space and under my skin in waves. In tremors. But I forced myself to keep going despite feeling his eyes pierce me. Each motion was a test – folding, checking, rechecking – while pretending I couldn't feel him cataloging every item. When I reached for a pair of hiking boots I'd secretly bought, Alex's nostrils flared, but he said nothing. We both knew this wasn't about luxury hotels.

It wasn't until I was past airport security that I could breathe a little easier. Neutral territory. *Finally.* I found a quiet corner at the gate and texted Alex and my parents that I'd checked in. Somehow the action felt different this time. It wasn't just a lifetime of hotel management making me report my status, and that realization made me uncomfortable.

"A mimosa, please," I ordered from a small bar. I didn't care that it was barely nine AM. The mediocre champagne tasted like victory.

Business travelers, families, and couples all rushed past. I wondered how many of them were choosing something, rather than just running away. How many were solo travelers like me – especially for the first time? The crisp edges of my new passport pressed against my palm, reminding me how quickly plans could change. Soon enough, Miami shrank beneath the plane's wing.

I'd done my own research, and planned on a day trip to Lake Atitlán, and a possible volcano hike at Acatenango. I was nervous about it all, but this was my shot to explore and live on my time. My terms. My pace. The flight was three hours from Miami to Guatemala City. Three hours of recycled air and airplane coffee and not having to manage anyone's expectations but my own – just enough time to watch a movie and not overthink my decision.

THE IMMIGRATION OFFICER barely glanced at my blank passport before stamping it. And just like that, I was officially in Central America. Wow!

My phone buzzed again: Alex's fifth message since landing.

The driver's name is Roberto. It'll be a black Mercedes. Don't take any other car, babe.

Oh, for fuck's sake! What I used to think of as helpful now felt like a kazoo at a funeral. I wanted to rest!

I silenced the notifications, remembering what the Solo Sisters Travel Group had said about Guatemala City's airport: *Ubers are fine, but they have a habit of canceling at night. Use the yellow taxis inside the terminal during the day. Don't stress about the chaos – the tourist help desk speaks English.* All good.

The arrivals hall hit me with a wave of Spanish announcements. A wall of drivers held signs, and there, near the center: "Mrs. Alex Jones – The Westin Camino Real." My stomach clenched.

"Ms. Baines," I corrected quietly, showing my hotel confirmation. "My...fiancé booked under his name...but I'm still Ms. Baines for now." The driver's eyebrows raised but he took my bag without another question about what to call me. "Soy, Alejandro." *I'm Alejandro.*

"Mucho gusto," I told him. *Nice to meet you.*

The car's interior could have been any one in Miami – same leather seats, same new-car smell, same complimentary bottles of water. But outside, Guatemala City sprawled in vivacious contradictions: modern skyscrapers and colonial churches, luxury brands alongside street vendors. I pressed my forehead against the cool window, watching a city that brightly dissented from Alex's stereotypes and expectations.

"First time in Guatemala?" Alejandro quizzed. He met my eyes in the rearview mirror.

"Si. Si. Is it that obvious?" I managed a small laugh.

Bashful, he demurred, "Well, most visitors go straight to Antigua." Alejandro navigated around a produce truck painted with vivid murals. "But Guatemala City has her own magic. ¿Habla español?"

"Sólo un poco!" I giggled. *Just a little.*

"Ahh...excelente, señorita." Clearly, he was pleased with even the smallest attempt.

I was happy with myself and couldn't hide my goofy grin at how fast I felt at ease despite it being my first time on a solo trip. Just then, my phone lit up. Alex again: *Remember what Marco said about luxury market research. The Westin's part of Marriott now – perfect example of international standards.*

"Are there any other places I should see besides the main tourist attractions?" I remained present with Alejandro.

"Si, Señorita Baines. It depends on what you like. If you like something fun and unusual, you could try Hobitenango. Or, if you're interested in our history, Zona 13 has our national museum right next to a beautiful zoo. Many tourists miss these places, but they are some of our city's best treasures. Muy bonita, señorita."

"Gracias," I noted his suggestions.

We rode the rest of the way in mostly silence. As we got off the highway onto regular streets, something caught my eye in a mall entrance...a Bitcoin ATM gleamed next to a Radio Shack storefront—a brand I hadn't seen in years back home. The juxtaposition was jarring. Guatemala wasn't stuck in the past as Alex assumed; it was simultaneously preserving what worked while embracing the future on its own terms. I continued watching Guatemala City's mix of modern and colonial architecture blur past until we pulled up to the Westin's dramatic entrance.

The hotel's distinctive triangular windows created a geometric pattern above the covered driveway. The moment I stepped out of the car, the contrast between the Jeffrey and this place hit me. Where our hotel aimed for intimate boutique luxury, this one was old-world grandeur. A gleaming revolving door welcomed me into a lobby that took my breath away. Soaring ceilings crowned with a massive stained-glass dome, floor-to-ceiling windows draped in flowing white fabric. A crystal chandelier cast dancing light across classical murals depicting pastoral scenes.

It was exactly the kind of international standard Alex wanted me to study. *What kind of vacation is this?* My mind tormented me with reminders that he'd steamrolled my trip to get away and pressed it into a business jaunt.

"Welcome to The Westin Camino Real, Mrs. Jones," the front desk agent greeted me in English. "We have you in one of our Vista Suites."

I smiled through gritted teeth. *Baines.* One part annoyed, but one part appreciative that Alex had probably insisted on the upgrade. But for the first time in years, I wasn't analyzing the check-in process. Hell, I was finally on the other side of the desk! My heart lit up.

That first evening, I made myself explore the property with "fresh perspectives" in mind, as Marco had suggested to Alex. The hotel staff moved with an easy grace, mixing international standards with distinctly Guatemalan coziness. At dinner, the waiter didn't just recommend the pepián; he insisted I try it with a side of loroco flower buds. It was a local delicacy his grandmother swore could cure heartbreak. "The chef sources them from women who have been growing them for generations," he explained through a translation device, his pride evident.

Then there was Martha at the spa, who described their signature cacao treatment. It was a ritual that began with beans sourced from women's cooperatives near Lake Atitlán. "They prepare everything the traditional way," she explained, demonstrating how the warm cacao butter was worked into tight muscles using ancient Mayan massage techniques. The Jeffrey's carefully experience luxury suddenly felt hollow in comparison. *Mmph.*

I took careful notes about "authentic guest experiences" and "cultural integration," playing the role of the diligent GM. It was surprisingly interesting, but something inside me yearned for more than just observing from behind a business lens. I wanted to meet these women, understand their traditions, see the lake where they gathered their healing ingredients.

By the end of day two, I'd had enough of structured observation. "I'm taking a car to Antigua," I told Alex during our morning check-in call. Before he could protest, I added, "The concierge confirmed it's the cultural capital, perfect for understanding authentic guest experiences." The lie came easy. Click.

"Buenos dias, señorita!" An older gentleman on horseback greeted me as my driver slowed down on the cobblestoned road to allow him passage.

I nodded affirmatively with a cordial smile. All around were beautiful buildings. Pinks. Browns. Blues. Yellows. Ancient bricks and stucco arches. Weathered walls against a mountainous backdrop. Not a corporate brand in sight. No luxury standards. Just life, energetic and unrehearsed.

During my official tour, I learned the city had been Guatemala's colonial capital until earthquakes forced its relocation in 1773, and that the pastel colors were strictly regulated to preserve its UNESCO heritage status. With a group this time, we also passed hole-in-the-wall taqueria stands and local cantinas with marimba music floating through open windows.

"See those shadows in the walls," our guide, Manuel, pointed to dark patches in the earthquake-damaged ruins. "The Spanish learned to build them twice as wide as normal after the 1717 earthquake. And notice how the buildings are low? Everything in Antigua was designed to survive tremors. These ruins tell the story of how humans adapt to living in earthquake country," he finished.

We wandered through markets where women in traditional huipiles sold handwoven textiles, past ruins of ancient churches where bougainvillea spilled over crumbling walls. After the bazaar, I found a quiet corner in Parque Central and pulled out my itinerary. Tomorrow's early wake-up call for a hike up Acatenango volcano loomed.

Hmm. I exhaled. My muscles were already complaining from walking Antigua's cobblestones, and the altitude made every breath felt like sipping through a child's straw.

"I'm tired," I whispered to myself. What I really wanted was one of those cups of mangos with Tajin spice on them. Alex would have a fit if he knew I was considering street food, but it all looked so damn fresh and good that I wanted it anyway. *Skip the hike.* My inner voice spoke up. *Eat the mango.* Do what you want—*even if that's just sleeping!* My thoughts were a trampoline of expressions. Even though the trudge was originally my idea, my body was protesting after days of "market research," that I'd never planned on doing this trip...and the ones that I had.

My fingers hovered over my phone before pulling up a different website. "Hobbitenango," I whispered the name like a secret, scrolling through photos of what looked like a fantasy world carved into the mountainside. I could almost hear Alex's voice: *You came all this way to visit a theme park?* But something about those whimsical doors and garden paths called to me. Volcano treks would always be there, but this... this was unique. *Do it.* I got up and walked to a street vendor for the fruit snack I wanted while deliberating. And finally, I decided to ditch the already-paid-for-hike for the Hobbit village. Tonight, though, I would rest.

6

THE SHAPE OF FREEDOM

The next morning, I requested Alejandro take a detour through an area that would show me more than my immediate surroundings and tourist havens.

"¿En serio?" He hadn't expected my assertion.

"Si, por favor."

"Con gusto, señorita. I will take you through Zona 14. It is not far from here. Very different from what most tourists see," he glanced at me through the rearview mirror with a knowing smile.

"And then, Hobbitenango, as you suggested."

Alejandro beamed! "Perfecto!"

My stomach fluttered. The sensation wasn't entirely unpleasant, more like the tickle of champagne bubbles than the usual gurgle of anxiety. I didn't know the last time I'd deviated from a planned route. Even this small shift in direction felt deliciously unfamiliar.

I watched the city transform through the car window. Steel and glass buildings rose against the mountain backdrop, anchored by Parque Las Americas' modern facade. Around another corner, street art of a massive white tiger prowled across a storefront wall. Its painted form leapt through stylized mountains in shades of turquoise and coral.

"There is a park up ahead: Plaza Berlin," Alejandro mentioned. "The view is spectacular."

"I'd love to see it." The words came easily now. "Let's stop."

The road wound higher until we reached a pine-shaded sanctuary carved into the hillside. Exercise equipment dotted a walking path, the kind you'd see in Miami's fancy waterfront condos, except this overlooked the entire valley. A few early morning joggers moved between the stations, but what drew me in was a man in a pink shirt and straw hat pushing a food cart across the plaza. How charming!

"I will wait here," Alejandro offered before getting out to open my door for me. "Take your time. Today is beautiful!"

"What is he selling?" I pointed at the man. "Atol...?" The words on his cart were too faded for me to make them all out.

"Atol calientito. It's a traditional corn drink."

Steam rose from the man's buggy into the cool air as he sang 'atol calientito!' The beverage perfumed the morning with hints of vanilla and cinnamon.

"You should try it," Alejandro cajoled. "With churros!"

"I will!" I grinned. I already knew I loved golden churros.

I chose a spot on the grass to watch shadows race across the city below. The vendor's melodic calls mingled with bird songs and distant traffic, creating an unexpected symphony. A young couple claimed a patch of grass nearby, spreading out a quilt without any apparent concern for their business clothes. They shared what looked like a homemade breakfast, laughing quietly together. No rushed coffee run, no frantic checking of phones. Just... being. It was beautiful.

My own phone chirped with Alex's daily check-in: *Don't forget to document the luxury indicators in each zone. Building materials, landscaping, security features...*

I reached for the device, then stopped. Instead, I closed my eyes and let the sun warm my face. The atol man's song grew closer, then faded again. I loved it. When I finally stood up, I knew I'd made the right choice about today's plans—to do whatever I wanted in the moment. Next up was Hobbitenango. Forget market research. I was eager to keep following my own curiosity, wherever it might lead. It was exhilarating!

"Ready?" Alejandro asked as I slid back into the car.

"Yes." I smiled. "To the magical village."

THE HOBBITENANGO SIGN loomed against clear skies. Its circular design glowed like a portal to another world. I half-expected a wizard to appear and announce I was about to be enraptured on an unexpected journey.

Alejandro was clearly amused by my wide-eyed expression. The path ahead wound through wild gardens. Each turn promising something new. I felt like a child entering a storybook, that enchanting anticipation of not knowing what comes next but knowing it would be wonderful. I was so excited that I damned near bounced on my toes!

A perfectly round blue door appeared first. And a riot of coral and cream flowers cascaded over its frame set into a hillside. I couldn't resist pushing it open, giggling at how I had to slightly duck to enter. *Creeeak.* The entry squeaked as if it were older than it really was. I knew this was a fake "village" but still. It was so charming.

The view that greeted me on the other side immediately stole my breath. Mountains rolled away in waves of green and blue. Clouds cast shifting shadows across their slopes. It was so astonishingly different from Miami's ocean views. Both were beautiful, but this was remote beauty I had never seen before.

"¡Venga, venga!" A local family waved me over to where they were taking photos with giant butterfly wings made of air plants and moss. The mother insisted on taking my picture, directing me with enthusiastic gestures to spread my arms wide. It was a treat to not worry about looking professional or polished. My sneakers got dirty. My hair wasn't dreamily in place because we'd driven over with the windows down. And my face was make-up free—I wasn't in the mood to put it on this morning. Among the few vendors vying my attention,

I just played along, letting myself feel weightless against the sky. I also bought a hoodie and enjoyed a quaint breakfast overlooking the lush valley. My God. This was heaven.

Stone paths led to more whimsical discoveries between the buildings. A giant hand sculpture emerged from the hillside—I couldn't resist climbing up. The basin sprawled below, making me feel both tiny and infinite at once. Two beautiful women nearby arranged themselves for a photo, but gave up halfway through. They were too captivated by the view to care about documentation.

A flower-draped swing near the edge of the property caught my eye next. As I settled onto its wooden seat, the mountains seemed to sway with me. Red and white blooms danced overhead while my feet traced arcs in the air. I hadn't been on a swing in nearly 30 years! The simple pleasure of it bubbled up in my chest until it escaped as laughter.

"¡Hermosa, no?" An elderly man paused beside me, gesturing to where clouds parted over distant peaks. He wore a woven bracelet that matched his granddaughter's, both of them carrying cups of something that smelled like chocolate and cinnamon.

"Increíble," I agreed.

He smiled and continued on, unhurried, while his granddaughter skipped ahead to what looked like a decorated bear statue.

I stayed on the swing a moment longer, letting the breeze carry away all thoughts of anything I didn't want. This wasn't a place for expectations or impositions. It was simply... joy. Pure, unfiltered joy.

BACK AT THE WESTIN, I sank into a plush armchair by my window. My feet pleasantly ached from exploring Hobbitenango as the sun painted Guatemala City's skyline in shades of amber and rose.

A guitar trio played flamenco-style music in the hotel's courtyard below and the melody drifting up like incense. I closed my eyes and let the music wrap around me. Unfortunately, my phone went off and Alex's face filled the screen.

"Hey," I answered, trying to keep my voice neutral.

"Finally! I've been texting you all day." His tone carried an edge. "I miss you..."

I struggled to say it back. "Mm hm."

"So...how's the market research going? Did you enjoy your hike? I thought for sure you'd send pics of the volcano."

I glanced at my notebook, still blank except for doodles of the Hobbit doors. "It's... enlightening," I managed. "And I ended up not doing the hike. Exhaustion won, so I did something more local."

"Oh really."

I was happy he asked about the adventure even though I didn't take it. Alex knew I loved hiking despite me hardly doing much over the last few years. One of our first dates was to Bill Baggs Cape Florida State Park. Alex being much more of a city boy than nature lover, did not enjoy it, but pushed through it because he knew I loved walking through the grass among wildlife, kayaking and trying to fish just as much as I enjoyed cocktails with him on Biscayne Blvd. "Yeah, I went to a hobbit village."

"A *what*?!"

As expected, he was flummoxed with my choice. But unexpectedly, he did not mock it. I told him all about it with much enthusiasm —I couldn't slow it down if I tried by this point, because the entire trip had just been so unique until now. I was amazed.

"Great! Listen, I've been thinking about your cultural immersion angle," eventually he'd had enough. "What if we did something like what you mentioned in the restaurants at the Jeffrey? Maybe a Miami heritage wing?"

The excitement in his voice made my stomach clench. He was already co-opting my experience, turning it into new project upon my return. Before I could respond, my other line lit up – Dad.

"Alex, can we talk later? My parents are calling."

"Sure, babe. Don't forget to document everything for the board presentation when you get back. Love you!"

"Me too." I switched calls, grateful for the interruption. "Hey, Pop!"

"There's my wandering girl!" My father's voice came through warm and rich. "How's Guatemala treating you?"

"It's amazing." The words tumbled out. "I feel like I've stepped into another world. There's so much culture. Great music. Amazing food...oh, my God, the food! And tomorrow I'm heading to the main place I wanted to see Lake Atitlán!"

"The one you said is world famous?"

"Absolutely."

"Alone?" Mom butted in. Her concern crackled through. "Nyla—"

"No. With a group," I comforted her.

"Okay, good! You know I worry!"

"I know, Mom. That's your job."

"Well, don't let your dinner get cold," Dad said. "But Nyla? I'm proud of you for doing this. I know you're being careful and it sounds like you're really enjoying yourself."

"Thanks, Daddy." My throat tightened. "Love you both."

After hanging up, I opened the door to find room service offering a covered plate that I definitely hadn't ordered. A note sat beside it: "Our chef noticed you enjoyed the pepián at dinner. He insisted you try our rellenitos de plátano. It is a traditional Guatemalan dessert made with plantains and black beans. A sweet ending to match your adventurous spirit. – Carolina, Guest Relations Manager."

Ooh! I loved surprises! I carried the dish to the balcony, where the guitar music had shifted to something slower and contemplative. The dessert's rich aroma mixed with night-blooming jasmine from the courtyard below. Each bite felt like permission to stay in this moment and let Guatemala seep into my bones.

Bloop, bloop! My phone flashed with a text from my sister Kendra: *Girl, I heard you're actually LIVING! Call me before bed – need ALL the details! PS: That engagement ring looked heavy AF in those photos...* ● ●

I laughed out loud, startling a dove from my balcony railing. Trust Kendra to cut straight through the pretense. I would get back to her soon. *Promise,* I told myself. Tonight belonged to sweet plantains and instrumental music. I wanted to enjoy being alone.

I pulled up the lake's location on my phone, tracing the route with my finger. Three volcanoes surrounded the water like ancient guardians. *Sigh.* A primal exhale escaped me. For the first time since landing in Guatemala, I wasn't thinking about Alex, expansion plans, the Jeffrey, or what anyone else wanted. Tomorrow, I would see the water that healed souls – and I'd see it my way.

7

INTO THE BLUE

The call time for the trek to Atitlan was at 5:15 am. The drive was three-hours and wound through mountains that grew more imposing with each turn. This tour was organized by the hotel and there were four others aboard the van: a retired couple from Seattle and two friends from Germany who'd met while back-packing through Central America.

I dozed off and on against the window as the van climbed higher, each curve revealing glimpses of dawn breaking over distant peaks. I'd forgotten to charge my phone overnight, but the dead battery actually felt like freedom. Ever prepared, I had backup power bank, but decided to leave my phone off while it powered up.

"Have you been here before?" The woman from Seattle – Linda or Lisa, I hadn't quite caught it – offered me a piece of banana bread. She'd been baking with locals the day before, she explained.

I was hesitant, never being one to take food from random people. But she wouldn't take multiple "nos" for an answer, and everyone else had indulged. Fuck it. *You took a probiotic and charcoal pill this morning,* my mind rationalized that saying 'yes' was easier than dealing with the fallout. Eventually, I relented, not wanting to be rude. "Mm-hmm." I accepted the bread with a grateful nod. *Damn, this* is *good!* It was still warm from whatever bag she'd had it in, and it was studded with chocolate chips that melted on my tongue.

"Seeee," the others teased. "It's delicious, isn't it?"

I affirmed with a self-conscious grin. It was.

The German backpackers compared notes on hostels, their voices a quiet stream of enthusiasm about someplace called "Free Cerveza." Their casual approach to travel and easy willingness to let plans evolve fascinated me. Four days before, they'd been in El Salvador.

Our tour van rounded another bend, bustled down an unkempt road and suddenly there it was – a sheet of liquid silver cradled by three massive volcanoes. The air left my lungs in a silent gasp. No website, brochure or YouTube video had captured the sheer scale of it.

"Holy shit," one of the Germans whispered.

The reality was both more *and* less than the postcards had promised. Yes, there was stunning natural beauty, but also poverty mixed with progress. Laundry hung from windows above internet cafes. Children in mismatched clothing played games on smartphones. It wasn't the pristine tourist paradise I'd imagined, but somehow that made it more compelling. More real.

Our driver, Manuel, grinned at our reaction in the rearview mirror. "Bienvenido a Lago de Atitlan!" *Welcome to Lake Atitlán!*

We descended into the main village, Panajachel, as the town stirred awake. My senses were heightened, and I noticed everything. An old, dusty, red pickup truck loaded with egg crates navigated the narrow street ahead of us. The driver called out greetings to early risers. Restaurant owners seemed to flag him down to signal their need of dairy for the day.

Manuel pointed out what he called a "chicken bus" – a decommissioned American school bus transformed into something whimsical with chrome details and intensely painted designs in orange, blue and cream.

The town was the most unfiltered place I'd ever seen. Dogs stood sentinel on tin rooftops, while sandal-clad children chased each other past stands being assembled for the day's market.

"Beunos días! Buenos dias!" The greeting seemed to come from all directions at once. I didn't know what which way to look.

"Thirty minutes until the lancha to San Marcos," Manuel announced, parking near a stretch of wooden docks. "Time to explore Panajachel first?"

I followed our group down a stone-paved street lined with vendors. The scent of corn tortillas and something sweet I couldn't identify wafted into the air. A too-thin dog trotted past, pausing to shake morning dew from its dusty fur.

The German backpackers had already wandered ahead, drawn to a narrow alley draped with textiles in every imaginable color. Linda – I'd finally caught her name – touched my arm and pointed toward the water. "Look at those boats!"

The lanchas, as Manuel called them, bobbed gently against weathered docks. Some were simple wooden vessels, others painted in brilliant turquoise and lime green with names like "La Paloma" emblazoned on their sides. Beyond them, the water stretched vast under cotton-candy cloud skies.

I followed a covered walkway, where blue and white streamers fluttered overhead like forgotten festival decorations. Vendors arranged their stalls with practiced efficiency. Textiles here, carved masks there, paintings propped carefully against weathered walls.

"These are hand-woven," a woman told me through Manuel since she didn't speak English. She gestured to a display of scarves. A little girl with dark eyes curiously giggled and peeked out from behind stacks of fabric.

I ran my fingers over the elaborate patterns, admiring the workmanship but moving on. The German backpackers were haggling cheerfully over coffee beans at a nearby stall, while Linda examined traditional blouses. Her husband documented everything with his camera—super touristy, but they were enjoying themselves.

That's when I saw it—a painting tucked between larger, more predictable-looking pieces. It wasn't the typical lake scene that decorated every other shop. No, no, no ...this piece captured something else entirely. It caught the way morning light hit the water, how the clouds wrapped around the volcanoes like sea foam clinging to Caribbean cliffs. But more than that, it captured the dignity of the place. The artist had somehow painted the feeling rather than just the appearance, showing both the tourist veneer and the real life beneath it. It made me think of the Jeffrey's meticulously curated luxury, how we displayed culture without really honoring it. This painting was different. It was honest. And gorgeous. I wanted it.

"Muy bonita, ¿no?" the gallery owner noticed my interest. She moved to take it down, but Manuel called out that our lancha was boarding soon.

"Si, pero. I will return," I promised but could tell she didn't understand the English words. "Regresso?" I guessed. I didn't know how to say it in Spanish and Manuel wasn't so close anymore. In my best miming hand gestures, I told her I'd be back, surprising myself with how much I meant it. The painting stayed with me as we made our way to the water. Waves lapped against wooden planks and boat engines rumbled to life.

As our lancha pulled away from Panajachel's shore, I noticed a woman kneeling at the water's edge, her hands working methodically through a pile of laundry. Tall reeds swayed around her like nature's privacy screen. The scene struck me like lightning. Here was someone carrying out their daily routine while tourists like me snapped photos of her and the volcano. The contrast felt important somehow, though I couldn't quite say why.

Our lancha ride was way too fast, bordering on reckless, but 45 minutes later, we arrived at the village of San Marcos. It was another town across the lake.

"My Lord, I'm glad we made it alive!" another passenger squealed.

Quietly, I thought the same thing. The jaunt was bumpy and splashy, but yes, we'd made it just fine.

San Marcos revealed itself in layers. A rocky path curved upward from the dock. Beautiful bougainvillea plants trickled over garden walls in deep pink cascades. An old dog with a graying snout dozed in a patch of sunlight. It barely lifted its head as our group passed.

I lingered behind as the others followed Manuel. A café tucked into what looked like a converted porch called out to me. Turquoise-painted chairs clustered around wooden tables, while dreamcatchers and macramé plant hangers swayed gently in the breeze. Local art covered the walls. Portraits in bold strokes. Masks that seemed to hold ancient stories. They all arranged against weathered wood and painted palettes in shades of blue.

"You can rejoin us after lunch," Manuel offered, noting my interest. "The nature reserve has a path that leads to a peaceful viewpoint."

Peaceful sounded perfect. The road was dusty and the altitude made breathing a labor, but the view more than made up for it. When I finally found the lookout platform Manuel mentioned, I understood why people came here seeking something deeper. The lake stretched out incredibly blue, framed by branches and vines woven into a natural railing. Below, lanchas traced white paths across the water's surface, tiny as water striders from this height. There were even signs for a trampoline and altar tucked in the trees. The former, I later saw was a wooden plank people used to plunge more than fifty feet into the water below

A burst of laughter drifted up from somewhere below – likely tourists emerging from one of the many "healing sessions" advertised along the path. I hadn't expected so many, especially speaking English, nor the amount of dreadlocked hippies treating the place like their personal enlightenment playground. Something about it made me uncomfortable, though I couldn't articulate why. Maybe it was how they seemed to take without giving back, consuming the culture like they—or *us?*—consumed everything else. Still, their sounds mixed with birdsong and rustling leaves in the thin mountain air as I closed my eyes, thinking about the woman doing laundry by the shore. She was part of this place. Us tourists were just passing through. But unlike others, I found myself wondering what I could offer rather than what I could take.

"Señorita?" Manuel's voice carried up the path. "Would you like to see the Mayan ceremonial sites?"

I opened my eyes, taking one last look at the lake. "Coming," I called back, but took my time descending. Some moments deserved to be savored.

The ceremonial site was more tourist-friendly than I'd expected – a cleared circle with concrete benches arranged in a spiral pattern. Admittedly, I was a little underwhelmed. And suddenly, a wave of unexpected heat washed over me, making my blouse cling uncomfortably. *The Miami heat never hit me like this.* I thought, fanning my face.

"This way back to the lanchas," Manuel gestured after much walking. "It's time to go back to Panajachel and then the City."

My muscles sang their own weary folklore as I navigated the descent, but I couldn't leave Lake Atitlán without that painting. The older woman was still in her shop when I rushed in, breathless...and feeling supremely out of shape. Not good. I'd have to fix that when I got home.

"Hermosa!" She outstretched her hands to me with wide eyes, likely not expecting a tourist to return. When she quoted the price – nearly three times what I'd mentally budgeted – I hesitated only briefly before pulling out my credit card. *This isn't a financially responsible decision.* Swipe. I bought it anyway. The signature in the corner was an elegant scrawl I couldn't quite decipher. Something about those clouds wrapping the volcanoes had captured exactly how I felt: suspended between earth and sky, between what was and what could be.

The sun was already softening toward afternoon as we headed back to Guatemala City. I cradled my wrapped painting, wondering what Alex would say about the spontaneous purchase. I tried not care. In fact, I was happy that was the first time he'd penetrated my mind in hours. Not having a signal meant I could take lots of pictures without seeing constant notifications from him. It was bliss.

Back at the hotel that evening, a call from my mom greeted just after I'd had a quaint dinner alone. "So? Was it everything you dreamed?"

"It's... different," I admitted. "Not as developed as the postcards show. But Mom, there's something about it—"

"Oh, thank goodness!" Her relief was devilishly enthusiastic. "I was worried you'd get caught up in some fantasy. Now you can come home and focus on the wedding and—"

"No, Mom, you don't understand," I cut in. It was just her on the line this time. "It's not perfect, but it's genuine. There's so much potential here. The way people live, how they blend tradition with progress..." I trailed off, realizing she would never understand how the lake's imperfect beauty had shifted something inside me. I still felt tingles when I thought about it.

The way a luxury retreat ran beside a simple fishing village, ancient traditions mixing with modern life. The contradictions had me in a chokehold and I didn't want to be released. It was like the water itself, everything here flowed together in ways that made sense, even if they didn't look flawless on Instagram and TikTok videos. Hell, it all made me wonder if I'd been chasing the wrong kind of perfection all along. I glanced at my engagement ring, then back at the painting. One represented a life arranged for display, the other showed beauty in all its messy reality. For the first time, I knew which one felt more "right." The realization settled in me like lake water finding its level after a storm. Inevitable. Clarifying. And strangely calming in its turbulence.

8

CARRY-ON REQUIREMENTS

The painting lay across my hotel bed with morning light catching its oils in ways that made the lake ripple. Twenty-four by thirty-six inches of truth I somehow had to get home. The concierge found me a sturdy carrying tube but getting it in felt like surgery—one wrong move and I could damage everything that mattered.

"Careful, careful," I whispered, easing the canvas in while keeping it aligned. My expensive clothes lay scattered around the room as casualties of my repacking strategy. Most would have to go in my checked bag. The painting tube would take up most of my carry-on allowance, but I didn't trust baggage handlers with something this precious.

A streak of cobalt blue paint smeared across my white blouse as I secured the tube's cap. That would have once sent me into a panic but now, I just dabbed at it with a hotel washcloth and smiled. It wasn't a big deal. I was only going home...a little different than I had left.

~

MIAMI INTERNATIONAL'S arrivals hall hit differently upon my return. The medley of languages. The colors. The comings and goings of everyone was palpable. I adjusted my grip on the painting tube, scanning for the exit signs. And that's when I saw him—not a driver holding a sign with my name. Nope. Alex.

He stood by the information desk looking like he'd stepped out of the Spring collection of a fashion magazine—business casual edition. A leather portfolio was tucked under one arm. Even from this distance, I could see his jaw was tight – the way it got when things weren't proceeding according to his plan.

"There's my wandering woman!" His voice carried across the terminal as he strode toward me. "I tracked your flight, and thought I'd surprise you. Welcome home!"

Home. Coming out of his mouth, the word ricocheted in my head like a stray bullet.

Alex's kiss landed somewhere between my cheek and ear as I tried to manage both my carry-on and the awkward tube. His eyes fixed on it. "What's that? And let me get your luggage, babe."

"Just a little something I found." I tried to keep my tone light. I had no time to think.

"It must be special if you carried it yourself." He reached for it, but I stepped back.

"It is." I noticed the portfolio he carried. "What's *that*?"

His face brightened. "Engagement party samples! I've been working with that planner you liked, the one who did the Roberts wedding?"

I had no idea who he was talking about.

"Since you weren't exactly available for consultation..." He let the words hang. "I thought we could look at venues over dinner. Get you back into the swing of things."

The painting tube suddenly felt heavier. I looked at Alex...really looked at him. Had he always been this eager to plan my life, and if so, how was I just now noticing?

"But first, let's get you home." His hand found the small of my back, guiding me toward the exit. "The car's right outside."

Now, his hand felt like it was marking territory rather than offering support. I shifted the art tube to put some space between us, pretending to adjust my bag.

"Thanks, but I can get my checked bag first—"

"Already taken care of." His smile was delighted. "I had Marco send someone, so we don't have to wait. It'll be delivered to the house."

This can't be real.

"You must be exhausted from your connecting flights."

I was tired, but not from the flights. From the realization that every choice, every movement, had been anticipated and managed. Even my absence had been choreographed.

The sunrays thudded into us as the automatic doors whooshed open. Alex's BMW idled illegally in the pickup lane, hazard lights blinking. A police officer approached but stopped short when Alex raised a hand in greeting. They knew each other. Of course they did.

"Wanna do takeout tonight? I'd love to hear more about your trip," he announced as we reached the car. He opened the trunk for my carry-on but frowned when I clutched the painting tube closer. "You want that in the backseat?"

"Yes." It came out sharp.

His eyebrows rose slightly, but he recovered quickly. "Whatever you want, babe." Alex helped me into the passenger, then slid behind the wheel. The portfolio of engagement party options bounced between us like a question no one wanted to ask.

As we pulled away from the airport, Alex's hand found my knee. The gesture was familiar, possessive. The ring on my finger caught the sunlight, sending tiny prisms dancing across the dashboard. I watched them scatter and thought of Lake Atitlán, where light played on water without anyone trying to control its pattern.

"So," Alex's voice cut through my thoughts. "Was it beautiful? The lake?"

"Life changing," I answered honestly.

"Wow...well, I'm glad you got to see it."

The car was quiet. No follow-up questions about why it was life changing or how—or about how I felt. Just...Dead...Space. Neither of us knew what to say next.

~

"SOMETHING IS OFF," I noted when I walked into my office the next day. With a piece of Guatemala under my arms—ready and waiting to be hung on a wall, I discerned my desk had been "organized." Files were relocated. The computer screen showed a calendar already populated with Charlotte meetings. And there was a sticky note in Marco's handwriting: "Cultural Integration Program Review – 10AM."

My private space had been invaded. Everything looked perfect, pristine, productive. And completely wrong. *Bzzz.* My phone jerked with a message from Alex. *Moved the 10AM to the main conference room. Investors want to hear about the Charlotte cultural angle first-hand.*

I stared at the message, remembering how the lake's surface had rippled under morning light. How everything there moved according to its own natural rhythms. I hadn't even had time to process what I might bring to the Miami location of the Jeffrey let alone the unbuilt Charlotte location. I rest the painting against a wall, thinking.

My shoulders tensed at the sight of emails popping up on my laptop—detailed notes about the Charlotte market, proposed budgets, an architectural preview. Everything was ready for my "input." The quotes around Cultural Integration Program made it clear – they'd already decided what my trip meant. But they had missed the point entirely. Guatemala wasn't about expanding the Jeffrey's brand. It was about discovering mine. At least to me.

The conference room doors were open when I arrived and voices spilled into the hallway. I caught snippets of Marco's presentation: "...authentic experiences..." "...cultural immersion..." "...luxury market penetration..."

He stood at the head of the table—my usual spot—gesturing at a PowerPoint. I felt sick watching them reduce my transformative experience to a marketing strategy. Not a single image captured the real magic of the place. The investors nodded along, taking notes.

Alex's face lit up when he saw me. "Impeccable timing! Marco's just walking us through the preliminary cultural program framework. Your experiences will add the necessary personal touch.

Visions of the pickup truck full of eggs, the dusty dogs, the Maya woman washing clothes in the lake...*no, no, no*. This isn't right. They wanted me to validate their sanitized version of Guatemala, to help them package and sell an "authentic experience" that was anything but authentic.

I brought my left fist to my lips, feeling the ring's platinum groove teeth marks into my skin. Like braces. Like a bridle. Nothing natural belonged in this room of sharp angles and shareholder expectations.

"I can't."

The room stilled. Marco's laser pointer blinked out.

"I won't."

Alex looked at me with utter shock, horror and disgust. His eyes bulged and nostrils flared.

"I need space. Excuse me." I walked out before I could be challenged, rushing outside for oxygen.

"Ms. Baines!" It was Clive, but I kept walking...not even sure where to. He called out again.

I sank onto a courtyard bench without words. It was hot and the air felt like soup. After the thin mountain air of Guatemala, the humidity drowned me.

"They don't understand," I said finally, Clive had followed me.

He didn't say a word, just listened to me babble about things he likely knew nothing about.

My phone chirped. Alex: *Where are you? We're all waiting.*

Another message on the relay. Marco: *I can finish the presentation if you need time to collect yourself.*

I didn't need any more help. I didn't want to make any more decisions about the hotel.

"Ms. Baines," Clive's voice was gentle. "Sometimes we see things different when we step away, you know? I mean, really tek some time. Your vacation—"

"Was not a vacation at all."

He listened, clasping his red cap between his knees. Clive looked ahead but kept his ears open for me. I didn't have much more to say but appreciated the soft silence between us. Standing, I smoothed my skirt. "Thanks, Clive."

The hotel corridors felt different when I went back inside. Alex's voice drifted from my office "...Yeah, this would look perfect in the Charlotte lobby. Really showcase our commitment to—"

"No." The word came out sharp as broken glass.

Alex turned from where he stood. "I beg your pardon?"

"That is not hotel property. It's mine. And I said no. It will not go to Charlotte."

"Jesus Christ, Nyla." His façade cracked. "What is wrong with you lately? I'm trying to help your career! Trying to expand our vision. Marco's been covering your responsibilities while you were off playing tourist at the *worst* fucking time—"

"Playing tourist?" My laugh felt dangerous. "That's rich, coming from someone who turned my vacation into another business takeover."

He stalked toward me, voice lowered and eyes intense. "I've given you everything. This job. Our home. A future! And you're acting like some god-damned teenager because what – I made sure you were safe? Because I kept things running while you took your little sabbatical?"

I yanked open my desk drawer, pulled out the memos. "You mean while you and Marco hollowed out my role? While you tracked my flights? While you turned my vacation into another expansion strategy?"

"Of course I did! Someone had to think about the big picture while you were taking photos of lakes and buying tourist trap art!"

The ring felt like ice on my finger. "Well, here's a picture for you." I slid it off, placed it on the desk between us. "The engagement is off."

His face darkened. "Wait. What?" Alex was stunned. "What are you talking about? You're just overwhelmed. Coming back to work too soon—"

"I'm talking about control, Alex. I'm done with it."

"Whoa, whoa, whoa, Nyla! You're being ridiculous. Where is this even coming from?" He had the nerve to look genuinely perplexed. "What, do you think you found yourself on some solo trip? You can't leave me!"

"Yes, I can." I walked away, tears on the brink.

"Ha! You really think you can do better on your own?" Alex laughed like a hyena with a fresh kill. "You're just going to end up right back where you started—alone, basic, and lost."

Pain. White hot pain. It surged through me as I reached the doorway. "We're done."

Marco, Clive, Ana, and several others were conveniently in the hallway as I stormed past. The investors had already left by then. Back outside, the sun hit like a spotlight, but I didn't flinch. My phone tremored. Voices called from behind me. And my mind was a tornado of thoughts. *What have I done? Where is this going? How will I make it?* Alex had a way of twisting things, making me doubt myself until I couldn't tell which way was up. But I didn't look back or in my bag. Instead, I watched a flock of ibises strut across the parking lot as I made my way to my car. Holy shit.

9

THE PRICE OF NO

"The Westin sent over their final invoice," Marco announced from my doorway, his usual warmth replaced by neutrality. "I took the liberty of processing it already."

Through everything, I'd forgotten that my so-called vacation was technically a company expense. I nodded, not trusting my voice. Good. *Now, get the fuck out of here, traitor.*

Marco lingered before turning away without his usual "¡Hasta luego!"

The morning crawled by in a haze of averted gazes and hushed conversations that died when I approached. Even Ana, who'd often brought me coffee, suddenly had urgent business elsewhere when I entered the break room. I poured my own brew, noting how the simple act felt like a demotion. But I couldn't do anything. While I was ready to take a break from Alex, I wasn't prepared with a replacement job. I hadn't thought that far ahead.

I felt like I walked on eggshells the evening before. This morning for our top-of-the-day huddle, Alex commanded the head of the table while I sat between Trevor from Security and one of our newer front desk agents. The message was clear: I was just another employee now. It hurt. Real bad. After all I had done.

"Let's review today's arrivals," Alex began. Marco handed out the room assignments, which was my job, until today. It burned, but I swallowed the flames, my nostrils exhaling the afterburn. The staff listened as Alex detailed the morning's priorities, transforming our routine procedures into executive mandates.

I sat quietly. Untethered. Each minute scorched away my authority. But the absence of my engagement ring grinned like a conspirator. Sure, I hadn't mapped out the escape route, but I'd found freedom in the freefall.

By afternoon, the hotel's rhythm had decidedly rewritten its loyalties. Staff who built their careers with my guidance now scurried to Marco or Alex. By late afternoon, I was over everything—guests and all.

The drive home felt longer than usual. Alex had texted that he was "working late," which meant I had a brief window of peace in our shared space. My own home had become enemy territory. It was edgy, with bursts of quarrels followed by gulfs of self-imposed muzzles to "keep the peace" until I "came to my senses."

My chest ached at the sight of his car missing from the driveway. Two years of morning kisses and shared dreams don't just evaporate because you finally see the cage they came in. Part of me still wanted to talk to him and hear the voice that used to make everything feel possible. The one that once whispered plans of our future over Sunday morning coffee and fresh fruit. The memory of his hands cupping my face, his smile when I mastered a new skill at work, the way he'd dance with me in the kitchen – all these moments now felt tainted, and they hurt to remember. The good times weren't lies. They just came with invisible strings I hadn't wanted to see. Damn it.

I hadn't told my parents about the broken engagement yet. My mom's number lit up my phone twice today, but I let it ring. I wasn't ready. She'd hear a strain in my voice and then, I'd have to explain everything. Dad would try to fix it. They would ask questions I didn't have answers to, like how I could still miss someone I needed to escape.

Kendra's last message still sat unanswered: *Girl, I heard you're actu-*

ally LIVING! Call me before bed -- need ALL the details! My sister would understand. She'd probably even cheer. But calling her meant making this real, and I wasn't sure I was ready for that level of real yet. Shit.

I parked in the driveway instead of the garage, leaving myself an exit. Inside, I moved through our rooms like a ghost. His cologne lingered in a closet we shared, and my throat closed up at the scent. Every photo of us felt like evidence of something that perished while we weren't watching. Or was it that innocent? I didn't know if I was inventing more genuinely shared joy than was there or not. The Alex in those frames smiled without agenda, loved without conditions—or did he? I was unsure.

White designer sheets mocked me from our bed. I grabbed a blanket and retreated to the guest room, the same one I'd hidden in before Guatemala. Before everything changed. My phone buzzed again – Mom. I stared at her photo until the screen went dark.

Tomorrow. I'd tell them tomorrow.

Tonight, I just needed to breathe through the paradox of missing someone who was both my best memory and greatest regret.

AT 5:00 the next morning, I arrived at the Jeffrey before the sun rose. I pulled into a regular employee space and steeled myself for the day. My laptop warmed on my thighs when I powered it up from my car instead of going inside. Instantly, my work e-mail gave me trouble. *Account access restricted. Please contact system administrator.*

System administrator. As if Alex were just another IT guy and not the man who used to trace constellations on my skin. I rolled my eyes at his pettiness. "Fuck it," I accepted my new role, knowing he could not outwit me.

I tried a few more things on my computer but everything required permission. What the fuck? Were we really doing this? Ugh! I closed my eyes and exhaled. Instantly, colorful reveries of Lake Atitlán filled the darkness behind my eyelids. Underdeveloped or not, I missed that place. Atitlan was where decisions seemed to flow as naturally as the water lapping against wooden docks.

A notification dinged: *Meeting request from Alex Jones - Priority: Urgent.*

Just days before, I'd watched a woman in Guatemala make business decisions over coffee, no committees required. Now here I sat, needing approval to order new guest soaps.

My phone lit up with a video call from Kendra. My heart lurched. It was time to stop dodging her.

"Nyla, what the hell? Why are you ghosting me, sis?" Her voice was drenched with concern. A bit of annoyance, too. I deserved it.

"I've been..." *What? Trapped? Lost?* "...busy."

"Mmhmm." Her eyes locked on mine and her voice carried years of sisterly skepticism. "Too busy to tell me why you're sitting in the Jeffrey's parking lot instead of running your morning meeting?" She placed a hand over her lips, red nails glistening against her light brown skin.

I whipped around, scanning the lot. "How did you—"

"Find My iPhone, sis. You never turned it off after I helped you track your phone at Ultra."

Of course. Kendra the corporate lawyer and professional sister never missed a detail. Not even the app not showing sneakers to indicate me walking around.

"The engagement is off," I said finally. "And I think I'm about to lose my job."

The line went quiet. Then: "I'll grab breakfast. Meet me at that Cuban place by your old apartment? The one with the good tostones?"

"I can't just—"

"Yes, you can. Text Alex you're taking a sick day. You sound terrible, by the way. Very hoarse." Her tone shifted to mock concern. "Probably shouldn't risk spreading anything to the guests," she winked, her beautiful lashes seeming to sweep in slow motion.

A laugh bubbled up, surprising me. Damn, when was the last time we shared a laugh?

"Thirty minutes," she said. "And Nyla? I'm proud of you. But we can talk about that in a bit."

I stared at my phone after she hung up. Through the windshield, the Jeffrey loomed like a castle I'd helped build but couldn't stand living in anymore. My fingers moved automatically: *Not feeling well. Taking sick day. Will update later.*

Send.

Guilt. Lots of it. The feeling rained over me in a cold rush. I hated to do that to my staff. My pulse quickened, and tears threatened again. My life was a tattered mess, and a part of me taunted that I had no idea what I was doing.

Just as I was reached for the ignition, a soft tap on my window made me jump. It was Marco.

After a moment's hesitation, I lowered the window halfway. "Yes?"

"Nyla," he began quietly. "I saw your out-of-office notification." He glanced toward the hotel, then back. "Listen, about everything—I need to explain."

"Marco, I don't want to hear—"

"Please." The desperation in his voice stopped me. "My mother... she had this little shop in our town near Havana. Good business, stable life. But she wanted more. She believed she could build something bigger in Cancún. Tourism was booming there, she said. She sold everything, borrowed money she couldn't repay." His shoulders hunched. "When it failed, we lost our home. Had to start over here with nothing."

Blank stare. *Why was he telling me this?*

"It's just...jefa, I watched you looking at those Guatemala pictures, planning a vacation—to you, but I already knew it would be more once you saw a different kind of paradise. Through stressed and overworked eyes, I saw that you might begin dreaming. And all I could think about was my mom. How alive she looked planning her dream." His voice cracked. "And how destroyed she was when it crashed. I thought—I really thought—I was protecting you from that. A stable partnership, a clear future..." He trailed off, the weight of his choices visible in his posture.

"So, you spied on me? And reported everything to Alex?" I couldn't stop them. Tears crawled out of my eyes, and they stung so badly I squeezed my eyes shut.

"Sí, pero lo siento!" *Yes, but I'm sorry!* Marco's voice was barely audible, but his eyes said it all. "I saw how you lit up researching Lake Atitlán. The same way mi Mamá glowed talking about Cancún. I thought..." He gulped. "I believed if I helped Alex keep you focused on what was stable, what was sure...that..."

"I just wanted a vacation, Marco. My God..." My voice cracked. "Just a week to breathe. To rest. To not answer to anyone and do what *I* wanted to do. Just. For. A. Few. Fucking. Days!" I'd never cursed at him.

"I know that now!" He shifted. "But fear makes you see ghosts everywhere. It makes you hurt people trying to protect them from shadows."

I wiped my eyes, anger and understanding warring in my chest. "You can't protect people from their own choices."

"No." He lowered his eyes. "I learned that too late. I was wrong, Nyla. I apologize."

Warmth fell over us. The sunrise painted the Jeffrey's windows gold behind him. My phone buzzed again—Kendra wondering where I was.

"I have to go."

He nodded, stepping back. "Nyla, for what it's worth... I hope you find what you're looking for. Even if it's not what any of us thought you should want."

I drove away without responding, watching him shrink in my rearview mirror. My hands were steady on the wheel, but my mind spun with the realization that sometimes the smallest desires could reveal the largest truths about the space you're given to exist.

Kendra was waiting. And for the first time, I had words for everything I hadn't known I needed to say.

10

BLOOD AND BALANCE

Kendra sat waiting at Abuela's, her slim frame draped in a charcoal suit. "Girl!" She rose the moment I neared the table. Hugs. I held longer than I normally ever would, sniffling.

"Big sis?" she whispered.

I couldn't answer. I just held on. Eyes closed. Breathing jagged. Nearly dropping my purse.

"Oh my...Nyla," she gently pulled back and looked directly into my eyes. "Hey, hey..." Kendra opened the space between us while still holding my hand. "It's okay. Whatever it is...it's okay." She nodded toward the table where her café con leche sat half-drank.

I slid into the booth across from her. "I'm sorry," I confessed. "I avoided you for too long."

"Why, Nyla?" Her face wrinkled in confusion.

A huff escaped me as I told her everything. From the engagement to my trip, to the fallout, to sitting in my car outside the Jeffrey instead of going in. I shared how Marco had lovingly betrayed me. How Alex unofficially had scraped out my role and how I'd given back the ring and was sleeping in the guest room of a house that suddenly felt like a museum of mistakes.

"I couldn't tell you before because...honestly, I didn't even know anything was wrong," I stared into the coffee she'd ordered for me, mindlessly watching the steam curl up. "And then, I realized saying it out loud meant admitting I'd let someone else design my life. You tried to warn me, didn't you? At your partnership celebration?"

"Huh?"

She didn't remember. I stretched my neck, hearing several pops.

"Oh....that comment about building your own legacy?" Kendra's fingers tapped the table. "I wasn't just talking about you, sis. But yeah, I felt it happening. At the same time, I didn't want to get in your business, especially without you asking me for my opinion. Plus, I never dreamed it could get this bad. Just thought he was annoying as shit – always trying to show everyone how together his life and business were. Ugh."

Her comment shouldn't have been funny, but it got a broken smile at me. We kept talking, and eventually, I felt better. When I mentioned having to transfer my last direct deposit to cover the Westin bill that turned out to *not* be covered, Kendra's whole demeanor shifted. Her lawyer face slipped on like armor and she was in protection mode.

"Start with the money," she said, cutting straight through business. "Always start with the money."

"What?"

"Bank accounts, investments, retirement funds – tell me everything is separate." When I didn't answer immediately, she set down her spoon. "Nyla. Please tell me you kept your finances separate."

Shame. Its bitter taste rose up like bile because I did *not* retain my independence. Foolish. *Oh my God.* Fear rattled my bones.

"Nyla." Kendra's voice dropped low, serious. "How tied together are we talking?"

"Everything." My legs bounced with nerves under the table. "Joint accounts, investment portfolio—"

Kendra's phone chimed loudly. She glanced at it and muttered a curse. "My judge moved up my hearing. Shit. I've got thirty minutes to get to the courthouse." She was already gathering her things. "Listen, I'm in depositions all day but come over tonight. We'll figure this out."

"Ken—"

"No excuses." She squeezed my shoulder as she passed. "And Nyla? Call me if you need anything before then." A kiss on the cheek and she was gone.

WHEN I GOT HOME, dozens of roses filled the kitchen island. Their scent overwhelmed me. A card nestled among the innocent blooms: *I'm sorry. Let's talk when I get back from Charlotte tonight. -A*

I stood there, staring at Alex's handwriting. The florist didn't write the note, he did. The gesture made me uneasy. My fingers brushed the velvety petals. White roses. Like our first date, when he'd shown up at the restaurant with a single stem and a self-deprecating grin about being "kind of traditional." God, he was so handsome with those blue eyes, brown skin, and killer smile. I couldn't find a thing wrong with him between his dashing style, intellectual conversation and silly wit.

I put the roses in water before moving through the house, discovering more peace offerings. My favorite Cuban coffee brand—the one you could only get from a tiny shop in Little Havana—sat by the coffee maker. Alex hated going to that neighborhood. And there, on the living room mantel, a new frame held a candid shot from our Atlanta trip. I was laughing at something off-camera, caught in a rare unguarded moment at the Porsche driving experience. Alex had been ecstatic the entire time. Fuck...the memories...

Don't fall for it. My gut sounded an alarm. *Don't fucking fall for it, Nyla!* Alex was dangerous. Little by little, it was still sinking in how his thoughtfulness was laced with manipulation. He remembered details. He knew what would trigger me. He knew everything.

Buzz. My phone went off. *Family dinner TONIGHT. Non-negotiable. 8pm sharp. Mom.*

"Shit." Kendra must have said something, forcing me to stop hiding. The realization immediately angered me, but I quickly dialed the feeling down. I knew she did it to help me. Damn it. There goes that sentiment again. I despised it but knew in this case it wasn't about control or manipulation. It was about support. *Okay.* I typed back. I couldn't hide forever. Plus, telling them in person was better than letting them hear anything else from Kendra, I told myself.

The roses watched as I changed clothes, their pearly petals already starting to brown at the edges. I left them there, beautiful and dying.

THE DRIVE to my parent's place in Miramar felt endless. Past strip malls and gated communities, muscle memory guided me through familiar turns until I reached their street. Motion-sensor lights clicked on as I pulled into their driveway, illuminating my mom's prized hibiscus bushes. Through the kitchen window, I could see Kendra already inside. She was probably helping Pop with dinner.

"There you are young lady!"

Hell. This already felt like a 'come to Jesus moment.' My mom's voice carried down the walkway. Her silver braids caught the porch light as she stood in the doorway. "Are you losing weight?" she quizzed before I'd even reached the steps.

"Regina, please don't do that!" Dad called from inside. The smell of grilled snapper and plantains wafted out—comfort food for uncomfortable conversations.

I found Kendra in the kitchen, chopping mangos. She was always his sous chef. Her eyes met mine over the fruit. *Sorry,* they seemed to say, but *you've got this.*

"So," Mom bustled in behind me. "Have you set a date yet? Because I was thinking spring would be perfect. The weather, the flowers—" She paused, finally registering my expression. "Nyla?"

Maybe Kendra hadn't told her anything specific. I had no idea what to think, say, or do anymore. Heck, I never thought I'd be someone who needed an intervention, but I felt like I was at the start of one. My world began spinning again. Nerves.

"The engagement is off, Mama."

She gasped. My father spun around like a soldier snapping to attention. The mango knife's rhythm stuttered then resumed softly. Kendra kept chopping, but I knew she was listening.

"What do you mean 'off'?" My mother's voice rose half an octave. "Did you have a fight? Because couples fight, Nyla. That's normal! Your father and I—"

"It's more than a fight." The words came easier now, practiced from my morning with Kendra. "Much more. And I gave the ring back."

"Really—"

"You did *what*?" She sank into a kitchen chair.

My parents' words collided.

"But...but everything was perfect! The hotel, the expansion plans, the—"

"That's just it, Mama. It looked like that because that's what Alex needed it to be. What everyone needed it to be." I glanced at Kendra, drawing strength from her presence.

"What's that supposed to mean, Nyla?" My father jumped in.

"It means most of my life is a lie and I didn't even realize it until now. And I don't want to pretend I'm happy living like this anymore." My voice cracked but held. "I'm afraid," The words broke something in me and a rush of tears poured from my eyes. "I don't want to be managed. I want to be loved."

"Managed? I thought that man adored you! Look at everything he's given you—"

"Mom!" Kendra came to my defense.

"Girls, come sit down," my father instructed.

"Yes, Daddy." Suddenly, I felt ten years old again. Head down, I followed them to the living room and explained... "Everything he's given me comes with conditions, Mama. The job, the house, even the ring..." I confessed all the details I could, feeling stronger with each admission.

"But are you sure, baby?" She asked, still unable to not see Alex as a prince. "I just don't want you to throw your future away. Look at how much I was able to grow and build with the help of your father. A good man—"

"If everything Nyla said tonight is true then all she's throwing away is the trash!" Dad was livid. "And he could never be compared to me or any other good man! Wait until I see that boy again!" He stood up. Paced. Rubbed his bald head. Rubbed his temples in shock and exasperation.

"I'm choosing myself," I slipped in, wanting her to hear me. "I need to be independent."

"Choosing yourself?" Mother threw up her hands. "Over what— security? Success? A good man who wants to give you everything? Independence?"

"Mom!" She clearly wasn't listening to me.

"You think I don't understand wanting independence? Girl, I wrote the book on it. But there's a difference between independence and isolation. Your father and I built our careers together. When he started his accounting practice, I graded papers at his office on weekends. When I was studying for my doctorate, he took care of everything else. That's what a real partnership looks like." She was on a roll. "Wait, wait, wait! I want to know! Is this about that trip? Did something happen in Guatemala? Because you've been different ever since—"

"Everything happened in Guatemala." A force buoyed my voice. "I finally had time and space to dissect my life. To listen to my own voice. To connect the dots."

"What dots?" My mother pressed. She barely let me speak. "Baby, I'm not saying stay if you're unhappy. I'm saying be sure you're not throwing away a partnership because you think you have to do everything alone. That's not strength – that's pride. Tell him to back off at work if he's piling too much on, but don't sabotage your future." She looked directly into my eyes, her own softening.

"I'm not, Mama," I whispered. "There's just…" I exhaled and decided to reveal details I'd initially held back. About how I had no say in almost anything. And about my passport…the police station, the posters I saw.

"Leave that man tonight," my father said.

Mom's hand flew to her mouth. "I...I didn't..." She came over to me, took my hand and apologized. She cried, realizing that full picture now. "Baby, why didn't you tell us sooner?"

"Because I needed to be sure. Not just about Alex, but about me." I squeezed her hand but didn't let her pull me closer. "And I need to handle this my way.

"You'll stay here," she started, already planning. "We'll help you—"

"I'm staying with Kendra."

"But—"

"She needs space," Dad said quietly. "To stand on her own feet."

"I do have a spare room," Kendra commented. "And good security. Plus..." She shot me a knowing look. "There will be no one else trying to fix things for her."

My mother flinched at that, but didn't argue. The silence stretched until Dad cleared his throat.

"The fish really is getting cold."

We ate. Not the celebration dinner Mom had probably imagined, but something more important—my first family meal that felt like truth. My mouth was no longer swallowing words, I was not hiding, but being myself again. Even if I wasn't quite sure who that was yet.

When I gathered my things to go home later, my father stopped me cold.

"I'm going with you." His voice carried the same steady authority. He was already reaching for his keys.

"I'll be fine, Daddy," I told him.

"Lord have mercy, you are not going anywhere alone!" My mom's words tumbled out like spilled dominoes.

"I think I need to do this myself." I confirmed. My voice emerged softer than intended, but it stilled them both.

Kendra set down her wine glass. "Let her go, Daddy." She caught my eye. "I've watched enough power plays in my boardroom to know one thing..." She smiled at me, shining belief in me. "The smoothest exit is the one you orchestrate yourself."

"I'm nervous about this now that I know more about him, Nyla. How will you face him alone? You don't have to. Let your father—" Mama's braids swayed as she shook her head. Her fingers twisted her wedding band – a nervous habit I'd seen a thousand times.

"Nyla?" My dad glanced at me, waiting for my decision.

"Pop, I need to do this. He won't hurt me." I hoped I were right... the thought hadn't occurred until the words slipped from my lips. Alex was a lot of things, but a physical abuser wasn't one of them. I believed that with my soul the more I thought about it.

Kendra stood, car keys already in hand. "I'll shadow you, sis. He won't even know I'm there."

The plan settled something roiling in my chest. Trust Kendra to know exactly what I needed – backup without rescue, support without surrender.

"Twenty minutes," I said, meeting my father's eyes. "That's all I need."

LIGHT from our house bled into Miami's ink-black sky. Alex's silhouette filled our doorway before I could get within steps of it.

"Jesus, I've been worried sick." His voice cracked perfectly. "Why wouldn't you answer your phone? And your parents – God, babe, what did you tell them?"

"The truth." I moved past him and the dying roses.

"Whatever you think happened with the passport, with work—" He reached for me. "I was trying to protect you. You must know that. I'm not a monster, Nyla! I'm sorry!"

"Don't."

"Please." His fingers grazed my arm. "Baby...talk to me! We make a great couple, babe. A power couple, Nyla. Not whatever story you have created in your head."

I headed for the stairs. His footsteps followed, too close.

"Eighteen more minutes," I glanced at my watch before pulling my overnight bag from the closet. "I'm getting what I need tonight. Kendra will help with the rest later."

"Oh, fuck no! Kendra?" Ice crystallized into his tone. "So that's where this is coming from? Your sister who can't keep a man longer than her latest case?"

Don't take the bait. I grabbed my toiletries, my hands steady. One drawer. Then another. *Do not argue with him.*

"Baby, stop. Just – look at me. I'm begging...look at me."

I did. His eyes shone with tears that could've been real.

"We built this. Together. Everything you are, everything you've become—"

"You think you created me," I mumbled.

His perfect face hardened. "I did! Before the Jeffrey, you were just another front desk greeter with community college dreams. I made you General Manager. I gave you a future."

Each word struck true, but I kept packing. Birth certificate. Various clothes. Empty journals that I should have been writing in.

"You'll come crawling back." His mask fell completely. "When your sister gets tired of playing savior. When you realize you can't hack it alone. When you miss winning with me—"

"Goodbye, Alex."

"You're not even gonna make it a month without me," he spoke through gritted teeth. "Mark my words."

I walked out. The night air was now streaked with rain.

Behind me, Alex's voice carried one last time: "I made you, Nyla. Remember that when you're trying to remake yourself."

I didn't turn around. The girl he'd "made" was already gone, leaving only the woman I'd always been, finally awake and walking away.

11

STRATEGIC DEFAULTS

Kendra's condo was an odd hybrid of fastidiousness and whimsy. The minimalist chrome and glass surfaces gleamed like a courtroom exhibit, while her balcony flaunted a jungle of mismatched planters filled with bright flowers, as if she'd tried—and happily failed—to keep her inner rebel in check. The walls held streamlined shelving units arranged with geometric shapes, but the items on them told a different story: a vintage gavel repurposed as a paperweight, a collection of brightly colored origami cranes, and a row of fat, cozy mystery novels with lurid covers. Beneath the coffee table, a heap of legal briefs jostled for space with a half-assembled jigsaw puzzle of Frida Kahlo's "Self-Portrait with Thorn Necklace and Hummingbird."

I sat cross-legged on Kendra's guest bed, surrounded by printouts of my work emails and bank statements. It was a lot. I felt couched between her detailed styling and hasty accommodation. A sleek desk lamp cast harsh light over my scattered papers, while a throw pillow embroidered with Ruth Bader Ginsburg's face offered unexpected comfort against my back. My few rescued belongings from Alex's house barely filled a corner.

"Found anything useful?" Kendra appeared. Clad in yoga pants and an old University of Miami t-shirt, she clutched two takeout containers. Her after hours look reminded me of the kid sister who once helped me sneak out to walk the beach at night with my high school crush.

"Just more proof that I was an idiot." I held up a performance review from last year. "'Exemplary attention to detail.' 'Natural leadership abilities.' 'Cornerstone of the Jeffrey's success.'" All Alex's words.

"That's actually perfect." Kendra settled beside me, passing over pad Thai. "Documentation of your value to the company strengthens our position."

"Our position for what?"

"Getting you out without losing everything." She twirled noodles around her fork with practiced precision. "Ever heard of FMLA?"

"Family Medical Leave Act? That's for like, having babies and stuff, right?"

"Or stress. Anxiety. Depression." Her eyes met mine. "Things that might arise from, oh, I don't know... discovering your fiancé has been systematically controlling your career and personal life?"

I pushed my food around. "But I can't afford unpaid leave, sis."

"It might be paid if you have a doctor certify the condition. Which, given everything, shouldn't be hard."

"Hm. But is it instant? What if there's a lag? I mean, I'll go to the ATM in the morning to take out as much cash as I can since I don't have another account to transfer anything into right now..."

Kendra hesitated. "I'd loan you money to bridge the gap, but..."

"But what?"

"Let's just say student loans from law school are a bitch, and big law firms aren't as lucrative at the junior partner level as people think." She gave a hollow laugh. "That view out there," she pointed to the skyline, "is eating half my monthly income. Chile, I'm one bad month away from moving back in with Mama and Daddy myself."

"I had no idea."

"And neither do they, so don't say anything." She laughed

nervously. "Plus, that's my point." Kendra shrugged. "We all maintain some kind of illusion. Don't be so hard on yourself, Nyla."

We continued chatting and planning my escape. By midnight, my path seemed clear: doctor's appointment first thing, then work, acting as normal as possible while setting the wheels in motion. Thanks to Kendra's connection with a college friend who'd become a psychiatrist, I landed an emergency appointment before work.

Dr. Shepherd took one look at my shaking hands and the dark circles under my eyes and said what I'd been afraid to admit: I was having an acute stress response. "Classic symptoms of workplace trauma and emotional abuse," she wrote in his notes. The words felt both damning and validating.

I looked down. Ashamed.

"Take care of yourself, Nyla," Dr. Shepherd handed me a signed note with neat handwriting. "And please come back if you need to," her voice was sturdy but kind. I folded the paper carefully and tucked it into my bag. Gratitude and dread pooled in my chest. *Who* was *I*?

The morning staff meeting at the Jeffrey crawled by. I focused on breathing evenly while Marco detailed occupancy projections. Alex was traveling again, thank God, but his presence lingered in every glance and whispered conversation that screeched to a stop when I walked past. During a lull, I submitted the FMLA paperwork to CorporateCover's online portal. Their automatic response promised a decision within 48 hours. Each second was a nervous tick.

At lunch, I drove to my bank's closest branch. The mid-day sun scorched the sidewalks, glaring off the mirrored glass towers like they were designed to blind you. Inside, the air-conditioning barely masked the sterile hum of the ATM machines.

"Afternoon," a security guard greeted me upon entry.

"Hi," I smiled before turning to insert my card. I punched in the code I'd used a thousand times before. The screen flickered. *Access Denied - Please contact your financial institution.* This can't be right. 5583 – I tried again. *Access Denied - Please contact your financial institution.*

My phone buzzed immediately after. It was Alex. *Had to implement*

*some security measures after suspicious login attempts. Just protecting our
assets, babe. Call me and we can sort this out together.*

I stared at the message until the words blurred. My eyes burned.
How utterly fucking embarrassing. Alex's casual "babe," enraged me.
My heart pounded in my chest like a bull wanting to charge through
a cage. Behind me, a line was forming. I pulled my useless card from
the slot and walked away. Fuck him. I wouldn't give Alex the satisfaction of calling, but I needed a solution. I didn't want to ask my parents
for money. Just the thought of my mother's eyes as she potentially
gave it to me was enough to want to avoid that at all costs.

I stepped outside still clutching the card in my hand. The sun
burned my face, making my makeup feel too tight. I couldn't tell if it
was anger or fear heating my cheeks, but I was hot.

The afternoon stretched thin. Every email required double-
checking. Every interaction felt loaded with subtext. By the time I
made it back to Kendra's, my shoulder muscles felt like they were
caught in a fist, squeezing tighter with every breath I took.

"He froze the accounts," I announced, dropping my bag on her
counter. My lips quivered in fear and fury.

"Already?" Kendra looked up from her laptop, glasses sliding
down her nose. "Damn. That's faster than I expected. Okay, new plan.
Start going through every record you have. Any accounts from before
him, any assets he might not know about. Anything that's just yours.
You gotta have something."

Anxiety ate me alive, and I felt like I was freefalling into a cavern
of whipping winds and rain. Not to mention I didn't like taking up
space in Kendra's place without having anything to contribute.

"Nyla? Did you hear me?"

"Yes." Barely. I pulled my laptop closer, starting yet another search
through years of emails. Work correspondence. Hotel vendors.
Nothing.

I rubbed my temples, hot tears building again.

"No luck?"

"No." Well, I did have a retirement plan, but I couldn't touch it
without a huge penalty and taxes, neither of which I could afford or

wanted. I'd diligently saved money in an emergency account for two years and Alex locked me out of it!

Kendra huffed out an exhale. "Check your personal email accounts."

Sales and junk. Social media notifications. Travel newsletters. I opened folder after folder, each one as empty of solutions as the last. Ugh. My pulse drummed louder with every click. Just as I was about to slam the laptop shut, a forgotten label caught my eye: Guest Feedback.

For a moment, I hesitated. Guest Feedback? It was a relic from my first job, a folder I hadn't touched in years. What could possibly help me there? But I clicked anyway. My breath stalled as I opened the file. Seven years ago. A guest had left me a compliment with the subject line: "Bitcoin tip – You'll thank me one day."

I had no clue how Bitcoin worked, if it was legit, or what I was supposed to do with it, but I opened the message to learn more. Instructions were in the email about setting up a digital wallet, along with a string of random letters and numbers that supposedly held 0.25 of a Bitcoin. Back then, it had seemed like fake Internet money, but now if the financial sites were right, that quarter coin could be worth over thirty thousand dollars. *If* I could still access it after all these years. It was worth a try. So, I went for it before going to bed.

I couldn't sleep for shit. Tossing. Turning. Sweating. Ugh. Eventually, I just laid there for a while until thoughts of Guatemala flooded back. What if I returned for a while? I knew it sounded crazy, but I couldn't stop thinking about it and it became a full-blown fantasy. The idea to make a list of pros and cons between the two locations came to me at 3 AM while Kendra slept.

STAY IN MIAMI
- Financial security
- Years invested
- Professional contacts
- Parents' approval
- Sibling support
- No language barrier

- Developed city

GO BACK TO GUATEMALA
- Freedom
- Lake Atitlán
- Fresh start
- Breathing room

THE "GO" column was shorter but somehow weighed more heavily. I pulled up my banking app, running the numbers again. Not enough. Between my retirement account (minus penalties), savings, and ...I still didn't have enough to leave for too long—not if I wanted to maintain most of the home standards I had. Damn.

Switching to my personal email, I opened a fresh document and began typing: *Documentation of Hostile Work Environment at the Jeffrey Hotel Date Range: March 30, 2024 - present Primary Parties: Alex Jeffrey (Owner/Operator), Marco Rodriguez (Front Office Manager).* New strategy deployed.

The facts arranged themselves. Meeting removals. Surveillance reports. Permission to travel rescinded then granted with conditions. Each bullet point stripped away another layer of doubt about what this really was. My palms began sweating but my keystrokes remained steady. Words had power. I'd learned that managing guest complaints. Now I wielded them like lockpicks, finding the weak points in my own gilded coop.

A message from CorporateCover HR Services popped up: *Ms. Baines, pursuant to your inquiry...*

I'd forgotten I'd already contacted them. Abigail from Corporate-Cover wanted to set up a call first thing in the morning. My throat itched. Making this official meant no going back. I agreed, and finally, went back to sleep. Finally.

∾

I GOT to work earlier than necessary. A flare of movement caught my eye. Marco. It was actually late for him. *Slacking already*. His yellow socks were visible even in the dim light. He paused when he saw my car, then deliberately walked the long way around to the staff entrance. Funny how we now orbited each other like planets thrown off course, maintaining careful distance to avoid collision.

The sun had fully crested the horizon now, burning away the last threads of night. Muscle memory pushed me to check my reflection, smooth my blazer, adjust my lipstick. The woman in the mirror looked surprisingly calm for someone documenting her professional demise.

Things went incredibly smooth, however. The call with Abigail was a quick formality and faster than I could process it, Corporate-Cover's approval arrived in my inbox like a salvation. I hadn't gotten my coffee yet when I saw it: *Leave approved effective immediately.* My shoulders dropped an inch. The FMLA approval meant protected and untouchable time off and a chance to think clearly. I needed it to figure out my next move. But Alex wasn't about to let me slip away that easily. His lawyer reached out within hours, not to challenge the leave – they couldn't legally do that – but to 'discuss parameters.' My salary would not continue; FMLA didn't require that. But the Jeffrey was "willing" to apply any accrued PTO—if I agreed to their conditions. *Fucking Alex...*

"The Jeffrey Hotel values discretion," his lawyer explained, her voice smooth. "Mr. Jones is prepared to be generous regarding compensation during your recovery period. Naturally, this generosity comes with the expectation of certain boundaries: limited communication, non-disclosure, and a controlled narrative."

He was thinking about the investment deal nearing closure. It figures.

I caught Kendra's eye across her kitchen counter. She'd insisted on listening in, her legal pad already filled with notes. "This is garbage. You know that, right? They're trying to box you in."

"Shit. Yeah, it seems like it," I confessed, rubbing the back of my neck. I was in a bind, though. I needed the money. I also needed space.

"They're holding your PTO hostage," Kendra's tone was sharp. "That's a leverage move. You don't have to accept it."

I shrugged, already exhausted from managing my new life. Just then, my phone chirped on the counter. The jingle cut through an awkward moment of indecision.

Kendra glanced at it. "Well? Who's that?"

"Just a social media notification," I spoke nonchalantly, but in reality, I was intrigued. I could tell it was from one of the woman solo traveling groups I'd joined and someone was answering a question I'd asked likely weeks ago. I ignored it. Couldn't think about that now.

"So, will you accept Alex's terms?"

"I don't know. Feels like I don't have a choice."

We went back and forth on my options and broke down every angle: signing the agreement meant immediate financial relief but came with Alex's strings attached. Refusing meant unpaid leave and an uphill battle to regain access to my accounts. I would sign the agreement and take the PTO, buying myself just enough time to figure out my next move. *Decision made.*

The fully executed copy appeared in my inbox minutes later. The speed of it all felt like Alex's final message: *See how efficiently I can make things happen when I want to?*

Later that night, I went back to my Facebook notifications and scanned the reply: *"Hey Nyla! Just saw your post about your first solo trip. You mentioned loving Guatemala. Are you thinking of going back? If so, let me know. I have a contact in Lake Atitlán who runs a beautiful B&B —super affordable and safe for solo travelers. She even hosts yoga and well-ness workshops if you're into that. Let me know, and I'll connect you two!"*

I stared at the message, my heart thudding in my chest. *Should I really go back?* The question lingered like an open door.

"You're thinking about it, aren't you?" Kendra glanced at my screen, then added, "Don't worry, I wasn't snooping. Just caught the photos when I looked up."

"Mm hm." I teased. I'd forgotten she could be nosy. "I don't know. It's not like I can just drop everything and leave."

"Shiiiit. Why the hell not? Alex is acting the fucking fool. You're on unpaid leave. What exactly is tying you here?"

Her words stung, but they weren't wrong. I looked back at my phone. *I was so at peace there.* Just the thought of it calmed me.

Peace. I hadn't felt it since I'd come back. I didn't need Kendra to push me. I could feel the pull of something bigger than my doubts and Alex. But my parents would think I was nuts. *Was I nuts?* I knew what I wanted to get away from, but what was I running to? Conflicting thoughts ran a relay race in my mind but not for long. Staying here wasn't the answer, and deep down, I already knew that. I didn't realize my thumb was moving until the message was already typed: *I'm in. Send the details.*

"Fuck it," I said aloud, hitting send.

12

FRAGMENTS OF FREEDOM

The crypto exchange website's warning flashed red against the white screen: *Once you enter your personal information, there's no going back. It would get more real.* My fingers hovered over the keyboard, doubt creeping in. The exchange's verification process could take days, but the alternative I'd found—a Bitcoin ATM nearby, would give me money instantly while eating nearly 20% in fees. Damn.

"You sure you want to do this now?" Kendra peered over my shoulder, reaching to adjust the screen. Steam from her coffee mug created a hazy barrier between us. She set it down with a clink punctuating the quiet between us.

I exhaled. "I don't know." I rubbed my forehead, fighting the urge to slam the laptop shut. The technical jargon about seed phrases and private keys made my head spin. One wrong move and I could lose everything. Again.

"A twenty percent difference in fees is worth $7,500," Kendra murmured, her practicality cutting through my hesitation. "That's a lot." She was right, but the thought of waiting days for verification, of being trapped here while Alex played more games with my finances didn't sit with me. My PTO money would take two weeks and I needed money now.

I closed the exchange website and pulled up the address of the nearest Bitcoin ATM. This was crazy, but since I barely knew what was sane anymore, it didn't matter. I'd rather be crazy than controlled. Sometimes freedom meant paying a premium for speed, besides, I could do both. Take a little for now and send the bulk to a new bank account. I copied down the private key—sort of like a password—and grabbed my purse, ready to turn digital promises into real escape.

The Bitcoin ATM shined orange and white in the corner of the convenience store. A few people were in there, including a drunk buying lottery tickets at the counter. He talked loud as fuck. A TV played sports highlights behind a bullet proof glass where the cashier stood. *The ghetto.* The place smelled like Krispy Kreme donuts and gas station hot dogs. Five minutes and several verification steps later, I walked out with a stack of bills that felt surreal. I couldn't believe this was the result of a random gift from a guest...magic internet money, alright. And I did silently thank him until I could sift through my email and surprise him with a real acknowledgement. The cash felt good in my hands. Like *liberation.* The rest of my funds would soon eventually be in a new account—I'd tackle that set up tomorrow. But for now, I had freedom.

The next few days were as intentional as I had ever been. Double-checking my leave papers so Alex couldn't claim I abandoned my job. Ignoring his calls. Ignoring his texts. Assuring my parents that I was doing alright. And running to discount stores to buy essentials to avoid going back to my old place with Alex.

"Wow," I had to chuckle at the $12.99 price tag while exploring a row of cotton tanks. "Never thought I'd be starting my life over at forty-four."

"Please." Kendra tossed two sports bras into our cart. "You make it sound like you're starting from scratch. You've got skills, savings, and a sister with excellent taste in practical underwear."

The store's massive selection suddenly felt overwhelming. There were so many choices. I'd gotten used to Alex's suggestions, his subtle redirections whenever I reached for something too casual or colorful. Now every decision was mine, and I had no idea what I actually liked anymore.

"Okay, essentials only." Kendra pulled out her phone. "I made a list: quick-dry everything, sturdy sandals, basic first aid—"

"Since when are you the practical sister?"

"Since I had to learn how to be for myself." She steered us toward the luggage section. "One carry-on, Nyla. That's your limit."

I **loved** this time with her! "Thanks, Kendra. I mean it. I've missed you," I caught myself admitting.

"Missed you, too, big sis. I really did," she gave my hand a squeeze and helped me finish shopping. Life was feeling good.

Kendra steered us toward the luggage aisle, scrolling through her list.

I reached for a sleek black suitcase that was practical but forgettable. Kendra snorted and yanked out a bright, mosaic-patterned bag. "This one. It's fun, and no one will mistake it for theirs."

I hesitated, fingers grazing the loud fabric.

"Okay, fine. Pick one that speaks to you," she told me.

I had no idea, so I went with her choice. "If I hate it by tomorrow, you're replacing it."

Kendra grinned. "Deal. But trust me, it's you."

As we headed for checkout, I took another glance at the bag. The boldness actually didn't feel wrong. She was right.

THREE DAYS LATER, I watched Guatemala City sprawl beneath the plane's descent. Miami faded quickly beneath me and soon enough, the mountains welcomed me. The airport was familiar. And the immigration officer barely glanced at my tourist visa before stamping it with a thud. Ninety-days. That's what he'd given me though I only planned to stay for 30. As much as I wished I could never go back, I knew I had to. There were no questions about my previous stay, no raised eyebrows at my quick return. I was just another gringa with a backpack and vague plans.

I wanted to spend the first few days back in the familiar city and check out a few museums I didn't get to see the first time. I also planned to spend every night mapping out my new future. Where would I go long term? What would I do? Where would I work? I had so many unanswered questions. But I also had time and space.

That first night, I sat cross-legged on my hotel bed with my laptop open to travel blogs and Facebook groups. The city lights twinkled beyond my window while I scrolled through posts from other women who'd found themselves in Guatemala for one reason or another. A photo of ladies in vibrant dresses dancing on a beach caught my eye. Their movements were caught mid-spin against a sunset sky.

"What's this?" I wondered.

If you're curious about Garifuna culture or need a break from the highlands, Livingston is a must! someone had written, attaching photos of palm-lined beaches, vibrant murals, and a lively drum circle. *Where Caribbean meets rainforest.* Oh? So, there *was* a rainforest? With Afro-Latin people? I was intrigued! The poster described a place where three cultures collided – Maya, Garifuna, and Caribbean – to create something entirely unique. I was shocked and instantly absorbed. Livingston's coastline was different than Lake Atitlá's shore. It was tropical and reminded me of home...just a little.

The social media post had dozens of comments: tips for boat rides, food recommendations, and advice to hike to the Seven Altars waterfalls. My toes curled on the carpet in excitement as I read on and watched short videos. Many of them looked rugged and under-developed, but I *had* to explore it! Something about my last trip to the country unlocked a level of courage in me to explore on my own that I didn't know I was capable of. Sure, I was a little nervous about going beyond safe tourist spots, but not afraid enough to not try.

My cursor hovered over the "Book Now" button. It would be an adventure because there were no flights from the airport nearest me. I would first have to travel four hours west to the Quetzaltenango Airport, then transfer to a flight heading north toward Livingston.

From there, the Afro-Latin people region could also include a 45-minute boat ride. Each step was a more remote and a little more adventurous. *You can do this*, I coached myself. The options were limited and expensive, but suddenly the museum visits I'd planned felt too...safe. Too much like the old Nyla, carefully researching and categorizing experiences. *Do it all.* My inner voice pushed me.

I refreshed the page, and the woman in the photo's yellow dress spun again. Her freedom called to something in the depths of me. *Screw it.* Three clicks later, I had tickets for the complex journey. The travel time should have deterred me, but instead, my skin tingled with anticipation. I felt like a kid who'd just convinced their parents to let them ride the biggest roller coaster at the park – that delectable mix of "should I really do this?" and "just watch me."

When the final email confirmation dinged my inbox, a laugh bubbled up. It was part delight, part disbelief at my own daring. The old me would have created spreadsheets comparing hotels and cross-referenced every TripAdvisor review. This Nyla was about to chase waterfalls with nothing but a backpack and a spirit of "why not?" Holy shit! I felt a tad wild and I liked it.

I wanted to text Kendra but hesitated. My decision felt impulsive and insane the more it sank in, but so was this entire trip. Shit, I was unemployed and homeless if I didn't want to return to Alex. Why would I spend my limited funds on this? I couldn't understand how I still felt happy in the moment with all the uncertainty. Was I a vagabond? Would this spark soon fizzle leaving me worse off than I was in Miami? Why did I just do that? "Stop, Nyla." I had to prevent myself from over-thinking again.

I started a message to Kendra, deciding to double-down on my decision to let go and live a little. *Sis, this is what I'm going to do...*I also found groups to do most of these adventures with to feel safer. *There,* I thought. *A gratified medium.*

Two days later, Caribbean heat descended on me as I stepped off the boat in Livingston. The first thing that struck me was the art. Oh my! A giant mural covered a white wall with striking faces of the Garifuna people. Natural hair, full lips, and deep brown skin all gathered beneath a towering traditional drum. Splashes of yellow, blue, and orange burst around them like a visual echo of music. The street art was alive.

The air was salty, but something sweet also barreled its way through. Plantains? I wasn't sure. The atmosphere pulsed with life as I walked along a narrow street crowded with vendor stalls. Tuk-tuks weaved through the chaos. *Beep-beeeeep!* Bright tarps stretched over tables piled with fabrics, handmade jewelry, and carved wooden trinkets. And someone was playing a drum in the distance.

The smell of grilled fish and pineapples mingled with the heat, making the whole street feel animated, sticky, and unruly. Restaurante Las Tres Garífunas caught my eye. Its sign was framed by greenery, and its thatched roof peeking out like an invitation to pause. Laughter, clinking dishes, and the irresistible scent of coconut and something fried wafted out. It wasn't just a place to eat. It was a place to *be*, and for now, that was exactly what I needed.

From the menu, I learned about the fusion of Guatemalan, Honduran and Nicaraguan—all countries that were home to Garifuna people. I ordered a plate of fried fish, coconut rice, and sweet plantains. The server suggested I try a local herbal rum called Gifiti, said to have medicinal properties. Cautious, but willing, I took a sip. *Whoa!* The earthy sweetness burned just enough to warm me from the inside out. It left me loose, relaxed, and a little curious about its supposed healing powers.

"Es bueno, sí?" The server—Itandi, according to her name tag—smiled as she cleared empty plates from the next table.

"Muy bueno," I agreed, then gestured at my throat. "Pero... uh, fuerte." My Spanglish kicked in. Sort of.

She laughed. "Strong, yes. But good for your spirit." Behind her, two women burst into dynamic conversation. I found myself leaning forward, trying to catch their words. It wasn't Spanish—the rhythm was different, deeper somehow, with sounds that reminded me of West African documentaries I'd watched. When Itandi returned, I pointed in their direction.

"That language they're speaking..."

"Ah, Garifuna." Itandi's face lit up. "It's language from our ancestors." She switched effortlessly between English and Spanish as she explained, her hands moving expressively. "We use many tongues here. Three languages, one people."

One of the women called out to Itandi in that melodic tone. She responded with a quick phrase before turning back to me. "They ask if you want to learn some words?"

Wow! I hadn't expected the warmth, but loved it all the same. "Si!" I nodded eagerly, the Gifiti drink loosened me up for sure. For the next twenty minutes, I fumbled through basic Garifuna greetings. The three women's patient corrections were punctuated by laughter and more stories. I had the time of my life! So free. So enchanted. So invigorated. I was exhausted by the end of the tour, but had zero regrets.

THE NEXT FEW days in Livingston flew by in a kaleidoscope of waterfalls, drumming, and more attempts at the Garifuna language. But as I lounged on the beach my last evening I watched fishing boats bob against the sunset and my thoughts kept drifting back to Lake Atitlán. To that piece of art that had first captured my imagination. I was ready to return. Like the adventure getting *to* the Afro-cultured part of Guatemala, the trek *out* was just as multi-faceted. This time, I made my way through with more ease and comfort. I could almost hear "Hold Us Together" by H.E.R. as I made every transfer. Sang and hummed it to myself, actually, smiling the entire time.

I eventually landed in Antigua for a night of rest before the early morning ride back to Lake Atitlán. There was no tour group this time. Just me and a personal driver.

Morning unfolded over the lakeside village like a whispered secret. Soft. Deliberate. Unhurried. The water shimmered in transient and undefinable colors, and the volcanoes' permanence seemed to mock the fragility of my thoughts. This beauty was always there. Finding a corner off the tourist path, I sat down to quietly take in the view. I inhaled the tranquility, letting the peace settle into the marrow of my bones.

My phone buzzed and Alex's face filled the screen. *No thank you.* I declined the call, but another message popped up instantly: *The lake looks beautiful from your location. Much safer than Livingston - smart choice, babe. But you should move to the more populated area by the Santander street market.*

My eyes pop open. I whipped my head around, terrified. What the? How did he...? Another message: *Just tracking you through Find My iPhone. For safety. I worry about you alone out there.*

My hands trembled as I turned off location services, but the damage was done. The invasion of my peace, my choices, my solitude, sent me stumbling to my feet. I needed to move, to hide, to breathe. Something! Alex's message threw my world off its axis. Shit.

I found myself in a small gallery off a side street minutes later. Its cool shadows drew me in just as a scruffy puppy trotted by.

"¡Bienvenido! ¿Puedo ayudarte?"

I couldn't make out the words, still in a panic from Alex's meddling in my business.

"Señorita?"

I stuttered, not getting a word out.

"Do you need help?" She switched to English. Her voice was gentle. Paint stained the cuffs of her white linen shirt, and a silver pendant in the shape of a butterfly rested against her collarbone.

"I just..." I gestured vaguely at nothing in particular. "Sorry. I needed to get off the street for a minute."

She studied me, head tilted. "You look like you need water. And maybe a chair." Without waiting for my response, the woman disappeared behind a curtain and returned with a drink and worn wooden seat. "Sit. Please. Sometimes the altitude can be difficult for visitors."

The simple kindness nearly undid me. I sank onto the stool, grateful for its solid presence beneath me. Fighting. I gulped and fought tears.

"I'm Mariana," she offered, keeping a respectful distance. "You can rest here."

"Nyla." I took a long sip of water and managed a smile. "Thank you. I'm not usually..." I trailed off, unsure how to explain.

She busied herself with a stack of canvases. The silence between us was comfortable rather than awkward. After a moment, she glanced up. "You know what's strange? These walls have seen more honest breakdowns than the confessional at the church." A half-smile crossed her face. "At least that's what my friend the priest tells me when he brings me coffee." Her hands stilled. "Where are you staying?"

"Panajachel, but..." I didn't want to admit I hadn't planned beyond escaping Alex's digital reach. But I did note how perfect her English was. *Interesting.*

Mariana read my shifting expression. "Panajachel can be intense for most tourists. It's suitable for quick visits, not for staying if you've never lived like this before."

Funny enough, I was already wondering how long I'd last in Panajachel because coming in for a day trip was proving vary different than staying several days. I noticed the stray dogs more. The church bells seemed to ring every few hours. And many of the passing cars had likely never been through an emission's test in their existence—the air was harsher when you slowed down. Suffocating at times. The grit was more obvious.

Mariana moved a canvas, revealing a painting of constricted streets winding up a hillside, dotted with small houses in weathered blues and sunbaked yellows.

"That is *beautiful*," I told her, drawn to the way shadow and light played across the scene. "Where is it?"

"San Pedro La Laguna. It's on the other side of the water." She gestured to the steep paths in the painting. "Most tourists stay by the lake, but the whole village climbs the volcano. The old neighborhoods up there still feel like they did when I was young."

I hesitated, thinking of my carefully researched Panajachel booking. But the painting pulled at something in me.

"I have family there," she added, almost as an afterthought while wrapping a small sculpture in brown paper. "Up in the older part of town. Different rhythm there. Slower." She paused. "If you're interested in staying a while, I know a place that might have a room. Simple, but clean. The owner makes amazing tamales for breakfast," Mariana continued.

The scraggly puppy from earlier had followed me in. It sniffed my leg and quickly settled near the door. Mariana glanced at it, then back at me. "And the dogs are less bold."

I laughed despite myself, feeling some of the tension from Alex's messages return. "Sounds amazing. But I've already paid for a week here and I don't think I can cancel without a penalty," I confessed. "Your English is great, by the way. Much better than my Spanish."

"Thank you. Eight years in Las Vegas. That's a long story for another day."

I nodded, understanding there was more there but respecting her boundary. As I stood to leave, a movement by the back caught my eye. A familiar swirl of colors. That same distinctive style as the hillside scene. My heart stopped.

There, propped against the wall, was a smaller version of the painting I'd fallen in love with on my first trip – the one I had impulsively bought before leaving. It had the same vibrant brushstrokes and depth of emotion, but with subtle variations.

"That one...is it a copy or..." I started, then stopped, suddenly uncertain.

Mariana followed my gaze. "Ah, yes. I do variations sometimes. Each one's little different." She tilted her head. "You've seen my work before?"

"Yes. I bought one the last time I was here." The connection clicked into place – why this gallery had felt like a sanctuary, why her art had drawn me in. "It's actually what made me want to come back to Lake Atitlán."

Mariana's expression immediately shifted in surprise. "En serio?" She even slipped back into Spanish, blushing.

"Sí." So did I, following her lead.

She smiled bashfully. "Then I should uh...I should thank you." Mariana cleared her throat. "It's not often my paintings bring people back to Guatemala. Not ever, I don't think." She reached for a business card. "This gallery is open most days, if you want to come back when you're more settled."

I took the card. Having a reason to return felt oddly good. "I'd like that."

She smiled with a slow, lingering grin. Curious, I guess.

The puppy whined at my feet, breaking the moment.

"Well, thank you so much for supporting my work. You should go...get some rest. The lake isn't going anywhere." Her voice was the finest silk.

I smiled. "You're right. Thanks again," I gestured to the water. "Have a nice day."

"You too, Ms. Nyla." She beamed.

As I stepped back into the late afternoon sun, I pulled out my phone. I meant to block Alex's number, but Mariana's business card stuck to my phone screen. Her Instagram handle was printed beneath the gallery information. I followed her without overthinking it then quickly pocketed both phone and card.

My heart felt lighter, despite Alex's disturbance. Or maybe because of it. His tracking me had sent me running into that unexpected moment of connection. It wasn't the history-rich communal warmth of Livingston, but something quieter, more personal.

I headed back to my hotel, the scraggly puppy trailing me halfway there before finding more interesting distractions. My week in Panajachel stretched ahead of me – too long and not long enough all at once. There was still much to experience, especially with the inexpensive boat rides to other villages, but mostly, I needed to finish strategizing how I'd go back to Miami. I was also running low on cash and didn't want to use a Bitcoin ATM I'd seen earlier. The fees were astronomical. I had to conserve my resources for the rest of my trip and give my body a break from all the exploring.

But first, I had a tracking app to delete and an ex-fiancé to block.

13

DOUBLE-TAPPING DISTANCE

Mariana's profile was a mosaic of artwork and lake life: close-ups of paintings in progress, sunset-lit gallery openings, and candid shots of her kayaking on the lake. I scrolled. Each image drew me deeper into her world until a recent post made me pause. To ensure I read it right, I tapped "See Translation."

Opening night at Casa Luz – celebrating indigenous artists of Lake Atitlán. Music, art, good company. All welcome. 7PM Friday.

The picture was of wooden masks and colorful textiles arranged against whitewashed walls. I checked the date. It was tonight. My eyes peered over the post as questions crowded in: *Would I be intruding? Was "all welcome" really meant for tourists? Did I even have anything appropriate to wear?*

A notification popped up: *marianaartista followed you from your reel.* What reel? I hadn't posted one in months, and Instagram didn't specify. Still, my pulse quickened as I pinched and zoomed in on her photos. I also took a screenshot of the event details for easy recall.

"You said you were staying in tonight," I told myself. But one more outing couldn't hurt. I felt like a bird finally let out of a cage and didn't *really* want to stop flying, even if my wings were exhausted.

I FaceTimed Kendra, pacing my hotel room while holding up the two outfits I'd brought that weren't hiking clothes or beachwear. And I decided against telling her Alex was digitally stalking me. Didn't want to talk about him.

"The black tank?" she suggested when I finally got the camera angle right.

"Too Miami nightclub."

"The flowered dress then."

"Too resort tourist." I sank onto the bed. "Maybe I shouldn't go. I mean, I only met her today, and it's not like she personally invited me. It's a public event but..."

"But what? You're literally following an artist's gallery opening in Guatemala. Isn't this exactly the kind of local experience you wanted?"

"I had a minor breakdown in her gallery, drank her water, and learned she used to live in Vegas. Hardly makes me part of the art scene."

"Okay, look." Kendra's tone shifted to what I called her 'little big sister voice.' "You're in that country to experience something different, right? This is an art event featuring local artists. It's perfect for you. And..." she paused, "you already screenshot the details, so clearly a part of you wants to go."

I groaned. "But what if—"

"Nyla." Kendra cut me off. "What's the worst that could happen?"

"I'm overdressed or underdressed. Nothing major." I glared at my phone screen. "I hate when you're right."

"I know." Her smile softened. "Hey, text me when you get back? Just... you know."

The unspoken concern in her voice made me glad I hadn't mentioned Alex. "I will. Promise."

After we hung up, I laid the flowered dress on the bed. With a few adjustments – my denim jacket and flat sandals maybe it could work. Less resort tourist, more... whatever I was trying to be here. Someone who showed up. Someone who tried.

I checked the time. There were two hours until the event. Just enough to shower, change, and talk myself out of going at least three more times. Still, I ventured out.

CASA LUZ SAT at the edge of the tourist zone. It had a weather-beaten exterior transformed by strings of copper lights to give its worn stones a sunset-like glow.

"No esta aqui, señorita!" *It's not here, Ms.* My tuk-tuk driver had gotten lost twice before finding it, finally. "Ah, por alla!" He squealed and pointed when we spotted it. *Over there!*

Inside, the gallery space was bigger than I expected, with high ceilings and exposed beams. Local artwork covered the whitewashed walls and it wasn't just paintings, but textiles and sculptures that glimmered with life in the dim lighting.

I wavered in the doorway, suddenly aware of how tourist-obvious my outfit was, despite my attempts to dress it down. Around me, people moved with the easy familiarity of regulars. A woman in a hand-embroidered huipil chatted with a man whose gray dreads were wrapped in a colorful scarf. Two teenage girls in jeans and random t-shirts arranged drinks on a table near traditional clay masks.

Mariana stood near the center of the room. Her blouse was alive with colors that dared you to look away. She gestured with a fluidity that seemed to draw people into her orbit. Her laughter was a low, unexpected harmony over the ambient music.

"¿Quieres un trago?" A server appeared at my elbow with a tray of small glasses filled with what looked like wine.

"Si. Gracias." I accepted one gratefully, glad to have something to do with my hands. The alcohol was sweeter than expected, with an herbal undertone that reminded me of the Gifiti from Livingston. The memory of the Afro-Latino people made me smile.

I soon drifted toward the nearest wall, pretending to study a series of black and white photographs while actually watching the room through their reflection. Everyone seemed to know everyone else.

Conversations flowed in Spanish with little English, punctuated by laughter and the jangle of glasses.

"You came." Mariana's voice startled me. She'd materialized beside me so quietly I hadn't noticed.

"I hope that's okay? I saw your post and—"

"Of course." Her smile was genuine but distracted. "Local artists need support. Speaking of..." She glanced over her shoulder where someone was trying to get her attention. "Enjoy the wine. It's from a small producer in Quetzaltenango."

She was gone before I could respond, pulled away by what looked like an important conversation. I sipped my drink and moved to the next photograph, trying to look like I belonged while feeling increasingly like I didn't. *This is silly.* My mind taunted me.

The room grew more crowded. Snippets of foreign phrases floated past: "...el simbolismo de los patrones tradicionales..." "...el financiamiento para el colectivo de arte..." "...preservar las técnicas indígenas..."

Each utterance reminded me how little I knew about this world I was trying to step into. The sweet wine turned slightly bitter on my tongue.

That's when I heard it – Mariana's voice carrying from across the room: "...exactly what we've been talking about. Many tourists come through and think they understand our art because they bought one piece..." She'd said it in Spanish, but spoke slowly enough that I could figure out her sentences.

My chest constricted. She wasn't looking at me, probably wasn't even talking about me, but the words stung anyway. I set my half-finished beverage on a nearby table, suddenly needing air. The copper lights that were initially so welcoming now felt like they were spinning, creating halos in my vision.

"Te vas pronto?" The server reappeared. I could only make out one word and it wasn't enough to make the sentence make sense. She spoke much faster than Mariana, and it all ran together.

"I'm not feeling well," I managed, already moving toward the door. "Great event though."

She looked confused, not realizing that I wasn't fluent in Spanish. I'd only said one word earlier, and she likely assumed I knew them all. Politely, she nodded and whizzed off. My body language probably said all that needed to be said.

Outside, the night air was cool against my flushed skin. I could still hear the music and chatter emitting from the gallery. Looking left and right, I tried flagging down a taxi. There weren't any Ubers available and the cab didn't stop. Fuck. I tried for a ride share again. While waiting, I noticed stars scattered across the sky like spilled salt. They were indifferent to my embarrassment.

What was I doing here? Playing a local when I couldn't even handle one art opening? The wall's rough surface grounded me as reality crept in. I was alone in a foreign country, running from one life without any real plan for building another.

My phone chirped from Uber: *Cars are now available.* Thank God. I quickly requested one before straightening up, brushing invisible dirt from my clothes. As I began towards the curb, Mariana's voice caught me. "Nyla? You're leaving already?" Something in her tone made me turn around completely. She stood in the doorway, the lights catching subtle gold threads in her blouse I hadn't noticed before.

"I should get back to my hotel. Early day tomorrow." The lie felt clumsy on my tongue.

"But the real party doesn't start until after the formal opening." She gestured inside. "A few of us usually gather in the back garden. More relaxed, I promise." Her smile was warm, almost playful. "Unless...you're too tired..." she stepped closer – just a little before breaking a full stride.

The invitation hung between us, beckoning. But my skin felt too tight, my dress too wrong, my presence too foreign. "I really should go. But thank you." I couldn't read her expression as I turned away.

The waiting Uber's headlights cut through the dark. Behind me, the gallery door closed with a soft click that somehow felt louder than a slam. Damn.

～

MORNING LIGHT BOUNCED off Lake Atitlán like broken glass, making my already throbbing head worse. I'd barely slept, replaying my awkward exit over and over. Something pushed me to go back and apologize. *You owe her nothing.* Yet, something else pulled me away. Maybe it was the urge to prove I was more than a gringa tourist or culture vulture. Perhaps it was just a desire to feel less alone. Regardless, I wanted to see Mariana again.

The gallery looked different in daylight. Just another old building with peeling paint. *Huh,* I mused. Not so magical after all. A bell chimed softly as I pushed open the door.

Mariana stood at a tall table, sorting through papers and envelopes. She'd traded last night's dynamic top for a paint-splattered t-shirt and her hair was twisted up with a fat paintbrush. She glanced up. Her expression cooled when she saw me.

"We're not really open yet," she announced.

"I'm sorry, I just..." Gulp. The practiced explanation perished in my throat. "About last night—"

"Don't worry about it." Her attention returned to her papers. "People pass through all the time. It's what you do, no?"

The dismissal was an unexpected blow. "That's not—"

"If you're interested in more art, I have pieces at various price points." She was professionally distant, nothing like the night before when she'd invited me to stay awhile. "Though the shops downtown might be more what you're looking for."

Well, damn. This wasn't how I'd imagined things going. "I didn't come to buy anything."

"No?" Now she did look up, one eyebrow raised. "Then why are you here?"

Because I'm lost. Because I'm scared. Because for a moment last night, you made me feel like I could belong somewhere. But I couldn't say any of that.

"I don't know," I whispered, then turned and walked out.

She didn't follow me this time.

The sun felt brighter. Harsher. My hotel was only a few minutes away but felt miles distant. Each step echoed with Mariana's words: *People pass through all the time. It's what you do, no?*

Inside my room, the AC hummed its artificial comfort. I sank onto the bed, still fully dressed. What the hell was that? I replayed everything from the day before to now and while staring at the ceiling. What did I miss? Soon, my phone rattled: Three texts from Kendra asking if I was okay. A voicemail from my mother that I couldn't bring myself to check. And if he wasn't blocked, I'm sure Alex would have been among the check-ins.

I was *exhausted*.

Everything I'd been outrunning finally caught up to me in that moment. Tears came without warning now. Not slow and hesitant ones. Hot, messy sobs that bent me double. With my face buried in a wet pillow, it sank into my soul that I was forty-four years old, sleeping in a sub-par hotel with a dog on the roof and roosters screaming in the mornings. Somewhere with no job, no friends, no home, and dwindling funds. I'd walked away from a life I'd spent years building, and for what? To pretend I could reinvent myself in a month? In a place where I could only handle elementary conversations? My body went hot now. Unsteady, too.

My breath came in hiccups. When was the last time I'd really let myself cry? The engagement? Before that...? I couldn't remember. I'd been so busy being strong, brave, and being *fine* that I hadn't allowed myself to feel the terror churning beneath it all. Even when it everything fell apart. I'd patched it up with hasty adventures instead of honest feelings...and examinations of those feelings. When things started to burn, I ran toward the lake, not to the truth I was too afraid to see. The truth would hurt. It would expose every crack, bump, and bruise. And I wasn't ready to face them, but now they were all I had left in that room. Everything bled out of me.

Both my hands found their way to my face, palms against my forehead while my fingertips squeezed my scalp. I kicked off the sheets as the room's basicness pressed in. *Basic*. Alex's voice rang in my head like an annoying alarm. I choked on a sob, broken only by my ragged breathing. I curled onto my side, not bothering to wipe my face. Outside, life went on – vendors calling their wares, children laughing, church bells drifting from somewhere nearby. But in here, everything I'd been holding together finally shattered. I was bleeding without blood.

14

RETURN TICKETS

After five days of cold showers, spotty WiFi, and roosters that seemed personally invested in preventing sleep, I retreated to the familiar comfort of the Westin in Guatemala City. The same one from my first trip. My bank account protested the expense, but my nerves needed the respite.

Riiing. My phone sat on the desk. Its screen was dark yet its presence was heavy. Dozens of missed calls and messages from my parents waited. They knew I was alive because I'd posted to my social media stories, but that was it. Kendra's texts grew increasingly worried: *Girl, you good? / Nyla, seriously. Call me. / Don't make me come get you...*

I'd responded with brief "I'm fine," messages. That was all I had after my meltdown at the gallery. All I had after realizing how far I'd jumped without looking. The hotel room's crisp sheets and reliable hot water felt amazing—like finally, God gave me a break—and I instantly felt calmer.

Riiing. It was Mom. She was done with texting. Fuck. It was time.

Thankfully, it was a regular audio call and not video. I couldn't handle them seeing me right now.

"Nyla?" She spoke immediately. "Oh, thank God!"

"Hi, Mama." My voice came out soft and steady. "I'm sorry I worried you."

"Worried doesn't begin to cover it! We haven't properly heard from you in days, and then Alex called—"

"Alex?" My shoulders collapsed.

"He's concerned about you, baby. Says you're using your medical leave to travel instead of rest. That you're spending money that no one knows where you got it from..."

Air left my lungs in a rush. "You *talked* to him?"

"Well, of course we did!" My mom's voice rose defensively. "You disappeared for days, posting pictures of some rural lake without answering our messages. Then Alex calls, so worried about you taking medical leave to—"

"He cut *off* my access to money, Mama! Did he mention that part?"

Silence quaked between us. Then, softer, she said, "He said he was protecting your joint assets until you were thinking clearly again."

Oh my fucking God! He got through to them.

I pressed my forehead against the condensation-filled window. Outside, construction cranes punctuated the skyline. A new high-rise hotel was going up across the street, its banner promising "luxury meets culture." The irony was not lost on me. *How would I ever get out of this?*

"Nyla?" My mom's voice wavered. "Maybe he has a point. This running off to a third world country...it's not like you."

"That's exactly the problem." My words came out through gritted teeth now. "The 'me' you know was carefully designed. It was also highly managed. That 'me' was created by Alex."

"Baby—"

"No, listen." I cut her off. "He didn't just hide my passport or freeze our accounts. He tracked my phone. He had Marco spy on me. He controlled everything down to what I wore to dinner." My voice was a grenade as I reminded her of everything. "And now he's doing it again, using your worry to manipulate me."

"We were just concerned," she countered, but I heard the doubt creeping in.

I was so fucking tired of being tangled in Alex's web. So fucking fed up with everyone thinking they knew what was best for me. So no longer willing to live like this.

"Nyla?"

Through the window, I watched workers laying the hotel's foundation and something clicked in my head. Something in my soul sparked embers. I needed to rebuild my entire life from the ground up, not just run away or try to duct tape the holes hoping they'd be strong enough to hold me together.

"I'm coming home," I said quietly.

"Oh, thank God!"

"Not because of Alex. Not because anyone thinks I should. But because I need to do this right." I stepped away from the window to get a good look at my reflection. I felt stronger. More certain. Like whatever I'd come here to find just appeared in full color. "I can't build a new life on a tourist visa and Bitcoin loot."

"Build a new... what exactly are you planning? Bitcoin what? You—"

"I don't know yet." My eyes caught on another construction site, this one advertising future office space. Guatemala City was really growing—changing. Lake Atitlán might be next. "But I'm going to figure it out," I finished.

The rest happened quickly. A message to Kendra: *Heading home tomorrow. Yes, I'm okay. Yes, I'm sure. No, you don't need to come get me. And...yes, I had a good time! I'll tell you about it soon, sis, promise. Trust me.* She did nothing to deserve my being curt, but I needed to learn to set and hold boundaries—even for those I loved.

As I packed, I took a habitual look at my social media that revealed Mariana's gallery. I pretended not to see it. But then, I did something that surprised even me...I smiled. Not bitter or wistful, but something softer. A memory of her voice floated to mind. Her eyes when she tried to get me to stay. I sighed, still holding the grin. Despite the ending of my trip, I really did enjoy myself. From the culture to all the people I met along the way, it was a clarifying month.

DAYS LATER, I was back in Miami. The seasonal heat and humidity ran up on me like a clingy ex-lover. I couldn't wait to get back into central air-conditioning. Back to some semblance of home.

Back at Kendra's, her spare room had become command central, with my laptop, legal pad, and coffee cup creating a triangle of purpose on the small desk.

"Damn!" she appeared in the doorway, already suited up for court. "You weren't kidding about getting organized." I'd told her all the details of my trip and my revelation at the end. She was supportive.

The wall above my desk displayed my battle plan: bank account applications, FMLA documentation, and a calendar marked with appointments financial advisor today, HR calls tomorrow, lawyer next week. My to-do list felt endless, but it also felt *good*...like I was finally doing something for myself.

"Want me to come with you to see Johnston?" Kendra offered, adjusting her blazer.

"No, but thanks. I need to do this on my own." I'd chosen Sharon Johnston specifically because she specialized in women rebuilding after divorce or separation. My situation wasn't exactly the same, but close enough. "Besides, don't you have that big tech merger case?"

"True. But text me after?" Kendra hesitated. "You know Mom's going to ask me how things are really going."

I nodded, understanding the subtext. Our parents were still walking on eggshells after the Alex situation, not quite trusting my judgment but afraid to push too hard. I understood why, but pressed Kendra to let me share what and when I wanted to. She agreed.

Two hours later, I sat across from Sharon Johnston in her Brickell Avenue office. The view of the bay behind her desk probably cost a fortune, but her direct manner was worth every penny.

"So," she studied the paperwork I'd brought, "you're telling me you have around twenty-eight thousand in cryptocurrency from a tip seven years ago?"

"Yes. More now since Bitcoin recently surged." I tried not to fidget. "I've already converted a little to cash, but…"

"You need help structuring the rest properly." She set down the papers. "And separating yourself financially from this joint account situation."

"Exactly."

"You're smart to come in now." She began typing notes. "Too many women wait until they're completely drained." She smiled. "Now, about these accounts your husband froze—"

"Ex-fiancé." My smart watch lit up with a note from Alex's work email: *Quarterly investor meeting next week. Your attendance is expected now that your leave is over.*

I swiped it closed. That was tomorrow's problem. Right now, I needed to focus on building my financial foundation. One step at a time.

"And this idea about Guatemala?"

"It's not really a plan yet," I confessed. "Just… something I can't stop thinking about. The lake, the people I met there—it felt different. Like a place where I could actually build something," I rambled.

Her expression softened. "That's not uncommon. Sometimes stepping away from everything familiar makes you see things differently. But building something abroad comes with its own set of challenges—language differences, legal systems, local customs."

"I know," I said quickly. "It's not something I'd jump into right away. I need to get stable here first."

"Good," she replied. "Start with solid ground. Then, if the idea still speaks to you, explore it when the time is right."

"That's the goal." I sat with her a bit longer to talk everything through, and soon, my appointment was complete. I felt so good!

Outside, I paused near the exit. Seeing people rush between meetings was triggering. Their faces were either set with purpose or stress. A few months ago, I was one of them. Proud of it, too... "winning at work". Good Lord, I actually thought that was the dream.

I was waking up now. Guatemala wasn't a real plan. It wasn't a concrete mission at all, but it wasn't impossible either. The thought lingered in the back of my mind as I waited for the valet to bring my car around; I realized something: I felt less afraid. Overwhelmed, yes. Uncertain, definitely. But not afraid. And that felt incredible.

I texted Kendra: *Meeting done. Grabbing coffee, then we'll talk. And yes, you can tell Mom I'm handling things.* 😊

The last part was even true. Finally.

15

THE SPACE BETWEEN

The Jeffrey's lobby trilled with morning energy as I crossed its threshold. My flats moved inaudibly against the familiar terrain, and my sport jacket felt stiff after weeks of casual wear. However, I held myself upright. It was time for strategy and my backbone was a pillar of steel.

"¡Buenos días, Nyla!" Marco called from behind the front desk. He was all smiles. "¿Todo bien?"

"Sí, gracias." My Spanish rolled even easier now, a small victory from my time away. I caught his slight surprise at the natural response.

"Nyla!" Ana emerged from the service corridor. Her normally pristine housekeeping uniform sported a coffee stain. "Thank God you're back. The Azalea Suite's AC is possessed, the wedding party from hell just checked in, and—" She stopped short, studying my face. "Something's different about you."

"Time away will do that," I smiled, feeling the truth of it in my bones. The chaos of a luxury hotel suddenly felt trivial after navigating Livingston's streets and Lake Atitlán's complex culture. Guatemala had a hold on me.

Before Ana could respond, Alex's voice shot through the morning bustle. "Conference room, folks. Five minutes!" He didn't wait for acknowledgment, disappearing into his office just as quickly as he'd emerged.

"And there it is," I said, more amused than anxious. Three weeks ago, that tone would have sent me scrambling. Now? Now, I understood the difference between urgency and emergency.

"He's been..." Ana's voice dropped to a whisper, still laced with a Latin accent. "Different, too. Since you left." She touched my arm briefly before hurrying back to her duties, leaving me to wonder what exactly that meant.

My office – or what used to be my office – had been transformed. My personal touches were gone and replaced by barren efficiency. The painting from Guatemala was conspicuously absent. But instead of panic, I felt clarity. Like everything else, this space was just a steppingstone now. Besides, I knew the source of that painting and still, it made me smile inside. Butterflies fluttered in my belly at the thought of her.

"Ms. Baines." Clive's Jamaican accent floated from the doorway. "De morning meeting can wait a moment, no?"

"It's good to see you, Clive. Yes." My appreciation for his steady presence had only grown since he'd helped me escape.

Clive stepped inside. "De place hasn't been quite right since yuh gone." Mirroring Ana's words, Clive's dark eyes carried a mix of wisdom and mischief. "Though I suspect dat was never the point, hmm?"

A laugh bubbled up, surprising us both. "No, I suppose not."

"You bring someting back with you," he observed quietly. "More dan just better Spanish."

"Perspective, maybe." I glanced at the bare walls where my art had hung. "Or just the courage to see things as they are."

"Sometimes experience in one place opens doors in another."

Alex's speech carried down the hall again, followed by the shuffle of feet heading toward the conference room. The morning meeting would start with or without me. *Oh well.*

"Ms. Baines," Clive spoke carefully, "before you go in dere..." He adjusted his name tag, debating if he should say more. "Nut'n." He decided against giving specific advice. "I think *you* will know exactly what you must do now dat you are back." He cleared his throat and gave me a kind smile. "Come. Let's get into dis meeting."

The conference room throbbed with daybreak chatter that drowned as I entered. Faces turned – some curious, others prudently blank. Marco's smile flickered. His eyes didn't move. They were like curtains hiding an empty stage.

Alex stood at the head of the table. His crisp attire was a reminder of everything I wanted to leave behind. "Welcome back, Nyla. I trust your leave was...restorative?"

The pause after 'was' carried just enough emphasis to make Trevor from Security and Ana exchange glances. But his attempt at control felt small now. Way too small.

"Very," I smiled, taking an empty seat near the door. "Shall we begin?"

Alex cleared his throat, shuffling papers with exaggerated care. "Right....so, the Charlotte deal is almost final, and we're looking at breaking ground within six months."

Charts and projections filled the screen behind him. Revenue forecasts. Growth metrics. Construction timelines. They were all perfectly arranged, just like him. But something was off in his delivery. There was a tension I'd rarely noticed before. And I wondered why some of the staff needed to see *all* of these details.

"Marco will oversee hiring for key positions," Alex continued. "And speaking of staff transitions..." His eyes found mine. "Nyla has graciously agreed to resume her duties while we determine the most effective structure moving forward."

Structure. The word buoyed in the air. I could feel eyes darting between us, waiting for my reaction. But now I just nodded, letting the moment pass.

Ana raised her hand. "About the Azalea Suite situation *here*..."

The meeting shifted into familiar territory: guest complaints, maintenance issues, staffing schedules. I took notes mechanically while my mind thought back to Clive's comforting energy and words. *Experience in one place opens doors in another.*

"That's all for now," Alex announced. "Nyla, could you stay a moment?"

The others filed out, Marco lingering until Alex's sharp look sent him scurrying. When the door clicked shut, the air felt suddenly thick.

"You look well," Alex said quietly. "Guatemala agreed with you."

I kept my voice neutral. "It did."

"The staff missed you," He organized documents again, not meeting my eyes. "The place wasn't quite the same." Something glinted across his face. Regret? Calculation? I couldn't tell anymore. That felt like progress.

"If that's all..." I smoothed my blazer.

Alex's response caught as if snagged on something unsaid, but he just nodded. "Welcome back, Nyla."

"Thank you."

Ten minutes after the meeting, I found myself following the rhythmic whir of industrial washers to the hotel's laundry facility. The compact space hummed with energy – all gleaming steel and precise organization. Ana stood at a pressing table, her fingers working delicately over a silk gown.

"Dios mío," she muttered, lifting the fabric to inspect a stubborn spot. "This is not coffee."

"Need help?"

She startled, then relaxed when she saw me. "Nyla! I thought you'd be stuck in meetings all day."

"Alex can manage without me." I moved closer, examining the stain. "Red wine?"

"Si. Mixed with champagne and lipstick. The bride's sister got a little too celebratory at breakfast." Ana's expert hands continued working as she spoke. "But that's not why you're hiding down here, is it?"

Lavender scented steam rose from the press between us. It was Ana's signature touch for delicate garments.

"What did you mean earlier?" I asked finally. "About Alex being different?"

Her hands stilled on the silk. "Since you left... it's like he finally realized not everything can be controlled." She glanced at me with budding smirk threatening to grow into a relieved smile. "Fi-na-lly! Even the perfect hotel has its quirks, regardless of his wish for it not to?"

Ana shook out the luxurious gown, examining her work with practiced eyes. "You know, my aunt runs a small hotel near Lake Atitlán." She said it as casually as sharing a recipe rather than a connection that made my heart skip.

"What? You never mentioned—"

"You probably forgot." She hung the dress and turned to face me. "It was a long time ago. But...I never provided the details..." Her voice softened with pride.

"What do you mean?"

"My family..." She smoothed her apron, a gesture I recognized as gathering courage. "We have a small hotel in San Pedro La Laguna. It's nothing like the Jeffrey—just a simple place built into the hillside. But the view of the volcanoes, it's better than any Miami sunset."

The name of the town struck me like lightning. San Pedro— where Mariana had suggested I stay, where she said the real Guatemala lived beyond the tourist veneer. My heart quickened. And of course, I could never forget the volcanos.

"What happened to the hotel?" I quizzed, suddenly desperate to understand this connection I'd overlooked.

"It is still there." Ana moved to another clothing rack. "When I started here, I kept it professional...just listed the basic experience on my resume. The Jeffrey has such high standards, you know? I didn't want to go into how different things are there." She paused. "But watching you come back from Guatemala, seeing how it changed you..." her eyes swelled with pride.

Ana, herself, was born in Miami and was mixed with Mexican heritage on her father's side. Racking my brain, I could honestly not recall any details about her family being from Guatemala. But it made sense. Her mother rarely came to hotel events, and Ana spoke Spanish with a different accent than our predominantly Cuban staff. These were details I'd registered but never pieced into, too caught up in my own world. Plus, it was none of my business.

She heaved a clump of clothes into a washing machine as she spoke. "My aunt says the biggest challenge now is balance, keeping our traditions while giving guests what they expect. Tourism is slowly changing things around some villages near the lake."

"That must be hard."

"Yes. Last month she called asking if I knew anyone with hotel experience who could help modernize things, but not too much." Ana's eyes met mine in the steamy air. "My family still wants to keep things traditional. It's a delicate balance. I actually told her about how you run things here..." She hesitated. "Well, that was right before everything happened with you and Alex. But now..." Ana's voice softened even more. "Maybe the timing wasn't so wrong after all."

My phone buzzed. It was another meeting request from Alex.

"Go, go, jefa!" Ana waved me off, before returning to her work. "But maybe we can have coffee later? I have photos. And..." she smiled, "I would love to hear more about your time at the lake!"

"Bye," I whispered with a grin before slipping out.

The rest of the morning dissolved into status quo work. During lunch, I found myself walking across the street to a hole in the wall café where Clive usually took his break. He sat alone at his usual corner table, newspaper spread before him.

"Mind if I join you?"

He looked up, smile crinkling his eyes. "Whaat! Pull up a chair, Ms. Baines."

"Thank you," I grinned.

It was a beautiful break and I learned so much more about Clive outside the Jeffrey's walls. He told me that he'd started in hospitality through some cultural exchange program a Caribbean hotel association hosted many years back.

"Learned my trade in Jamaica, then came here." His sucked his teeth slightly and then drifted into a nostalgic smile. "Sometimes de best way forward is to look back first. I still keep in touch with dat network, you understand? Good people doing good work." Clive adjusted his name tag thoughtfully. "Including some interesting projects with UNESCO. Helping small hotels stay competitive without losing their soul, if you follow me." His speech went a tad more formal. More serious.

I did. "Tell me more," I said, and for the first time since returning, I felt truly awake.

Clive didn't have a ton of relevant or up-to-date details, but what he shared was enough to boomerang visions of the building cranes I'd seen on my final night in Guatemala City.

"Ms. Baines, I didn't have all de answers when I started either," he told me. "But you learn by jumping in. Dat's where de magic happens." He relaxed again.

"Hmm. How did you know when it was time to leave?"

"When stayin' felt harder than leavin'."

"That simple, huh?" I glanced at my coffee, as if the answer might be in there.

"It can be."

My time with Clive helped me to think about creating a tangible plan to perhaps go back to the lake for two months, maybe longer. It was enough. He did say the programs and cultural differences could be difficult to adapt to, "but it's nothing somebody like you can't handle," he added.

"Thank you."

We wrapped up faster than I would have liked but I was galvanized by the chat. Later that day, I swung by my parents and caught them up on everything. I told them more about how I felt and shared how I'd devised a plan for independence. I left out my deeper Guatemala dreams to save myself the headache of that sensitive topic, but when I was back at Kendra's, I couldn't help but squeal a little of them out again. She was cautiously happy for me and that was fine. There was one more thing I'd been avoiding, however, and that was returning to the home Alex and I shared for more of my personal items. I dreaded it, but forced myself.

Our house looked different as I pulled into the driveway. Grass was overgrown and dead leaves scattered across the walkway. *What the hell?* It dawned on me that Alex had no idea who any of our household vendors were or what intervals they came in. He probably made a mess of everything when he froze our accounts. Serves him right!

Through the window, I spotted boxes from his favorite meal delivery service piled on the kitchen counter – the ones I always said were overpriced and under-seasoned. I huffed, goading myself, "Go in."

I'd timed this for when Alex would be at the hotel, but his BMW sat in its usual spot. *His meetings must have ended early.* The garage door rumbled open as I parked. He had heard me pull up.

Suit jacket discarded and tie loosened, Alex appeared in the doorway. He still managed to project control. "I had a call from our investors. They're impressed with how we're handling everything."

Only when I didn't respond did I notice a glass of scotch in his hand. Sunlight glinted on it as he raised it. His hands slightly tremored. Alex never drank during the day unless something was really wrong.

"I had a feeling you'd come by this week," he tried again. His voice was quieter now, cracking a little. Alex looked around, self-conscious of everything and then, almost sheepishly, he spoke again, "I didn't realize how organized you had everything with the auto-payments and such even at home. But I'll—"

"It doesn't matter," I cut him off. I didn't care about what chaos he'd brought on himself, although I found myself feeling guilty—or just unsettled by seeing him like this. Pitiful.

He ran a hand through his hair and a hollow laugh escaped his lips. "The hotel's a mess without you being in it like you were, Nyla. Everything is." He gestured at the delivery boxes, the pile of unopened mail. "Turns out you managed more than just the front desk. A lot more..."

"You'll figure it out." I stepped past him.

"Maybe." He took another sip and followed me. "Your clothes are still where you left them. I haven't touched them... I couldn't..." He caught himself. "The painting's in your office now. I had it put back where you wanted it....Nyla?"

I hoped Alex wouldn't follow me down the hallway, but he surely did. His footsteps raced behind me, but I kept pacing toward our bedroom for my things. I was clearing out a drawer when he finally spoke again.

"I didn't realize just how much you handled around here." His voice was warmer than I'd ever heard it before. I didn't look at him, but I could feel his presence. I could smell his cologne. "The house...the hotel...me....babe?"

I glanced at him briefly before swiftly turning back to my packing. He was too handsome. Too surprisingly honest. Too much like a needy puppy. I had to look away. "I think you managed just fine without me, Alex." *Don't fold, don't fold, don't fold*, I thought. Not the clothes, but my resolve. I willed myself to stay firm.

"Did I?" He gave a reverberant laugh, gesturing at the broom and dustpan by a window, the mismatched bedding. "Look around, Nyla. It turns out I couldn't even keep the sprinklers on schedule."

I pressed a shirt into the suitcase and didn't answer.

"You don't have to say anything," he continued. "I know I made this impossible. You were the glue holding everything together, and I...I took that for granted." He kicked the air.

The words dangled in the space between us. For a second, I wondered if I'd misheard him. Alex never admitted fault. Never. The words made my heart hurtle, and I fought back a tear and sniffle.

I zipped the suitcase halfway before answering. "What do you—"

"You're not taking your Louboutins? The Birkin bag?" Alex stopped my words, gesturing at the accessories that had once felt like achievements.

"Keep them. Sell them. Doesn't matter."

His confusion was almost worth the fortune in leather and snake-skin I was leaving behind. Almost. But he quickly recovered. "I mean... they're yours. Whatever you want to do with them."

The uncertainty in Alex's tone made me ultimately stop and stare at him. I'd never seen this expression painted on his before. It was like he was *finally* seeing me instead of his vision of me. And I was a stranger to him.

"What do you want, Alex?" Stupid question. I knew what he desired: me. But I was exhausted with him. With everything!

He paused long enough to expose his unguarded expression. "I don't want anything," he huffed. "I just...I needed you to know that I see it now. What I did. Who I became."

I honestly didn't know how to respond. I didn't trust him. Didn't know if I could believe him. Damn it, tears were threatening to fall, but I fought them back. Still, a sniffle escaped me. Something in his voice pulled at a thread I thought I'd cut loose. "Why are you telling me this now?" I asked with instant regret. I'd prepped myself to not engage with him more than necessary, but failed. Fuck.

Alex leaned against the doorframe, his shoulders slumping like they carried a weight he would be forced to bear. "Because I know I pushed you too far. And I'm sorry, Nyla." His voice dropped to a boyish whisper. "I'm trying to do better." He flailed his arms

My stomach twisted, and I gripped the handle of the suitcase tighter. Six weeks ago, I might have melted at those words. But now, they felt late.

His vulnerability was real, or at least as real as Alex could manage. I could see it in the way he avoided my eyes, the way he rubbed the back of his neck like he was bracing for rejection. He wasn't asking for a second chance. Not directly. But I knew what this was. Alex wasn't ready to let go of me, control, or the life we'd built that suited him more than it ever fit me.

"It's funny, isn't it? You leave, and suddenly everything falls apart."

"You'll be fine, Alex," I said, keeping my voice neutral. "You always are."

Regret sputtered across his face—I was sure of it now. "You don't have to pretend you don't care. I know you do." He proclaimed.

There he is again. I laughed, more from exhaustion than amusement. "Caring about you doesn't mean staying, Alex. It doesn't mean coming back."

His jaw clenched, but he didn't argue. Now *that* caught me off guard. It confused me.

I closed the suitcase and slid it off the bed, pausing by the dresser where one of my necklaces lay in a shallow dish. It was a simple silver chain with a small charm my dad had given me years ago—something I hadn't worn in a while but could never leave behind for good. I slipped it into my pocket.

As I moved toward the door, Alex straightened up. His hand twitched like he wanted to reach for me but thought better of it. "Nyla...if you ever change your mind—"

"I won't." I stepped past him, pausing briefly in the doorway. "But I hope you do."

I didn't wait for his response. I just took my bags and walked out. The air felt lighter as I stepped outside with more of my things. But as I took a few more steps, I noticed the quiet—a kind of stillness that settled over the house, the neighborhood, everything. Quiet.

I glanced back one last time and saw him. He was still standing there, staring at the space I'd left behind.

"Goodbye, Alex." The words flew out of my mouth before I could cage them.

He did not respond, but he gulped and furrowed his brows—not moving as I tossed my things in the car and left.

Next was work. I had to let that go, too.

My last day at the Jeffrey felt surreal. Ana hugged me tight, slipping me her aunt's contact information. Clive adjusted his red pocket square before tipping his hat. I pulled him in for a quick squeeze too. There was no way I could not embrace him after the role he'd played, even if understated. Even Marco managed a genuine "Buena suerte, jefa," to which I simply responded, "Adios."

16

UNBOXING DREAMS

The luggage from my place with Alex felt like air in my hands compared to the heaviness of everything I struggled to leave behind. Kendra opened the door for me. Before bringing in my small boxes, I touched the resignation letter in my bag. I'd written it early that morning, revising it over coffee until every word was precise and professional. No emotional language. No hints of our personal relationship. Just the essentials documented and proper, the way Alex had taught me.

"The Jeffrey Hotel Group LLC

Attention: Alex Jeffrey Jones

Re: Formal Resignation"

Two weeks' notice, though we both knew I had enough vacation time to cover it. It included my formal notice, last day of work, and offer to help transition my responsibilities. I'd handed it to Alex earlier that day, watching his face as he read it. His expression had shifted from confusion to anger to that careful blankness I knew too well.

"You don't have to do this," he'd said finally. "We can work something out."

"I do. And we can't."

"But...but..." He'd looked at the letter again, then at me. "You're really leaving?"

"Yes."

"What about me?"

"Alex."

"Please."

"ALEX!"

He grunted and slumped. I noticed his foot anxiously tapping the floor before he blew out "Fine. Goodbye, Nyla."

The three words rattled my chest even now while I was back at Kendra's. But earlier, I had walked out for the last time...making progress with moving on with my life.

My last day at The Jeffrey felt surreal, honestly. It was the abrupt end to so many things. So many dreams. So much – what I thought – unfinished business, but oh well. Ana hugged me tight, slipping me her aunt's contact information. Clive adjusted his red pocket square before tipping his hat. I pulled him in for a quick squeeze too. There was no way I could not embrace him after the role he'd played, even if understated. Even Marco managed a genuine "Buena suerte, jefa," to which I simply responded, "Adios."

Now, I was standing in Kendra's doorway with the small haul of my most personal things—the rest would have to go in storage, that moment felt like crossing a crucial threshold.

"Girl, are you moving in or opening a boutique?" Kendra's voice pulled me back.

"Depends. You in the market for overpriced baggage?" I shot back, hoisting a duffel past her.

She smirked and stepped aside. "Alrighty. Welp, the guest room's still yours as long as you need it." Kendra eyed me with all of my things, and I could almost hear that old Erykah Badu song of the same vein..."*Bag Lady*," *you can't hurry up...cause you got too much stuff*.... I know she was being silly about the boutique, but my own self-awareness plus the line gave me a flash of knowing that I had more purging to do. And I wouldn't overstay my welcome.

"There's more in the car!" I yelled. Relief, uncertainty, exhaustion, and the tiniest seed of hope all jumbled together in a messy bouquet inside me.

Kendra groaned dramatically. "Mm hm." Still, she hustled behind me, grumbling about needing hazard pay for sister duties.

"That's not everything from the house," she observed, eyeing the modest pile.

"No. Most of it stays."

"Stays? Nyla, those are your things!"

"Are they? The clothes Alex picked out? The art he approved? Even my office supplies came from his preferred vendors." I sat on the edge of the bed. "I'm only taking what's really mine."

"Like what?"

I opened the nearest box. "Photos from before him. Grandma's locket. Books that I chose." My hands found a small wooden box. "Daddy's letters from when I was in college."

She nodded silently. Positively. Kendra got it. When we finished hauling everything in, I dropped onto the nearest chair, cracking open a bottled water and an overripe banana. The day felt simultaneously slow and fast, but it was moving either way. As evening approached, Kendra watched me arrange my few possessions in her guest room. Without a word, she sprawled across the bed, pushing aside the pile of clean laundry I hadn't folded yet. She stretched out like a cat claiming territory and completely at home in the chaos.

"You know what's wild, Nyala?"

"What's that, baby sis?"

"This is the most relaxed I've seen you in years."

"Really?" I paused, a book in my hands. "Says the woman destroying my attempt at organization."

"Yeah. Even with everything up in the air you seem..." She searched for the word, still lazily moving her arms through my clothes. "Calmer."

I hadn't thought about it that way, but she was right.

"Hey, remember when we used to talk about opening our own business? Before you met Alex?" She giggled.

"The beach bar idea?" I sniggered. "God, we were going to call it 'Sisters' Sips.'"

"Hey, that name was genius!" She grinned, throwing one of my shirts at me. "Okay. Maybe it wasn't. My point is maybe you're finally getting back to *that* girl. The one who had wild dreams."

"Maybe."

"I think so."

"Mm hm. Anyway...care to explain why you still have *this*?" She tilted the box toward me.

I squinted. "Is that my high school dance team uniform?"

"Yup. Tacky sequins and all."

"Shut up! It's vintage. You wouldn't understand."

Kendra gave me a look, half-amused, half-curious. "Is this really everything? From the car, I mean."

I swallowed the bite of banana. "Everything I could grab for now." The words spilled out quickly, too quickly.

She didn't push, but I could feel her watching me as I took another bite—like she could see all the pieces I hadn't brought with me. The ones I wasn't ready to face yet. "Okay. And sis?"

"Yeah?"

She stared at me. Smiling. "I'm proud of you for standing up for yourself. For going after what you want—even if it's crazy as shit."

Bashfully, I thanked her.

"Come on, I'll make us a real meal and you can tell me all about these big Guatemala plans of yours."

They still weren't big or firm plans, but I did have something simmering now.

THE NEXT MORNING, over strong coffee and the beginnings of a strategy taking shape in my notebook, I finally called my parents. Mom answered on the first ring.

"Well, there you are! I was starting to wonder if you forgot how to dial your mother."

"Of course, not, mom. Been reacclimating. But I'm okay. I'm still at Kendra's." I took a deep breath. "And I've made a decision."

There was a pause, then Dad's voice came on the line. "We're listening."

I told them everything—about the epiphany at the gallery, the sense of connection I'd felt to the people and culture of Guatemala, and my growing realization that I couldn't keep living a life that didn't fit.

"I know it sounds hasty," I said finally, "but I need to do this for me."

Another long pause filled the line. Eventually, my mom's words poured into it. Her voice viscous with emotion but resolved. "Nyla, if this is what you need, then we support you. Fully."

Relief cascaded over me. "Thank you. That means everything!" My father and Kendra must have gotten through to her. I knew they were all worried, but finally backing off. I was grateful. I really did *need* this...whatever "this" was.

Over the next few days, I threw myself into deeper research and planning. Ana and I touched base, and her insights about running a small hotel in San Pedro La Laguna fueled my growing sense of purpose. *What if I could build something there one day? How far away did 'one day' need to be? How much money would I need? How sound or ridiculous was this idea and plan to go back to Guatemala for an extended stay?*

I reached out to UNESCO, eager to learn more about their current sustainable tourism projects in the region. The responses trickled in, full of ideas and potential collaborations. And with each one, I felt my nebulous dreams starting to take a more solid form.

One evening, scrolling through photos from my trip, I lingered on a particular shot. It was of an elderly woman weaving at Lake Atitlán. Her wrinkled hands moved with grace while tourists hustled and local shop owners passed. I remembered how she'd caught my eye and smiled, beckoning me closer to show me the pattern emerging on her loom. That moment had struck me. I loved the

quiet pride she'd shown in her craft and her easy generosity in sharing it.

"Earth to Nyla!" Kendra waved her hand in front of my face. "Your
food is getting cold."

"Sorry." I set my phone down. "Just reminiscing about my trip...
and thinking about something one of my employees told me today
about her family's hotel."

"Oh?" Kendra settled into the chair across from me.

"Yeah. Apparently, they're at this fascinating crossroads. Tourism
is growing around the lake I love, but they want to preserve what
makes the place special." I pulled up the notes from my conversation
with Ana. "The hotel's been in her family for three generations. Her
aunt manages it now, but they need someone who understands both."

Kendra's brows furrowed. "Someone like you, you mean? Girl!
You're about to work for pesos? I can't with you!" She cackled.

"Quetzales."

"What?"

"Nothing."

"Fine. Carry-on. Are you interested?"

"Initially, yes. But..." I hesitated, remembering the peaceful pride
in that weaver's eyes, the way Mariana's gallery felt both contempo-
rary and timeless. "The more I learn about the region, the more I
realize I want to build something of my own. Something that bridges
both worlds but in my way."

"And this interests you because...?"

"Because it's real." The words tumbled out. "At The Jeffrey, we
manufactured experiences. Here's a place actually living them. Plus,
UNESCO's developing a sustainable tourism initiative for the region.
Their local coordinator was interested in me when I mentioned my
background."

"Okay, but practically speaking... What about visas? Real, livable
income?" Kendra shifted into lawyer mode. "Have you really thought
this through?"

I pulled out my research binder—color-coded tabs and all. "Guatemala offers investment visas if you put enough capital into a local business. I've been running numbers..." I walked her through my calculations, showing how my wild cryptocurrency gains plus careful budgeting could sustain me while I explored opportunities.

"First of all, I hope you don't keep that Bitcoin on an exchange. I've heard horror stories, and I'm not even into crypto. Second of all, if you plan on using it over time, you need to convert it to cash or stablecoins now before it crashes again for another four years."

"I'd planned to. And since when did you become a crypto expert?"

"Since I saw those motherfucking gains, you made!" She cackled. "And good for you. Now," she paused. "Look who is finally using those spreadsheet skills for herself instead of Alex's projects." Kendra grinned.

I had no rebuttal. No wit to trump her with, so I just smiled and exhaled.

I dove back into research mode later that night with tourism statistics. Property regulations. Visa requirements. Each answer spawned three new questions. The more I dug, the clearer it became that I couldn't plan this from my laptop in Miami. I needed to be there and really understand how everything worked on the ground. UNESCO may or may not be helpful with me wanting to build something from scratch.

Later that evening, my phone jangled with a message from Ana: "My aunt would love to meet you when you return." I responded with genuine warmth but kept it vague. Ana's family's situation had opened my eyes to the possibilities, but their path wasn't mine.

Two weeks later, I had a skeleton of a plan. My cryptocurrency gains would cover initial expenses while I explored opportunities. A tourist visa would give me 90 days to lay groundwork. After that...well, that would depend on what I discovered.

"You're really doing this," Kendra said one evening, watching me book my flight.

"I really am." I clicked *purchase*. My pulse quickened at the finality of it. "Scared as hell, but I'm doing it."

Bloop Bloop! My phone clanged again with another alert. It was Alex. He was back on his usual cycle of trying to win me back. One minute with sweet words, the other with bitter jabs like making fun of me for how I used to sit in my car before going inside work. *What a waste of time. Did you meditate before you shit?* I could almost see him rolling his eyes as his javelins of insults and compliments slid into my mind. *You should come back and stay with me. I can make it all beautiful for us again. And you're so amazing at everything. You're perfect, babe. Come back, Nyla.* His voice recoiled around my mind.

I ignored him. Right now, my focus was on what lay ahead. Lake Atitlán was waiting, and this time, I wasn't going as a tourist. As I made notes, something clicked into place. Every skill I'd developed at the Jeffrey, from the attention to detail, the crisis management, the ability to make guests feel special, even my ability to navigate between English, Spanish, random Creole from Haitians and Jamaican accents like Clive's—could serve a different purpose. I was on a mission to build the next chapter of my life. Maybe.

I DREAMED of Lake Atitlán that night. Not the picture-perfect postcard version, but the real one. My mind's eye could see morning mist rolling off the volcanos as I inhaled and exhaled deeply. Entrancing sound carried across the blue waters. Everything was so, so, peaceful, and I woke up reaching for something I couldn't quite name. But my body remembered the feeling of possibility that had first gripped me there.

Over breakfast, I pulled up my travel photos, letting myself sink into specific moments: The random dogs on rooftops, carefree children running in the uneven streets, and an elder doing laundry in the lake. The way Mariana's paintings captured not just the water's beauty, but its soul. The Bitcoin ATM next to a hole-in-the-wall nail salon, a wild symbol of how Guatemala balanced tradition with progress. Images from the Black culture I'd found in Livingston were mixed in with the more Latin images. All of it stole my heart. So much so that I made a note to begin online Spanish lessons immediately. I wanted to get better and front-run my inevitable communication barriers.

Bzz. Bzz. My phone vibrated and lit up with another UNESCO update about their sustainable tourism initiative. It was confirmation they needed "people like me."

"Morning!" Kendra breezed through, orange juice in hand. "More Guatemala planning?"

"Yeah...Just thinking about how different everything feels there."

"You've really done your homework this time." Kendra settled across from me, gazing at my scattered notes. "This isn't just running away anymore, is it?"

"No." The certainty in my voice surprised us both.

"But what about your career? Just because you and Alex are done doesn't mean you can't rebuild right here. Why so drastic, sis?"

My phone dinged. An Instagram notification: Mariana had posted a new gallery opening. *When did I set up notifications for her page?* The image showed Lake Atitlán at sunset, but it was her caption that caught my eye: "Some places call to you until you answer. Some dreams won't let you rest until you fly into them."

You're absolutely right, I thought.

I recalled spending time at her gallery that one afternoon, how she'd offered water and understanding when I was crumbling in confusion. How different it felt from Alex's controlled kindness. Even our awkward ending held more truth than years with him.

"You're smiling," Kendra observed.

I fixed my face. Suddenly self-conscious and a tad embarrassed.

"Wait a minute." She pressed.

"What?" I looked down.

"Wait a fucking God damned minute!" Kendra paused for dramatic effect. "Nyla?"

"What?"

"Ooooh, Nylaaaa!"

"What!?" I stifled a bashful laugh.

"NYLA BAINES!"

"WHAT, KENDRA?"

"Is there a man in this backwoods-bougie ass lake town? Is that why you want to go back?" She looked me dead in my eyes.

"What? Fuck no! *Hell* no!" I chortled. Stunned. The last thing I wanted was another man.

Kendra glared at me suspiciously.

"I swear to God, there isn't."

She tightened the smile on her lips, but her eyes were still probing. "Okay." She rested her chin in the palm of her hand while staring at me, but soon, she jumped up. "Mm hm."

"Anyway..." I showed her my flight confirmation. "Three weeks. That's how long until I go back."

"To stay?" Her eyes bulged.

"To explore properly. For 90 days. I can sustain myself while I research opportunities. I'm not diving in blind this time."

"And after the 90 days?"

"That depends on what I find...how I feel..."

"Interesting." She looked at her watch. "Oh shit. Girl, I've got to go. Can't be late today. Talk to you later!" Kendra popped up and darted out the complete opposite of how she'd calmly strolled in. And again, I was alone.

I waved her off and went to fix myself something to eat before heading to the Jeffrey to grab a few things that I'd apparently forgotten. Alex and I were on cautious but professional terms. Somewhat cordial in front of staff, but still obviously fractured. It was so weird, but thankfully, he didn't bother me too much while I was there. He was too busy prepping to go to Charlotte. Construction was in progress at his new property and he was clearly in his element there. I can't lie, a part of me did have dreams about taking over the Miami location while he built his empire but those goals now felt like origami cranes. They were precise, beautiful, and empty.

As I packed the last of my Miami life into storage boxes later that night, I looked at the painting from my first trip—I'd removed it from my office at the hotel. The clouds still wrapped the volcanoes like smoke, but now I saw the shape of change, beautiful and inevitable. Lying in Kendra's guest bed with a cool and empty side next to me, I went back to Instagram...typing a simple comment under Mariana's last post: "The lake still calls. This time, I'm really listening."

The cursor blinked, waiting. *Send or delete?* I needed to make up my mind on communicating with her. I didn't even know why it felt so hard.

Send. I tapped the button and placed my phone face-down on the nightstand.

Three weeks later, I settled into my seat on the Guatemala-bound flight, a real plan in my carry-on and determination in my heart. The flight attendant's welcome announcement washed over me in Spanish I understood almost every word this time. I did eventually start those online classes. Did I have doubt about it all? Yes, I did. Could I be making the biggest, dumbest mistake of my life? Quite possibly. Was I walking into it with my head up and shoulders back? Yes, I was. Sometimes you have to trust what pulls you more than what holds you. Fuck it. If I failed, I still had my family's support.

17

TOURIST MAPS DON'T
SHOW POWER LINES

The shuttle from Guatemala City lurched around the final curve, and Lake Atitlán spread before us like spilled ink between three gigantic volcanoes. My heart jumped into my throat. This was real. *Holy shit.* I'd actually done it. Again! Third time's the charm!

"Primera vez?" The driver caught my wide-eyed expression in the rearview mirror.

"No," I managed, clutching my backpack closer. "Tercera vez." I was proud and ecstatic. Ninety days. Ninety days. Oh my fucking God, I was going to be here for 90 days!

The lake looked familiar yet fresh, like running into an old friend who'd gotten a makeover. It made me smile. This time, I was here to explore building something, and my hired car wound through Panajachel's narrow streets. Unlike my previous visits, I'd arranged to go directly to the small casita I'd found through Ana's family connections. It wasn't much—just a simple house next to a local family's home—but it was a start. And the price was right, even if my instincts still screamed for room service and concierge assistance.

After dropping off my bags later that afternoon, I ventured out to Café Loco, one of the spots I'd learned about in a Facebook group that said locals and expats often mixed. The aroma of locally roasted coffee drew me in, along with the promise of reliable WiFi. I needed to check in with Kendra and my parents anyway.

"¿Café?" The barista's greeting was warm but unhurried.

"Sí, por favor. Um... grande?" I pointed at the largest cup size. My tired brain refused to construct better Spanish. *Need to work on rolling your R's,* my inner voice lectured me.

A group of women occupied the corner table. Their conversation drifted in Spanglish. A little of this. A little of that. One had a yoga mat propped against her chair, while another spread papers covered in what looked like business plans across the wooden surface.

"Ayyyy!" The familiar call of African-American culture stood out immediately. I had to admit, it caught me off guard, but I would not complain. "You should join us," one called out as I searched for a seat.

The group was diverse, and consisting of five women. Most of them were drinking and jolly as hell.

"We're planning a lake tour for tomorrow," another one called out. "Checking out some of the smaller villages. Fresh eyes are always welcome," she told me.

I hesitated. The old Nyla would have politely declined, retreated to a safe distance. This was so random. So spontaneous and in my face. But...I wasn't here to play it safe anymore. *What should I do?*

I held my coffee closer, studying the group while pretending to look for a seat. Two appeared to be backpackers, their sun-weathered faces and well-worn Chacos telling familiar traveler tales. The Black woman who'd called out wore a beautiful head wrap and bangles that clinked musically when she gestured. Another had that distinct digital nomad look: MacBook covered in political and queer stickers with light blue glasses perched on her head. The fifth woman remained absorbed in her papers, only occasionally looking up to nod or comment.

"I'm Jade," the woman in the head wrap announced. Her smile was infectious, her accent hinting at Atlanta or maybe Houston. "And you look like you need more than coffee. Did you just get in today?"

"That obvious, huh?" I smiled back, my shoulders relaxing slightly. "I'm Nyla. And yes." Wow. I always thought it was hard to make friends as an adult.

"Pull up a chair," one of the backpackers offered. Her accent was distinctly Australian. "Unless you're one of those super organized types who already has their whole trip planned?"

"Actually..." I started, then paused. How exactly do you tell a group of travelers you're attempting to build a life where they're vacationing? "I'm here for a while. A few months, at least."

That caught the attention of the woman with the business plans. She looked up, reading glasses sliding down her nose. "Really? Work or..." she left the question hanging.

"Or," I answered, settling into an empty chair. "Still figuring out the details."

Jade's bangles jangled as she reached for the coffee pitcher. "Girl, aren't we all? Top up?"

The conversation flowed easier than I expected, though I kept catching myself before sharing too much. My plans still felt too fragile and too personal to share with strangers, even friendly ones who reminded me of home. Still, when they mentioned tomorrow's tour hitting some of the smaller villages I hadn't visited yet, my curiosity piqued.

"We're taking a private lancha," the Australian explained. "Much better than those tourist boats that try to cram in twenty people and steer like maniacs."

The business plan woman, Mikayla, I learned, finally set her papers aside. "I'm checking out potential locations," she said cryptically. "Always good to have new perspectives."

I recognized that careful way of not quite explaining yourself. I'd been doing the same thing since I sat down.

The women's easy laughter and fusion of Spanish and English filled the café as the afternoon arched toward evening. I nursed my coffee, letting their chatter about village markets and sunset spots envelop me. They clearly knew the area, even if some of them were just passing through.

"So, you'll join us tomorrow?" Jade quizzed me. "Ten AM at the dock. We're hitting Santiago first, then working our way around."

I weighed the invitation. A day on the lake would help me get oriented, see how things had changed since my last visit. *Do it.* My inner voice pushed me. "Count me in," I finally said. "But I should head out now. Still need to get my bearings in the neighborhood."

"Alright. Be safe!" We exchanged WhatsApp info—that was so much more popular in Guatemala than in the States, so I quickly adapted—and I headed out.

Walking back through Panajachel's lively streets, I took a different route than I'd come. That's when it happened. I passed Mariana's gallery. Unmistakably. In the window, I spied a new piece that instantly drew me in. Mariana had a way of building depth through layers of paint. She somehow made a flat canvas feel alive. *This is beautiful,* I thought. The image beckoned me to stand there longer than I meant to, studying how she'd created the fog's ethereal effect. The gallery was still open, but I wasn't ready to see her again. Kind of still embarrassed from the last time, I guess. So, no. Not yet.

Tomorrow would be about exploring the lake's villages with fresh eyes. But seeing Mariana's art reminded me that I'd really come back to find my own way of capturing this place's essence. I turned toward home...my temporary home, anyway just as street vendors packed up their wares.

"Buenas noches," a few offered me. *Good evening.*

I nodded and smiled, eager to wind down with a nice warm shower and deep sleep. What followed was my first real night in the casita. Between fireworks, music, barking dogs, and roosters, it felt like the village had a personal vendetta against sleep.

"Fuck..." was my first and only word upon awakening, but I was still excited about the boat trip with my new acquaintances.

Each village had its own personality: Santiago's traditional market sprawled up steep streets while San Marcos' New Age vibe attracted yogis and healers. San Pedro felt most like home, its mix of local life and foreign influence creating something uniquely its own. But reality set in fast once I was back in my casita. By day three, the power outages became routine. They were always at the worst moments, like when trying to video call Kendra. And the internet was a joke, despite my landlord's promises of "quality connection."

"¡No hay luz!" my neighbor called through the wall, like this was perfectly normal. Which, I was learning, it was.

I opened every blind to let natural light in. Trying to adapt without complaint. And when the electricity returned hours later, the internet refused to cooperate. The "high-speed connection" promised by my landlord turned out to mean "it sometimes works if the weather's good and not too many people are online." Shit! This is what social media posts don't show you about "expat life".

Even simple errands became adventures in miscommunication. At the local tienda, I thought I'd successfully asked for eggs and coffee but somehow ended up with instant chocolate milk powder and something that looked like pancake mix.

"No, no... huevos?" I tried again, making awkward chicken motions and "Os" with my hands that sent the shopkeeper's kids into fits of giggles.

"Ah, ¡huevos!" She disappeared into the back, returning with exactly what I needed. "¿Algo más?"

I stared blankly.

"Más?" She tried again with a gesture to other things. Her smile was patient.

"Ooooh! No, más. Gracias." I didn't need anything else.

I kept pressing forward through it all. But day five brought several issues simultaneously, a bit of mold in the bathroom I somehow didn't notice during the first few days. My landlord was apologetic and blamed it on the intermittent rain—essentially saying was a part of life. A "Es normal." To be exact. Maybe it was normal here, but I couldn't work like this. Not if I wanted some semblance of comfort and more developed world's standards. Something had to give.

My head throbbed as I went for an afternoon walk, the

cacophony of man and nature's sounds all around. A child chased a puppy past me, both of them kicking up dust from the unpaved road.

"¡Cuidado!" Someone shouted just as a motorcycle zipped past, forcing me to jump aside. My grocery bag tipped, sending an egg rolling down the cobblestones. Meanwhile, my phone buzzed with a message that wouldn't download.

This wasn't Miami. No concierge to solve problems, no Alex to smooth things over with his connections. Just me, stumbling through each day, trying to build something real in a place that felt surreal. What the actual fuck have I done?

After a week of cold showers, a gaggle of roosters and dogs, and spotty WiFi, I finally gave in and visited the Bitcoin ATM near the dock. The fees were criminal, but I needed reliable internet more than I needed the extra cash. *A mobile hotspot would solve at least one problem*, I thought.

"You're doing it wrong," a female voice said behind me just as I was about to complete the transaction.

I turned to find Mikayla from the boat tour. "There's a better exchange in San Pedro," she continued. "Less fees, more privacy. Want me to show you?"

"Lead the way." I was ready to do whatever to make this work. And I was thankful for her showing up at just the right time.

The lancha ride to San Pedro was fast, choppy, and probably unsafe. Freshwater soaked my jeans as we bounced across the water. Mikayla pointed out landmarks I'd missed on the tour: a hidden beach, a cluster of luxury villas under construction, a small hotel being renovated.

"That's Dulce's place," she said, gesturing to a whitewashed building set back from the water. "She's from one of the oldest families around the lake. Started out renting rooms to backpackers, now runs these transition programs for people trying to settle here." Her tone shifted slightly. "Smart woman. She saw the changes coming before anyone else did."

"I see," I responded, making a mental note to research this "Dulce" woman.

"But money is quietly finding its way in this region," Mikayla continued, raising her voice over the boat engine. "You can either fight it or figure out how to make it work for everyone," she added.

Before I could ask what she meant, the lancha heaved, sending my phone flying. I caught it just before it hit the water.

"First rule of lake life," Mikayla chuckled. "Nothing here goes according to plan."

Jesus Christ.

We docked in San Pedro just as clouds started gathering over the volcano. The cryptocurrency exchange turned out to be a small office above a cafe, run by a woman who switched effortlessly between Spanish, English, and what sounded like German as she helped various clients.

"See?" Mikayla gestured at the rate board. "Almost half the fees of that flagrant tourist trap in Pana."

"You were right. Thanks so much again!" The money gave me life and confidence back.

Thunder rolled across the mere. We'd need to head back soon if we wanted to beat the storm. But something about this place made me want to linger.

"You never said what kind of business you're planning," I ventured.

Mikayla's eyes narrowed slightly. "Neither did you."

Just then, someone in a dusty black pickup truck with a megaphone strapped to the hood rolled through. If I'd seen this in Miami, I'd say it was ghetto as hell. But here, it was normal.

"Welcome to real Atitlán life," Mikayla announced with an edge to her smile now. "Hope you're ready for it."

Thunder cracked again, closer this time. Mikayla glanced at her phone. "Last lancha leaves in twenty minutes. Unless you want to spend the night in San Pedro?"

"Nope." I pocketed my newly acquired hotspot. "Still getting settled in Pana."

"Gotcha." She gathered her things. "Take your time figuring out where you fit. It'll happen. And you can call me anytime. I'm happy to help! I've been here for a while. Well, between here, Antigua, and the city."

We hurried down the steep street as the first fat raindrops fell. A group of travelers rushed past, heading the wrong way for the dock.

"Over there!" Mikayla called out, pointing them in the right direction. She turned back to me. "Look, some of us meet at Café Loco every Wednesday. Expats, locals, people trying to build a community here. No pressure, but it might be helpful."

The boat's motor was already running when we reached the dock. Through the gathering storm, I could see lights flickering back on in Panajachel.

"Why are you helping me?" I asked as we climbed aboard.

Mikayla secured her laptop inside her waterproof bag. "Because someone did the same for me when I first came. Besides," she grinned, "looks like you could use a friend who isn't trying to sell you healing crystals or yoga retreats."

Ha! I appreciated the gesture more than she knew. Mikayla was at least a decade older than me, Caucasian, and carried the kind of glow that comes from a life spent outdoors—bronzed and softened like driftwood under the sun. Loose strands of blonde hair framed her face. They were wild from the lake breeze. Still, there was a grounded warmth in her sharp wit and steady gaze that made me feel safe, as though she understood exactly what I was running from.

18

LOCAL KNOWLEDGE

D ulce's property stretched toward the lake like a cascade of descending terraces woven with creeping vines. Each level offered a different view of the volcanoes. The main house was a masterwork of local stone and wooden beams that probably predated Guatemala's independence. *Wow.* I decided to take a tour.

"My great-grandfather built this place." Dulce's explanation carried history without sentiment. Her English was perfect even if punctuated with a Spanish accent. "It's always been more than a home. Now it's a legacy."

I followed her through an open courtyard where beautiful bougainvillea spilled over stone walls. A youthful Maya woman arranged flowers at a table while another swept a light layer of volcanic ash from the tiles. One nodded respectfully as Dulce passed. The other didn't make eye contact.

"We cater to long-term guests," Dulce said, leading me to a balcony where the lake glinted in the early afternoon sun. "People searching for something. Anything. Whatever. It doesn't matter. We're here for them." Her laugh was musical but measured. "Mikayla mentioned you worked in hospitality?" She paused at the edge of the terrace. In her crisp white linen dress and jade jewelry, she embodied effortless authority.

"I did. In Miami." *I did more than "work in it" – I practically ran a location*, I thought, but held back. The air tightened. Mikayla had told me this was a good place to hang my hat for a while since I didn't like the Airbnb I was in. Maybe she had her reasons.

"Ah, Miami." Something flickered across her face. "That's nice. Very different from here though."

Before I could respond, she moved again, pointing out guest rooms. I noticed how the staff anticipated her movements, doors opening before she reached them, fresh coffee appearing as we passed the dining area.

"The monthly rate includes daily breakfast and dinner," she said, then added with careful emphasis, "Many find it helpful while they figure out their next steps."

The way Dulce said it made me wonder exactly how much Mikayla had told her about me. Mental note: share less.

A bell rang somewhere above us, and she smiled. "Perfect timing. Join us for dinner? The other guests would love to meet you."

"I appreciate the tour," I said, keeping my tone professional. "But I have a few other options to explore."

Dulce's smile stayed fixed. "Of course. Options," her voice dipped. "Though you might find those... other options less accommodating than they appear, especially long-term."

"Thank you." I smiled and left.

Outside, the lake breeze carried the scent of rain and coffee from a nearby café. Dulce's place was nice, but not quite was I was looking for. I had no idea what I wanted, but I knew it wasn't that.

Making my way back to my existing lodging, I caught up on messages. Mikayla had sent details about a tourism position at a vocational school. Room and board included. The place looked better than where I was and something about it felt right even if it were a humongous step down for me. It felt more right than Dulce's! So, I decided to check it out.

~

THE NEXT DAY, I took a tuk-tuk up a steep, winding road to the school Mikayla had mentioned. The ride rattled my bones, the metal frame creaking with every bump. *Skinch skinch, skinch* was all I could hear from the bouncing springs.

The building sat on a hill and its walls were plastered with painted murals. There were chips here and there in the dwelling, but overall, it was in good shape. When we stopped, I stepped out onto cracked cement and took it all in. It was a compact building. Bright murals of jaguars, tigers, and other big cats stood as a backdrop for steaming mugs and smiling servers. Inside the courtyard, students practiced carrying trays loaded with empty glasses, their laughter mixing with the scrape of chairs being dragged into a semi-circle. I felt like I'd landed in a college time capsule, but in a completely different world.

A handwritten sign taped to the door read: "Seeking Hospitality Professionals. Room and Board Provided." Hand. Written. Good Lord.

"Buenos dias! Soy Antonio!" a guy painting a wall greeted me enthusiastically. His smile was bright and he had a shock of dark curly hair.

I nodded with a smile.

The director met me in the hallway. Her name was Martha and she extended a firm handshake. Her silver hair was pinned neatly back. "Bienvenido, Nyla! You are exactly the type we've been waiting for," she said, gesturing for me to follow her into her office. The room smelled of lemon oil and a stack of paper menus sat on the corner of her desk.

Martha got straight to the point: "We need someone to teach practical skills—guest relations, event setup, things they can take into the field. You'd also have a private apartment in the staff residence. Does that interest you?"

I asked about noise, mildew, Internet and everything else I could think of, and she had a confident, decisive answer for every question.

"There would be no problems with any of that. We are small, but

professional. And we have backup generators with modern ameni-
ties. Antonio, who you probably saw on the way in, is always a phone
call away to fix most things," she continued selling me. "You'll also
have your own kitchen and workspace. The staff wing is separate
from student housing, of course. And many of our international
faculty stay with us long-term."

Wow. I had *not* expected *this* opportunity. The apartment she
showed me was tiny but thoughtfully designed – exposed beams,
local textiles, a private balcony with lake views. Finally, a space that
felt both authentic and livable.

"You can start next week," Martha offered, "if this suits you."

I watched sunlight dance across the polished wooden floors,
already imagining my laptop on the built-in desk, morning coffee on
the balcony. "Yes," I said. "I think it does." I nodded, more intrigued
than I'd expected. Now this felt like a foothold!

I WAS ecstatic later that night! Small wins. They felt amazing, and I
was proud of myself for not hightailing it back to the comforts and
modernity of Guatemala City. I almost broke down and did it. But
instead, that night I found myself having a solo, celebratory meal at a
quaint restaurant with a live guitar player. I now had a job and a
comfortable place to live. Small wins.

My plate of pepián barely registered as I inhaled the food. I was
hungrier than I'd realized. With the sauce still steaming and the
rice perfectly mounded, I shoveled it in my mouth without a care of
who might be watching. The restaurant's evening crowd ebbed
around me in waves of Spanish and laughter while I toyed with my
fork.

Bzzzt. A video call notification lit up my phone. Ugh. It was Alex.
Without looking closely, I accidentally accepted rather than declined
the call. Shit.

"Nyla?" His face filled my screen. Damn, he looked sharp. Beautiful beard shape up. Piercing blue eyes.

My spoon clattered against ceramic. "Damn it." I scrambled to end the call, but my fingers slipped on the screen.

"Babe, wait! Please, please, please! I just need to know you're okay." His voice fractured. I could see that he was working late at the Jeffrey. Nothing had changed there.

"I'm fine," I spoke loudly over the music. "But I can't do this."

"Can't do what? Talk to someone who loves you?' A muscle twitched in his jaw. "Look at where you are – eating alone in some run-down café, Nyla. You deserve better than this."

The server approached with fresh tortillas. I politely waved her off, but not before Alex caught the exchange.

"You can barely communicate there! Come home. We can fix us."

"You don't get to decide what is best for me anymore, Alex."

"I'm sorry. Babe, please. The hotel's struggling without you. I'm str —" He stopped to compose himself. "I've been thinking about your ideas. The cultural programs you wanted. We could implement them all. I can give you more paid time off. Whatever you want, Nyla. Would you at least consider it?"

A burst of music erupted from the kitchen: marimba and guitar tangling together in joyous chaos. I was starting to *love* the unplanned magic here.

"No." I smiled, really seeing him now. Seeing us. "You'd package it, sanitize it, turn it into another Jeffrey Experience. That's not what I want anymore, Alex."

"What do you want then? I'm listening."

"To build something of my own." I watched his face contort. "Goodbye, Alex."

"Nyla—"

Click. I ended the call. My hands shook as I blocked his number, but my chest felt lighter.

"¿Todo bien?" The server reappeared. Concern creased her forehead.

"Sí." I smiled. "Mejor que bien." *Better than okay.*

"Ahhh perfecto! ¿Quiere postres?"

"Si, por favor." Yes, I would love dessert!

The server beamed and hustled off, leaving me alone with the pleasant ache of certainty. The live guitar shifted into something slower, more intimate, and that's when I noticed one of Mariana's paintings behind the musician. *This woman is everywhere*, I thought, then wondered if it were more like the phenomena of liking a certain car and then suddenly noticing that brand everywhere. I wasn't sure, but I did know her art was becoming as much a part of my landscape here as the volcanoes themselves.

The server returned with flan drowning in caramel sauce. As I savored the first bite, my phone lit up again. This time it was a WhatsApp message from Mikayla. I swiped down to preview it: "Heard you're moving to the school. Smart choice. But there's something you should know about that neighborhood..."

I clicked it open, my spoon freezing halfway to my mouth.

19

NEIGHBORHOOD WATCH

Mikayla's warning turned out more complicated than I expected: "That area is ground zero for the lake's culture wars," she told me. Dulce's tourism crowd versus the artist community. And your new boss, Martha, plays both sides," she gossiped through a WhatsApp call.

It was the next morning, and I was packing my things—prematurely readying to leave the unfitting casita for good! "What do you mean?" Mikayla seemed to know about everyone despite sharing little about herself.

"Meet me at Café Loco for lunch. I think there's someone else you should get to know."

I thought for a moment. "Okay, fine."

That "someone" turned out to be Elena, a local art gallery owner who had watched the neighborhood transform over the past decade. She sat across from us now wearing a bright red scarf and black camisole. Elena stirred honey into her tea.

"So...you've met Mariana?" Elena's eyes sparkled with interest. "She's become quite the voice for preserving local arts. Ever since she came back from Vegas..." She exchanged a meaningful look with

Mikayla. "Well, let's just say her ex-partner's big ideas for 'moving Atitlán forward' didn't align with her vision for the community."

The casual mention of an ex-partner...*a woman? Or business partner?* You never knew these days, nor should it have mattered. Still, the word settled something I hadn't realized needed settling. *Hmph.* But before I could process it, Elena continued: "Now Mariana's leading the resistance against outside developers. Which makes your arrival...interesting," Elena finished, looking directly at me. Her dark eyes were too curious. Or maybe mischievous.

"Interesting?" I set down my coffee. "But I'm just teaching at the vocational school."

"Yes, but..." Elena's smile turned knowing. "Teaching hospitality. To locals. Who'll work in the exact kinds of places Mariana's fighting against."

"That's not—" I started, but Mikayla cut in.

"The school walks a fine line," she explained. "They prepare students for tourism work while trying to preserve local traditions. It's a balance not everyone agrees with." She tossed back some fried grasshoppers that were on the table. I refused trying them. Couldn't do it. I wasn't ready for insect decadence just yet.

A waiter approached with fresh pastries. "Todo bien?"

"Si. Si." We sang in unison.

"Nyla, there's a community meeting tonight about local development." Elena slid a flyer across the table. "Mariana usually leads them. You should come. It might help you understand what you're walking into."

Mikayla shot her a sharp look. "Elena..."

"What? She should know the neighborhood dynamics." Her innocence felt practiced. "Besides, Mariana could use some alternate viewpoints."

I picked up the flyer and ran my fingers over the yellow border. The meeting location was just two blocks from my new apartment.

"Think about it," Elena said, rising. "Oh, and welcome to the neighborhood!"

THE COMMUNITY MEETING was held in an old church hall. High windows. Long shadows. Scratched up wooden floors. I slipped in quietly, choosing a seat near the back where a scatter of shades provided cover. Spanish and English buzzed throughout the room— mostly Spanish. There were locals and a few immigrants arranged in loose circles of conversation.

Mariana stood at the front, gesture-talking with two older men while referencing some papers spread across a folding table. She looked good in her paint-splattered jeans and a loose white shirt. And her hair was twisted up with a pencil again. Something in my throat tightened at the sight of her. What was it about Mariana's aura that constantly arrested me?

"Bienvenido!" Elena appeared beside me. "I'm glad you came."

Mariana called the meeting to order before I could respond. Her Spanish flowed faster than I could follow, but her passion didn't need a translation. She clicked through slides showing before-and-after photos of lakeside villages, each one documenting the creep of modern development.

"We're not against progress," she switched to English, her eyes scanning the room. "But it needs to happen on our terms, preserving what makes Lago de Atitlán special." Her gaze landed on me, recognition glimmering across her face. Her lips twitched. Was it shock? Intrigue? Dismay? What did that mean? For a moment, the room held its breath. Well, at least I did.

The discussion that followed was heated but controlled. I caught fragments of Spanish, watching how Mariana handled opposing viewpoints. She was firm but fair, nothing like the dismissive woman from our last encounter. When voices rose about jobs and development, I found myself wanting to speak up but held back. I wasn't ready yet. Not here, not in this language, not in her space.

After the meeting, I slipped out quietly. Elena caught my eye and nodded, but didn't try to stop me. Thank Goodness. I'd gotten what I needed to get that night. At least I thought so. And I needed to decompress.

THE WEEKEND PASSED, and my first week at the vocational school whizzed in a blob of lesson plans and fumbled Spanish. The students were patient with me, often helping with words I stumbled over. They were also eager to practice English. Beatriz, who was barely nineteen, wanted to manage a boutique hotel. Edgar dreamed of his own restaurant. Each morning, they arrived eager to learn. And I was still mind blown that I'd randomly ended up teaching hospitality in one of the most far-flung places of Central America. This was not my plan, but hopefully, it was a stepping stone along the way. I couldn't beat the free apartment and cultural immersion, that's for sure.

"Profesora," Beatriz caught me after class one day. "Can I practice my English with you?"

It soon became a routine: English over coffee before class, Spanish during lessons. Other students joined. We talked about more than hospitality: their families' histories of all of Guatemala, their hopes for staying in their community while building something new.

By my third week, I was catching more of the rapid-fire Spanish in the teacher's lounge—especially the slang—and it made me feel good! Martha nodded approvingly when I managed entire conversations with the maintenance staff. Gradually, the language was becoming mine, not just something I borrowed.

That came in handy one day when the classroom's ceiling fan rattled ominously during my lesson on table settings. Antonio appeared in the doorway with a wrinkled hat on his head and wounded squirrel perched on his shoulder, both heads tilted at the same angle as they studied the fan.

"He's a rescue," Antonio explained. "But this…" Antonio glanced up, "is very dangerous." He reached for his tools.

The students giggled as the man talked to a bandaged-up squirrel about proper maintenance. I caught myself smiling too. There was something strangely endearing about their double act.

"All fixed, profesora," he announced later. "Though your AC might be next. I will check it next week. And that squeaky door of yours. I'll bring lubrication for the hinge."

"Gracias, Antonio!" I thanked him. It felt good to have a handyman on demand.

The days got easier and more pleasant with each hour. When another community meeting came around, I felt ready to contribute. This time I sat closer to the front. The same discussions arose, but this time, I thought of Beatriz's fierce determination...of Edgar's careful plans.

"And what about jobs?" A voice rose from the back. "Our children need opportunities."

I watched Mariana's shoulders tense slightly as she began responding. Without planning to, I found myself standing. "There can be both," I spoke up. My voice carried more confidence than I felt. Heads turned. Mariana's expression was unreadable, but I remained focused on her. "Development doesn't have to mean destruction."

Once again, our gazes locked and held. I fought the urge to look away. Unblinking. Unflinching. Holding. Energy passed between us before she continued her presentation. I have no idea what it was, but I knew that it happened. So did she. And I couldn't help but facilitate it.

One of the older men cleared his throat and asked, "And you are?"

"I teach at the vocational school," I answered, then added in careful Spanish, "Soy profesora de hospitalidad."

Mariana's eyebrow rose with a hint of a smile. My Spanish was better than during our last meeting, though still far from fluent.

"The school that trains our youth to work for outside developers?" Someone yelled out.

"No, no," I responded, switching back to English. I continued softly. "I teach them skills so they can choose their own paths. Maybe work in tourism, maybe start their own businesses. But always with respect for their community."

The room grew quiet. Mariana studied me. "Gracias, Nyla. Muchas gracias," she eventually said, then turned to address another question.

My heart was racing as I sat down. Elena squeezed my arm. "Not bad for your first meeting," she whispered.

People broke into smaller groups after the formal discussion ended. I gathered my things, unsure whether to stay or go. That's when I heard it.

"You've reeeally been practicing the language."

I turned to find Mariana behind me. My breathing stopped. "Yes," I confessed. "But I still have a lot to learn."

"Don't we all?" A hint of a smile played at her lips. "Your perspective tonight was unexpected. Your presence, too. Welcome back." Her eyes lingered on me.

"So you *do* remember me?" A big exhale escaped me.

"Yes, of course. You're not easy to forget," Mariana smiled warmly.

I blushed. "And was my perspective *good* unexpected or *bad* unexpected?"

"That depends." She tilted her head. "Are you still just passing through?"

The question carried weight from our last encounter. "No," I said firmly. "I'm here to stay for a while. To build something."

"Is that right?"

"Yes," my voice softened.

"Interesting." Mariana echoed Elena's earlier word, but without the edge. "What kind of something?"

Someone called her name from across the room before I could answer. She glanced over her shoulder, then back at me. "Until next time, Nyla."

Elena just looked at us. And then floated away. I'd been so caught up in Mariana's presence that I hadn't noticed Elena was still lingering for it all. Lord, I hope I don't become the next talk of the town. I might already be.

I watched Mariana walk away and took in a few necessary deep breaths. The revelation was as jarring as the charged air. Whatever I decided to build here, I knew now it would have to navigate the space between defense against new-age colonizers and future possibilities.

And somehow, that felt exactly right.

A WEEK LATER, an old pension stood three stories tall in front of me. Its walls were a faded turquoise and semi-visible behind thick, climbing vines. I'd first noticed it on my walks to school. It was impossible to miss with its wide balconies and direct lake view. But today was different. Today, there was a "Se vende" sign in the window. *For sale.*

Mikayla's network had tipped me off about the sale before it went public. "A local family is retiring," she'd said. "None of their kids want to take it over."

The price was surprisingly reasonable, probably because the place needed serious work. But I could see past the cracked paint, wild courtyard and busted windows. It had potential.

That dream lasted exactly forty-five minutes into my first meeting with a Miami investor that I hoped could help.

"Look, Nyla," Nigel's voice crackled through WhatsApp. "You know I respect your expertise, but Guatemala? After everything with Alex..." He paused. "Let's just say certain people have concerns about your judgment right now."

Certain people. Of course. I ended the call and stared at the building's weathered facade. Alex's influence. Again.

"Typical tourist, no?" A familiar voice made me jump. "See something old and immediately want to buy it to capitalize on it?"

I turned to find Mariana leaning against a nearby tree.

"Actually," I said, "I was admiring how the original tiles are still intact under that awful green paint someone added on the corners."

Her eyebrow rose slightly. "You know about Guatemalan tile work?"

"I've been learning. My students' families share stories about the craftsmanship that went into these old buildings." I gestured at the guesthouse. "Like those balconies designed to create natural air circulation, not just decoration."

Mariana stepped closer, really looking at the building now.

"Those balconies..." I traced their outline in the air. "I can already see morning light hitting them while guests enjoy coffee, birdsong and solitude..."

Mariana's presence offered warmth in the cooling evening air as she inched closer. "Do you always see more than just the surface?"

I turned to face her and saw that she wasn't looking at the building anymore. She was looking at me and the intensity in her gaze caught me off guard.

"I've spent too long seeing only what others wanted me to see," I admitted. The words tasted metallic. They were honest in a way I hadn't planned.

"And now?"

"I'm learning to trust myself and my vision now." I gestured at the wild courtyard. "Like here. Most people would see chaos and neglect, but I see..."

"The spaces between things." Mariana knelt beside a broken fountain where moss had claimed the stone. "That's where the real story lives." Her fingers tracked patterns in the velvet green. "In my paintings, I spend more time on what isn't there than what is. The shadow behind a volcano. The breath between waves."

She glanced up with an unguarded expression. "Once, in Vegas, I had a gallery owner tell me to paint 'prettier sunsets.' So, I gave him a canvas of pure darkness with one point of light. Told him it was the moment before the sun slept." A wry smile played at her lips. "He didn't get it."

I giggled. The image of her quiet defiance made me want to know more. "I used to sneak extra food to the hotel kitchen staff during their breaks—at my old job in Miami. The owner had this strict policy about 'employee meals,' but I couldn't stand watching them serve elaborate dinners on empty stomachs."

"A rebel with a cause." Her eyes sparkled. "My students at the cultural center are like that – they save half their art supplies to share with kids who can't afford classes."

"You teach?"

"Twice a week. Though mostly I just provide the space and watch them create their own rules." She stood, dusting off her knees. "Last week, this eight-year-old decided all the trees in her painting should be purple. When I asked why, she said 'because trees are tired of being green.'"

"And what did you say?"

"That she should paint an entire forest of tired trees." Mariana smirked. "Sometimes the best thing we can do is give people permission to see the world differently."

Her words caressed a wound I'd been nursing. "I spent years making sure everything looked perfect from the outside. The right clothes, the right smile, the right opinions..."

"And look at you here now...seeing beauty in broken fountains while making friends with judgmental artists." She met my eyes. "Life has a strange way of leading us home."

My phone buzzed, startling me. We both glanced down at the lit screen.

"Bad timing?" Mariana asked, her tone neutral but curious.

"Just... Miami trying to remind me it exists." I slipped the cellular into my pocket. "But I'm here now."

"Mm." She studied me for a moment longer than was comfortable.

The sun was setting now, painting the walls in shades of amber and rose. Mariana took a step back, but her eyes seized mine. "Come to my studio tomorrow evening? I'm working on something that lives in the spaces between things. Would love to know what you think of it..."

There was more in her invitation than just art, I could feel it. "I'd like that."

I watched her walk away. Her words settled into me like ink into paper, and I wanted to bleed into her thoughts...to flow where her silence pooled. Somewhere in the distance, church bells began their evening clangs. Dogs still barked in the distance, and zooming tuk-tuks all came back into my sensory awareness. Had it been that loud throughout our conversation? I couldn't remember. My phone stayed dark in my pocket, but I could feel Alex's message waiting like a shadow at noon. Tomorrow, I decided. Tomorrow I would face whatever I needed to regarding him.

20

GHOSTS IN GLASS HOUSES

"You sound different." Kendra's voice carried that nosy little-sister certainty through my cell's speaker.

"Different how?" I adjusted my blouse. It was the third one I'd tried on. A gallery visit shouldn't make me this nervous, but it did.

"I don't know. Like you're actually enjoying yourself in that dusty, dog-riddled lake town." A pause. "Still no mystery man making you smile?"

"For the last time, no." I laughed, though something fluttered in my chest at the question. "Not everything's about finding someone, Kendra, especially after letting go of Alex."

"Mm-hmm. Then why are you changing clothes at seven PM on a Tuesday?"

I froze midway through reaching for my earrings. "How did you know?"

"I didn't—not for sure—but I can hear hangers clicking, big sis. And you've got that distracted voice you used to get before dates." She paused again. "You know, the ones you actually wanted to go on."

"It's not..." I stopped, unsure how to explain something I barely understood myself. How could I tell her about Mariana's invitation, about the way time bent when we talked? About the current of possibility that I felt whenever she was around? "It's just an art gallery visit. Professional networking."

"Right. At night. In what's probably your third outfit."

"Fourth," I admitted, then caught myself. "But only because—"

A notification lit up my phone: *Still in Guatemala? We should talk. A big favor, please The Charlotte project needs your touch. -A*

"Nyla? You there?"

"Yeah, sorry. Just..." I swallowed. "It's Alex again. New number."

"Oh, for fuck's sake! Do you want me to have him legally threatened? Because I totally can."

"No, it's fine. I'm heading out anyway." I grabbed my bag, suddenly eager to be somewhere else. "Love you."

"Love you, too. And Nyla?"

"Yeah?"

"Whatever, or whoever, is making you smile like that? Keep them."

I ended the call and caught my reflection in the mirror. Was I smiling? The woman staring back looked nervous, excited, and alive. She also looked *nothing* like the old version of myself I'd been in Miami. Yes, I was smiling.

The walk to Mariana's corridor took exactly twelve minutes. It was cool out, and I clutched my blue scarf to my neck. I appreciated not having to drive everywhere...heck, not having to drive at all. Small town life was so different. There was no part of me who missed being stuck in traffic on Florida's turnpike.

Through the windows, I could see Mariana moving between easels, adjusting something here, stepping back there. She worked with such focus, such grace. Such—

"Nyla."

The voice behind me stopped my heart. I knew its cadence, its depth, its ability to reshape reality. But it couldn't be. Not here. Not now.

"This is quite a change from the Jeffrey, isn't it?" Alex stepped into the lamplight wearing travel-worn khakis and a polo that had seen better days. His stubble and rumpled appearance couldn't hide the tension in his jaw. "I can't fathom how you could love this place."

The door opened behind me. "We're actually clos—" Mariana's voice cut off as she registered the scene. Her eyes moved between us, taking in Alex's stance and my rigid posture.

"You must be the artist," Alex said, with the fakest smile I'd seen all year. "I've been admiring your work in Nyla's office. Though she never mentioned knowing you personally."

"That's because it wasn't relevant," I found my voice. "What are you doing here, Alex?"

"Checking on an investment." He stepped closer. "The Charlotte property's almost ready. The board's looking for someone to lead our cultural integration programs. Someone who understands...local authenticity." His speech pattern made it sound dirty.

Mariana's hand tightened on the door frame. "The gallery is closed." The steel in her voice made both Alex and me swivel. "Whatever business you have can wait until morning."

Alex's laugh held no warmth. "I didn't fly all this way to be dismissed by a—"

"She said the gallery's closed." I raised my voice and spoke more strongly. "And I'm not interested in your offers. I don't work for you anymore."

Alex stepped back. He adjusted his shirt. "We'll talk tomorrow, Nyla. When you're thinking more clearly." He glanced at Mariana. "Interesting technique, by the way. Using shadows to hide imperfections."

"We won't," I snapped. I'm going back."

"We'll talk!" Alex screamed and spun around.

After Alex walked away, silence crammed the space he'd vacated. I couldn't look at Mariana, couldn't bear to see judgment or sympathy in her eyes.

"Come inside," she said finally. "I think we both could use a drink."

I debated. My hand still trembled against my scarf. The last thing I wanted was pity, but when I looked up, Mariana's expression held a quiet fury that made her brandy eyes simmer with heat.

"That man," she muttered, moving behind her small counter, "has excellent timing. I was just about to break my one rule about drinking alone while working." She pulled out a dusty bottle and two clean coffee mugs. "Unfortunately, I don't have proper glasses here."

The normalcy of her irritation made me laugh. It was so different from concerned platitudes. "Coffee mugs are perfect, actually." I settled onto a creaky wooden stool. My eyes followed her delicate hands as she poured. They were steady, certain, flecked with dried orange paint.

"This is Mezcal," she explained, sliding one mug over. "From my cousin's farm. Have you ever heard of it?"

"No."

"Well, I hope you like it," she offered. "He'd be horrified to see it served like this."

"Then we won't tell him." I wrapped my fingers around the ceramic, breathing in the smoky scent. "I'm sorry about that."

"Don't." She stopped me, not unkindly. "That's not why I invited you in."

"I know, you'd already asked me over but…"

Mariana took a sip, then suddenly grinned. "I wanted to show you something I've been working on. It's terrible."

"Terrible?"

"Spectacularly awful. I've ruined three canvases trying to get it right." She headed toward a corner draped in cloths. "Coming?"

Beverage in hand, I followed. Curiosity overtook my lingering unease. The painting she unveiled made me choke on my drink. It was a riot of clashing colors and misshapen forms that somehow managed to be both violent and oddly mesmerizing.

"You're right," I said, tilting my head. "It's horrible." *Did I really just say that?* I put the Mezcal down. It was too soon for this much honesty.

Her startled laugh ricocheted through the gallery. "Finally, someone who doesn't try to find meaning in my mistakes." She leaned against the wall, studying me instead of the art. "Most people would've lied."

"I'm done with lies," I spoke confidently, despite Alex's presence still haunting me. I picked my drink back up and tossed it back. *Oof.* The booze burned warm in my chest, loosening words I hadn't meant to share. "Even the pretty ones."

"Good." She raised her mug in a toast. "To ruining perfectly good canvases and telling uncomfortable truths."

Mariana said it like failure and honesty were things to celebrate rather than hide. The words shifted something in my spirit and I found myself telling her about my first week at the hotel. Years ago, when I'd accidentally sent an entire wedding party to the wrong beach. "I was so afraid of admitting my mistake that I hired a water taxi to ferry them back before anyone noticed."

"Did it work?"

"The bride got seasick. It was a disaster." I smiled at the memory. "But you know what? The groom later told me it was the most memorable part of their trip—because they were able to laugh about it later. Sometimes the worst moments..."

"Make the best stories," she finished, eyes crinkling.

"Yes. Plus, I'd done a ton to make it up to them and their guests – all free. All top notch."

Mariana nodded approvingly before suddenly straightening up. "Wait here."

She disappeared into her office, returning with something clutched behind her back. "Close your eyes."

"Why?"

"Because I'm asking nicely." When I complied, I heard her moving around, then: "Okay, look."

A small canvas sat on her easel. Unlike the chaotic piece from before, this one showed a simple scene. It was of a coffee mug on a windowsill with steam rising in mesmerizing spirals. The backdrop was of the lake and volcanoes. But the steam twisted into impossible shapes, forming tiny dancing figures that seemed to move if you looked too quickly. And there was an outline of a woman.

"It's not finished," she said. "I started it the morning after you ran out of here last time." She tapped her hands against her thighs. "Anyway, it's yours if you want it. As an apology for probably overcharging you on the first one—I know I didn't personally sell it, but vendors do that to vacationers."

The painting blurred slightly as I stared at it. I could see the places where she'd struggled, the edges that didn't quite meet. But because she'd noticed how I took my coffee that morning, how I'd watched the lake through her window. She'd seen me, really seen me, even as I was running away.

"I love it," I said softly. "But I'm not sorry about what I paid for the first one. It was worth every quetzal...even more now that I know you."

Mariana moved closer. I did, too. She reached to adjust the canvas angle just as I leaned in for a better look, and our hands brushed. The contact was brief but electric. Her fingers were warm against mine and my breath became jagged in my throat. My stomach quivered. Neither of us pulled away immediately. I could hear her exhale softly as her eyes locked on mine. Slowly. My lips parted as I began retracting my hand.

That's when we heard it. Marco's voice drifted through the gallery windows. *Marco?* I knew I wasn't mistaken, but was perplexed at why he would also here. *No way.* "El señor tiene una visión para la comunidad..."

My heart sank. I definitely knew that voice and unique way of selling someone else's dreams. And I knew exactly whose vision Marco was translating.

"Your friend from earlier is persistent," Mariana said quietly, filling in the now awkward moment.

"Ex-boss, and not a friend." The mezcal turned sour in my mouth. "But that is one word for it." Outside, Alex's voice cut through the evening air, all business confidence and trained charm.

"Think of the opportunities," he said. "Marco, explain about the cultural preservation fund—"

"¿El fondo para preservación cultural?" Marco's translation carried that same eager-to-please tone I remembered from the Jeffrey. The tone that had once made me trust him. *This is fucking insane!* A foreign blend of angst and rage twisted in me, but I tampered both down in front of Mariana.

"They're talking to Hugo Francisco," Mariana moved to the window. "He owns half this block."

I joined her. Through the ash-covered glass, I could see Alex and Marco with an elderly man. Even in the dim light, Alex's posture emitted authority. He'd changed into a sharp shirt to replace his travel-worn look. Marco stood beside him with a notebook documenting everything. The perfect assistant. *Ugh!*

"Some things don't change," I hissed and rolled my eyes.

Mariana glanced at me sharply. "You know the translator?"

"Yes. He used to work for me. With me." The distinction felt important. "Before I learned what loyalty really meant to him."

Outside, Marco's voice grew more animated as he detailed whatever ridiculous promises Alex was making. The same voice that had once apologized for betraying me, explaining about his mother's failed dreams. Now here he was, helping Alex chase me down—ready to facilitate whatever sociopathic schemes would get me back to Miami.

"Your ex-boss brings back up to a casual visit?" Mariana's tone was pierced with an edge.

"A little more than former employer, unfortunately. And Alex doesn't do casual anything." I wrapped my arms around myself, suddenly cold despite the mezcal's warmth. "Everything is strategy with him. Even people."

Hugo Francisco was nodding now. He gestured expansively as Marco translated something about "reuniones mañana" – *meetings tomorrow.*

"Well," Mariana said, moving away from the window. "Tomorrow should be noteworthy."

The easy intimacy from just moments ago had vanished. I could almost see her walls going back up. The artist and community defender were replacing the woman who'd shared bad art and good booze.

"Mariana—" I started.

"It's late." She began gathering the coffee mugs. "And apparently there are important business meetings tomorrow."

"I'm not part of whatever he's planning," I argued.

"You aren't?" Her eyes met mine. "He seems to think you understand 'local authenticity' quite well when he was 'checking on his investment.'"

"You don't understand." The way she threw Alex's words back at me stung. "And that's not fair." My shoulders slumped.

"No?" She sighed, some of the hardness leaving her face. "Maybe not. But fairness isn't usually part of these developments, is it?"

The voices faded outside. I watched Alex hand Hugo Francisco a business card through the window.

"I should go," I whispered, though everything in me wanted to stay and explain.

Mariana nodded, already turning away. "Probably best. Sounds like tomorrow will be busy for everyone."

I moved toward the door, then stopped. "The painting—"

"Keep it." She didn't turn around. "Consider it a souvenir of Lake Atitlán."

But it's not even done.

I left without responding, slipping out a side door to avoid Alex and Marco. The evening air had lost its earlier magic, and the walk home felt longer than twelve minutes. I was hurt. Angry. Confused. So many things. Too many things. A rogue tear threatened to fall through it all. Still, my life was a mess no matter how much I tried to clean it up. Fucking Alex! Fuck Alex! I needed to get rid of him pronto and for good!

Behind me, I heard Marco's voice one last time: "Mañana será un gran día, Hugo Francisco!" *Tomorrow will be a great day!*

I wasn't so sure about that.

As I walked home on near-empty streets, I noticed most of the shop doors were shuttered. I pushed my hands deeper into my pockets, walking faster to outpace the thoughts chasing me. I just wanted to be home and behind a locked door, where Alex's shadow couldn't reach me.

Nearing my place, I heard a soft whimper that stopped me in my tracks. I looked around, not seeing anything at first. And again. I heard the soft cry of an animal. Lord, don't let it be a racoon or something else I didn't need tonight!

Rrru. Rrru. It came from a dark corner near an overturned trash bin. I squinted into the shadows and saw a small shape, trembling but alert. Another whimper came, louder this time. I stepped closer – like the idiot in scary movies – crouching down as the dim light revealed the source.

"Oh my!" It was a puppy. Its fur was tangled and matted, patches of dirt clinging to its tiny frame. Wide and uncertain eyes locked onto mine.

"Hey there," I said, keeping my voice low. My knees hit the pavement as I knelt, trying not to spook it. "You lost, little one?"

The puppy backed up, bumping into the wall behind it. Its ribs showed beneath the grime, and its tail tucked low. It didn't growl or bark—it just watched me, unsure whether I was friend or foe.

What if this was a trap? My logic and Miami wits snapped me up and a step back. *What if it's not?* It took another step back. But...I pulled an energy bar from my bag and tore off a piece while looking around. There was no one around and a bright streetlamp gave me a clear peripheral view. "You hungry?" I held it out, my hand steady. The puppy sniffed the air but didn't move. I set the food down between us and waited.

"Hola, professor!" I heard in the distance. It was one of my students, waving and smiling. *Good sign.*

"Buenas noches!" I called back.

Minutes passed. The street began rumbling with a few cars and other pedestrians. Finally, the pup crept forward. Tentative and shaky. Its nose soon touched the offering, and it ate in cautious bites. Every few seconds, its eyes darted up to me.

"You've had a rough day too, huh?" I let out an unsteady breath and sat back on the ground. The cold seeped through my jeans, but I didn't care. For the first time in hours, I wasn't thinking about Alex or Marco or Mariana. Just this tiny creature in front of me.

When the puppy finished the last crumb, it looked up at me, its eyes wide and expectant. I stood, brushing off my hands. "Sorry, little one," I said softly. "That's all I have, and I can't take you with me."

It didn't follow when I got up and walked away. I glanced back once to see it still sitting there, small and alone in the shadows. Guilt penetrated me, but I kept going. I wasn't in a place to save anything.

When I reached my building, I caught the soft *pad-pad-pad* of tiny paws behind me. I turned. There it was, a few feet away, watching me with that same tilted head.

"Really?" I sighed, jamming my old school skeleton key in the knob. I stepped inside my first-floor apartment. I couldn't believe the dog caught up to me and followed me home.

Later, lying in bed, I heard more sounds—a soft scratching at the door for several seconds before it went quiet. I peered out the window. The puppy was curled up on a doormat, a tiny ball of fur under a light.

I leaned my head against the wall. "Damn it." I whispered. "What am I going to do about this fucking dog?"

The next two days passed in a whirlwind of classes and avoiding thoughts of Alex's appearance. But each night, like clockwork, the scrabbling would return. By the third evening, the puppy looked different. She was clean this time. Had a botched haircut, too. I'd learned from my students that she'd been wandering around the property since the first time she followed me home and the rest of the staff had liked her enough to clean her up and feed her real food regularly. Still, she seemed particularly drawn to me.

"You can't stay here," I insisted, but the dog sat there on my "Bienvenido" mat, tail thumping hopefully against the floor. Her eyes were big and bright in the dim light. Behind her, a bolt of lightning split the sky. She shuddered. Anxious. Shit.

I sighed. "Fine. Just until the storm passes."

The pup bounded in like she'd been waiting for an invitation all along, immediately finding the spot by my desk where she'd napped during yesterday's rain. I hadn't meant to let her in then either, but somehow she'd wormed her way past my defenses. Much like everything else about Guatemala.

Eeep Eeep. She looked up at me with complete trust, letting out adorable puppy sounds. "Sit over there, doggy." I ushered her over to a corner away from my workspace. As I sat down to cull through my email, a flashback of the carefree canine on the beach in Dania flashed like a polaroid reel. How far I'd come since that so-called wedding proposal night.

The puppy's head settled on my foot, her warmth seeping through my sock. Rain fell in sheets outside. It beat against the windows in a rhythm that was becoming as familiar as Miami's ocean waves. I glanced down. Her haircut really was terrible. One ear looked longer than the other, and patches of her golden-brown fur stuck out at odd angles. But her honey eyes were bright and unquestioning.

"You need a name," I found myself saying. "I can't keep calling you 'doggy' if you're going to keep showing up."

I closed my eyes, letting the rain wash over my thoughts. When I opened them, the puppy had rolled onto her back, paws cycling an invisible bicycle in the air. The little ragamuffin was totally at home.

"Ha! What do you think about Luna?" I asked her. Like the moon that kept pulling at my tides even when I tried to resist.

Her tail thumped against the floor. Good enough. Luna stretched, her bungled coiffure making her look like she'd lost a fight with scissors. But she didn't seem to care how she looked. She was too busy being exactly who she was.

∾

MORNING SLAMMED into my apartment like a brass section gone rogue. Seriously, not only was there not a gentle dawn, students' voices echoed across the courtyard. A clatter of kitchen prep from below and the metallic whine of the backup generator kicking in filled the air, too – and then there was an actual, fucking marching band playing terrible music somewhere close by. At 8:00 AM.

I hadn't slept. My skin tingled with leftover adrenaline. And my muscles coiled tight as copper wire. I. Was. Rigid. Plus, Luna was gone. Fuck my life...

Classes could wait. I punched out a message to Martha about needing personal time, then paced my small living room. I wanted coffee, but the coffee maker sputtered and died mid-brew due to another power outage that outlasted the generators. Perfect timing.

"Don't worry!" Antonio's voice carried through the darkness. "I know this building's moods. She just needs a little attention."

I loved the way he spoke.

Antonio worked by flashlight, telling stories about the school's history until I told him I had to take a call. I didn't, but I wanted a little silence. Funny enough, my phone lit up shortly after. Kendra. Then Mom. Then a Guatemala City number I didn't recognize. I ignored them all, but my fingers itched to call someone, anyone who could make sense of Alex materializing here like a nightmare in pressed khakis. Just not any of *them*. Antonio eventually left and gifted me a flashlight. Finally, I had a few minutes of silence. Just a few...until a knock at my door stopped my stride. Three sharp raps that screamed ...*him.*

"Nyla." Alex's voice carried through wood and plaster. "I want to talk."

From below, I heard my students arriving for morning practice: the screech of chairs, laughing voices mixing Spanish and English. Their normal routine felt surreal against this moment. My legs felt like overcooked spaghetti. *Pull it together, Nyla. Fuck, Alex.*

"Five minutes," Alex continued, his tone softening to that familiar dangerous warmth. "That's all I'm asking. Please, babe. I flew four hours for this conversation."

"I didn't ask you to." This motherfucker was unhinged! His presence catapulted me into a new mental space. I was afraid but furious.

"Right. Because running away is solving everything." Metal clinked. Something hit the doorknob. "Teaching at this... place, gallivanting with so-called artists, playing local in this dump – you are better than this, Nyla! You know it. I know it!"

Each word landed like a poker chip on felt. Too precise. Too calculated. Meant to raise the stakes. But something in his voice was ragged. Desperate in a way that made the hairs on my arm stand at attention.

I yanked the door open, letting the harsh fluorescent hallway light do the work of keeping him at bay. "That's what this is really about, isn't it? Not business. Not development. You can't stand that I'm building a *life* without you!"

Alex started a patronizing, dramatic slow clap as if I were giving a theatrical performance. His blue eyes were ice cold. Veins bulged in his neck. His jaw was tight. "Bravo, Nyla. Bravo." His clapping stopped abruptly. "Such conviction. Such independence." He stepped closer, cologne and coffee breath mixing in the stale hallway air. "But we both know you'll run out of money eventually."

"Go away."

"Or what? You'll call the police?" He glanced around the institutional hallway, lips curling. "Here?"

"I mean it, Alex." My voice came out steadier than I felt. "Leave."

He shouldered past me into my apartment. "Nice place." His tone dripped acid. "Very... petite." Alex picked up a hand-woven scarf I'd draped over a chair. "There's no way in fucking hell you really left me and our life for this...local *color*."

The door was still open. Students' voices drifted up the stairs. I could call out. Martha's office was just down the hall. But something in me refused. "No." I stepped between him and my small living space. "No, Alex. And I don't owe you any more explanations of why I left."

"I made you, Nyla. Everything you are—"

"Is mine. My choices. My mistakes. My life. You are nothing to me anymore!"

His face contorted, skin pulling tight across his cheekbones. "You ungrateful fucking b—" He lunged forward, fingers clamping around my biceps like a steel trap.

I jerked back but he yanked me closer. My shoulder screamed in protest. The odor of cologne and sweat stench choked me. "Let. Go." Each word scraped my throat.

"Or what?" His breath hit my face, hot and sour with rage. He slammed me against the wall hard enough for picture frames to rattle. Pain spider-webbed across my back. Alex laughed. A dark, psychotic lark from his belly. He kept squeezing me.

"Let me go!" I thrashed against his grip. "Son of a bitch!" I kneed him in the balls but didn't make full contact. Just enough to piss him off more. "Let me go!"

His other hand found my throat and the pressure made me see white. "Look at you!" He spat. "You think these people care about you? You're nothing without me. Nothing!"

Blood roared in my ears. I clawed at his fingers, lungs burning. Tears cascading. I wanted to scream but had no air. I struggled in his grip like a puppet dangling from taut strings. Through the fog creeping at the edges of my vision, I saw movement in the doorway, but my vision flickered black. *I. Need. Air...*

"¡CABRÓN!" Antonio's voice boomed through the hallway. "¡Quita tus manos de Nyla!"

Alex's grip loosened for a split second. I drove my knee up, catching him in the groin again. He doubled over with a grunt. I stumbled sideways, gasping for air.

Antonio charged in like a bull. Coiled muscle and righteous fury had arrived as I clamored for air. His fist connected with Alex's jaw without another word. The crack echoed off concrete walls. Alex staggered but swung back, catching Antonio's temple.

They crashed into my desk. Papers scattered like startled birds. "¡Pendejo!" Antonio spat blood. "You think you can come here and—" His next punch sent Alex reeling.

"Stop!" I screamed, but my voice came out raw, broken. "Someone call—"

More footsteps thundered up the stairs. Martha. Two other maintenance workers. Their voices blurred together in a storm of Spanish and English. Alex and Antonio went blow for blow, but Antonio had more might. More endurance. More will to protect me than Alex did to destroy me.

"¡La policía!"

"Get him out!"

"¡Dios mío, Nyla!"

"¡Llame a la policía!"

The maintenance workers pinned Alex's arms. He thrashed, t-shirt torn, blood trickling from his split lip. "This isn't over," he snarled. "You hear me? This isn't—"

"Yes, it is." My throat ached but I forced the words out. "Touch me again and I'll have you arrested for assault. I bet they'd love a pretty boy like you in Guatemalan jail."

His eyes popped wide – the first real fear I'd ever seen there. The workers dragged him toward the stairs, his designer sneakers scuffing against the concrete.

My legs gave out. I slid down the wall. My body trembled like a leaf in a hurricane. Antonio crouched beside me. His knuckles were raw, bloody and swelling.

"La clínica," he said softly. "We should have you checked."

I nodded, unable to speak. My arm throbbed where Alex had grabbed me. Bruises already blooming.

Martha pressed a cold cloth to Antonio's temple. "I've called the police," she said. "He cannot come back here. And I will look into private security for the building. I am sorry, Nyla."

"No." The word surprised me. "Por favor. It's not your fault at all. And let him run. He won't risk being arrested here." I touched my throat gingerly. "But document everything. Take pictures. If he tries anything else..."

Antonio helped me stand. My legs shook but held. Through the window, I watched Alex jump into a car waiting in the parking lot. Gravel sprayed in his wake.

"Gracias," I whispered to Antonio. To all of them. "Gracias a todos," I sniffled.

He shook his head. "Familia," he said simply. "We protect our own. I better never see him near you again. Or he'll regret it for the rest of his life." Antonio looked at me so protectively. So sweetly. I wanted to sink into him for the security. For the kindness and the no-strings-attached-masculinity that he offered. But I didn't, of course. I couldn't. I was still processing.

Martha wrapped her arm around my shoulders, steadying me. "Come. Let's get you both to the clinic."

I leaned into their support, letting the tremors subside. Alex had shown his true face at last. But he'd also shown me something else – that I wasn't as alone as I'd thought. That I found a new family here, in the place he'd tried to dismiss as beneath me.

My throat would bruise. My arm would ache. But I was finally, truly free.

From somewhere in the school, applause erupted. Students were celebrating something in their morning practice. The timing made me laugh like a maniac, a sound caught between triumph and relief. I pulled out my phone and typed a quick message to myself so I could remember the exact date and time when I physically wrote it in my journal: "It's done. Really done this time."

Later at a small storefront clinic, I sat on crinkly paper while a doctor documented my injuries in careful Spanish. Martha had insisted on accompanying me. Antonio ducked out after ensuring we made it safely. Like most men, he insisted his injuries were minor and would heal on their own. "No es nada," he winked. *It's nothing.* He'd left only after making Martha promise to call if we needed anything. His caring nature touched me more than I could express. I don't think I'd ever had a man protect me like that besides my father. I was grateful.

The doctor's gentle fingers probed my throat, her frown deepening at my winces. She spoke to Martha, who translated unnecessarily. I caught enough to understand they wanted me to stay for observation. Just in case of swelling.

I shook my head, immediately regretting the movement. "I just want to go home."

Martha squeezed my hand. "Then home we go. But you're staying with me tonight."

I started to protest but stopped at her stern look. Maybe I didn't want to be alone after all.

21

AFTERSHOCKS

The next few days passed in a haze. Martha insisted I stay with her, hovering with the protective instinct of a mother hen. I accepted because I was too shaken to argue.

"He won't come back," Martha assured me over coffee on the third morning. "My contacts say he left the country yesterday. Straight to Miami."

I nodded in relief though it warred with lingering fear. The physical marks would fade, but the memory of his hands on my throat felt branded into my nervous system. Every unexpected noise made me jump. I was constantly on edge. Never in my wildest dreams did I imagine Alex would do that to me. The truth of it hurt more than the physical aches and embarrassment.

One night, I found a few sheets of paper to journal, something I hadn't done since those first confused days after leaving Miami:

I can still feel his hands on my throat. The bruises are purple now, like toxic flowers beneath my skin. I keep touching them to prove they're real... that it really happened. I should have known better. Should have seen it coming when he showed up here...

My pen stopped. Shame burned through me. How could I have

been so stupid? How had I not seen this side of him lurking during all our years together? The questions churned in my stomach, along with the knowledge that I could never tell my family. They'd blame themselves for not protecting me and blame Guatemala for somehow causing this when Alex had shown his true nature all on his own.

"You can stay longer," Martha cut through the thoughts exploding in me.

"I need to go back to my place. I can't let him win," I affirmed. Otherwise, I'd drown in self-recrimination.

Antonio checked on me daily. His shielding nature was both touching and necessary. My apartment felt smaller somehow, but it was mine. I changed the locks and Luna became my constant shadow. She always knew when I needed quiet company. Bigger now, she'd curl up next to me while I worked, her steady presence more comforting than any words could be. I found myself talking to her in soft tones, sharing fears I couldn't voice to anyone else. She'd just look at me with those understanding eyes, offering unconditional love when I felt most broken.

A week passed. Then another. Slowly, I emerged from my self-imposed isolation. The bruises washed-out to yellowed memories, but I still wore high-necked blouses and scarves. I wasn't ready for questions. Not ready to explain.

Martha insisted I take enough time to physically heal before returning to the vocational school. I told the students I'd caught a nasty flu, which wasn't entirely a lie given how my body felt. Who knows if they believed it. It didn't matter. When I finally returned to classes, their enthusiasm for learning helped rebuild my confidence. Each properly folded napkin and each correctly served dish became a small victory was a proof that I could still make a difference here. I welcomed that.

Mariana noticed something was different. How could she not? I'd been slow to respond to her texts and hadn't been out nearly as much as I was before the showdown with Alex. I'm sure she'd heard through the grapevine what happened. News made its way around this little town. But she kept her distance, respecting my obvious withdrawal without pushing for explanations. Her concern showed in small ways – sunflowers left at my door, gentle waves from her gallery window. Sometimes they made me feel good. Other times, they made me feel ashamed. I should have never let things get so bad!

I appreciated Mariana giving me space, even as I longed for her closeness. But maybe the timing was a blessing. My world had been once again knocked from beneath me, and I had to find my footing again before exploring whatever was growing between us. Upcoming festival preparations provided a welcome distraction. Planning meetings and vendor arrangements kept me busy, slowly drawing me back into the community's rhythm. Life continued.

One evening, as I reviewed permit applications, a message from Mariana lit up my phone: "Miss seeing you at Café Loco. When you're ready, your usual table waits."

The text brought tears to my eyes. She wasn't pushing, wasn't demanding explanations. Just letting me know she was there, and that normalcy was possible again. I needed that. Maybe it was time to step fully back into my life. After all, I hadn't come to Lake Atitlán to hide. I'd come to build.

My hands shuddered as I got dressed to head out these days. *Focus.* I kept reminding myself. *Focus. And breathe.* I'd been trying to stop my nerves from reacting as though I were on a rollercoaster going down a mountain that never stopped dropping. My stomach constantly clenched and quivered, but I had to keep moving. Had to prove to myself more than anyone that I wasn't broken. My student's eager faces fought to anchor me in the present. Their questions about proper wine service and turndown protocol felt absurdly normal and absolutely vital after Alex's intrusion. But they also felt good. They made me feel needed and valued.

Now, as afternoon light slanted through Café Loco's windows, I was finally out of my apartment.

"¿Más café, señorita?" The server's gentle question pulled me from my thoughts.

"Sí, gracias." I pushed my cup forward. The café's usual buzz of conversation wrapped around me like a wool shawl. It grounded me in the present.

My phone vibrated. Mom. Again. I'd been avoiding her calls again, but my fingers hovered over the screen. It was time.

"Nyla?" Her voice carried that familiar mix of worry and reproach. "I've been thinking about you. This whole situation... teaching at a charity school? Baby, what are you doing out there?"

I closed my eyes, letting the café's ambient noise wash over me. The clatter of cups, snippets of Spanish conversation, a guitar being tuned in the corner. This wasn't a commune. This was real life... messy, authentic, *alive*.

"I'm building something, Mama."

"But—"

"No buts," I cut her off. "I know it's hard to understand, but I'm not lost. I know exactly where I'm going."

She sighed. "Well, you do sound different. Stronger maybe." A pause. "Are you... are you seeing anyone?"

My eyes drifted to the window. I caught sight of Mariana leaving her gallery. Our eyes briefly met and she smiled. A gentle, tender smile. I lifted my coffee cup in a small salute, and her grin widened.

"Nyla?"

"No, Mama. Just made some nice new friends."

After hanging up, I pulled out the notebook I'd been filling with business ideas and cost estimates. The "Se vende" sign on the old building still haunted me, but now it felt less like an impossible dream and more like a challenge to overcome.

The café door chimed. Mariana walked in. She looked beautiful in the fading light. For a moment, I thought she might turn away to a table of her own, but she didn't. She walked over instead.

"How are you?" The question left her lips in a rush.

"Better than yesterday. And last week." I felt so embarrassed even though I didn't tell her anything. I knew she knew. I could see it in her eyes. "I'm better. And thank you for the sunflowers."

"They follow the light," she said softly, her hand resting near mine on the table. "Even on cloudy days, they know where to turn."

I swallowed hard. "I'm learning that too."

A silence.

Everything unsaid charged the air between us. This woman...this woman *always* knew what to say. What to do. How to make me *feel* without feeling stupid. "Would you like to sit closer?" I tapped the back of the chair next to me.

"Of course...and..." she touched my knee. "You look different."

"Different how?" Suddenly, I became self-conscious.

"Like someone who's finally stopped running." A smile crossed her face. "Ms. Nyla...you look stunning." She let her gaze linger. Her bottom lip curled in and under a soft bite.

I shuddered. Oh my. Oh my, oh my, oh my...

"And I'm so sorry about how I reacted that night," she finally spoke again. "I should have been more patient with you. More open to listen—"

"You were protecting your community. I understand that now better than ever."

"And what about you? Do you feel protected?"

I gulped. The question was loaded. "I do."

"All parts?"

"Sí. My spirit. My soul. My heart. Everything, Mariana. My being and my dreams," I confessed and pushed my notebook toward her. "I'm more than ready to move forward."

It was true. From Antonio to Martha to Luna and to *myself*, most importantly, I felt protected and stronger. Ready. Ready to architect my new, independent life.

She flipped through the pages, her expression thoughtful. "These are good ideas. Ambitious, but good." Our conversation flowed easily again. It was light and fluid. Perfect. "You'll need local support though."

"From people like you?" The words slipped out before I could catch them.

A smile played at her lips. "Maybe." She turned another page.

"There's a municipal meeting tomorrow about development permits. Do you want company?"

The offer hung between us. Before I could answer, marimba and guitar music spilled in from the street. They twined together in the darkness, pulling people out of corners to bond, dance, and drink in public. Someone had set up an impromptu party in the plaza.

"Dance with me?" Mariana stood, holding out her hand.

"What?" I was genuinely shocked at her spontaneity.

"I want to see what you've got, Ms. Nyla! Come. Dance with me," she repeated. I loved how she said my name.

Still, I hesitated. Nervous about being touched in public, but I gave in. It felt too necessary not to. This was really happening...whatever "this" was. "Okay," I responded sheepishly, and went for it.

Mariana's fingers were tender against mine as she led me outside. Kids, elders and couples were already festively strewn about. Laugher and melodies wrapped around us as we found our rhythm together. I was a pretty good dancer, but hadn't done it in so long I couldn't remember the last time. As I lost myself in the moment though, I felt more and more at ease. More and more present. Dancing in the streets was a first, and I loved even just the thought of it!

"I warn you...I'm rusty," I confessed as Mariana's hand found my waist.

Her laughter melted into the melody. "Somehow I doubt that." Mariana's eyes scintillated with challenge. "Show me what Miami girls know about dancing."

The marimba's wooden notes tumbled like rain while guitar strings wept sweetly beneath them. Everyone around us moved in their own orbits. Some followed traditional steps while others simply swayed to the pulse of the music. The scene was hypnotic.

The music shifted. Faster now. My body remembered rhythms I thought I'd forgotten. We moved together, testing boundaries, finding synchronicity. When Mariana spun me, my skirt flared like flower petals opening to sunlight. I couldn't believe how carefree I felt. It was thrilling!

"Not so rusty after all," Mariana called out, pulling me closer as the tempo slowed. Her breath was warm against my ear, and her lips could touch my lobe if she wanted them to.

A young girl weaved past us, her braids flying. We had to step apart to avoid collision. The moment broke like sugar glass. Sweet and sharp.

"Your turn," I told her, catching my breath. "Show me how they dance in Guatemala...or Vegas."

"Oh no," Mariana grinned. "I save my Vegas moves for the second date."

Date? Neither of us pressed it, but I registered it. Instead, we kept dancing as stars emerged above the plaza. Each new song was a conversation without words. My heart high jumped in my chest.

When the music slowed again, Mariana stepped back slightly. "I shouldn't have said that," she whispered. "About the date. I'm sorry, Nyla. Things are complicated enough for you right now."

"Is that what you really think? Or what you think I need to hear?"

She studied me for a long moment. "Both, maybe." The plaza's lights cast shadows across her face and her hand dropped from my waist but lingered near me. "You're still processing a lot. And I know I'm not exactly everyone's favorite person in town right now either."

"Because you fight for what matters?"

"Because I don't compromise easily." A hint of her usual confidence returned. "And neither do you, it seems."

The music shifted again up tempo again, but we stayed in our quiet bubble. "So...what happens next?" I asked.

"Next, we figure out how to get your business permits." She smiled, professional mask sliding back into place. "One battle at a time."

But as Mariana made space between us again, she licked her lips and sighed. "Buenas noches, Nyla. Whew...I should get going." Her words were breathy.

As I watched her walk away, my skin tingled where she'd touched me. The plaza rotated with life. And here I was, in the middle of it all, discovering that freedom meant more than just escaping Alex. It meant allowing myself to want things I'd never knew I could.

~

THE NEXT AFTERNOON, I stood before the looming building I'd been drawn to despite its condition—deciding to skip the municipal meeting to ensure I wanted this place. Notebook in hand, I circled it slowly while furiously scribbling. Sagging balcony. Overgrown vines. Exposed beams where the roofline should've been solid. Every flaw made my stomach uneasy.

I glanced down at my notes. "Structural reinforcement?" I muttered, underlining the words twice. "Roof repair. Plumbing over-haul. Maybe the whole damn thing." My pen hovered, then dropped to my side. The building wasn't looking like a dream so much anymore. It looked like a nightmare.

"Still torturing yourself over this fixer-upper?"

I turned to see Mikayla coming up the overgrown path. She looked the same as when I'd last seen her, two weeks ago—tan, windswept, and grinning like she'd just hiked a volcano. Which, knowing her, she probably had. But I *still* didn't know what she did for a living.

"It's not torture," I said, trying for humor. "It's... thoughtful evaluation."

"Uh-huh. You keep telling yourself that." She swung a water bottle from one hand and gave the building a critical once-over. "It still looks like a mess."

Mariana arrived next, carrying a cloth bag stuffed with snacks and folders. She kissed my cheek in that Latin greeting kind of way, before walking over to greet the neighbor who was kneeling in her vegetable patch nearby. The older woman, Señora Lucia, squinted at me, then at the building, then back at me again.

"She says the plumbing's ancient," Mariana translated after a quick exchange. "It all needs to come out. And the roof leaks. A lot."

"Oy," I mumbled, jotting it down. Just what I'd feared.

Señora Lucia said something else. Her tone was skeptical. Mariana hesitated before smiling. "She wants to know if you're rich."

I cackled. "Rich in ambition, maybe!"

Mikayla wandered past us, into the weed-filled courtyard. She brushed vines aside with her boot. "So," she called out, "do you even know what permits you need? Or who's going to fix all this?"

Señora Lucia stepped closer, looking from me to the building. She spoke again, her voice softer this time.

"She says she's seen people try to fix this place before," Mariana translated. "But none of them stayed."

My notebook felt like stone in my hands. I glanced at my writings. There were so many questions and not nearly enough answers. "I am serious about this," I said, though my voice wavered. "I just... have a lot to figure out."

Señora Lucia nodded once, as if testing me, before retreating to her garden.

Mikayla sighed and leaned against the rusted gate. "You've got a lot of guts. I'll give you that. But guts won't pay for a new roof."

I wanted to snap back and defend myself, but she wasn't wrong. I moved closer to the building, to the broken window I'd peered into before. I closed my eyes and tried to picture what it could be instead. Laughter on the balconies. Travelers swapping stories over coffee in the courtyard. Music from a speaker tucked into a corner. For a moment, it felt real.

Then my journal slipped from my hands and hit the ground. The sound startled me out of the vision. I picked it up and held it tight against my chest. I wanted to believe in this. In myself. But as I looked back at the building, all I could think was: *What if I can't do it?* Mikayla and Mariana both turned to look at me.

"What's on your mind?" Mikayla quizzed. "You look like you're about to throw up or cry."

"Neither. I just...this was supposed to feel right, you know? Like when you just *know* something's meant to be?"

Mariana gave me a thoughtful look. "It doesn't feel right anymore?"

"I don't know." The words tasted bitter. "I thought it would be hard, but manageable. Now it just feels like I'm trying to build a sandcastle during high tide."

Mariana's voice was soft. "Nyla, you don't have to decide today. Maybe you need to step back for a moment and take some time to see all your options."

I shook my head. "If I step back now, it'll mean I was wrong. Or like I'm giving up. And I don't know if I can handle that."

"It's not giving up," she said. "It's taking a breath. That's different."

Her words were a caress.

Mikayla clapped her hands together, breaking the tension. "Well, whatever you decide, you're not doing it alone," she said, slinging an arm around my shoulders. "If nothing else, I can swing a hammer. Not well, but I can swing it."

I laughed, even though the knot in my chest hadn't gone away.

"There's another place I heard about," Mariana said casually. "Not far from here. Smaller, but in much better shape. Maybe it could work for your dream."

I didn't know what I wanted anymore, but Mariana's naming my dream made my heart leap.

"I'll think about it," I said quietly.

"That's all I'm saying," she replied. Mariana paused, brushing a stray vine off her sleeve. "By the way, you should come to the art festival next weekend. It's a big deal here. It might give you a better sense of the people and energy you're building for."

I blinked. "The art festival?"

"Yeah. There are flyers all around."

"Oh, man. I've been so immersed in this, but I vaguely remember reading one."

"It's a tradition," Mariana said with a faint smile. "Plus, a good excuse to take a break from all *this*...thoughtful evaluation." She gestured toward the sagging roofline.

The idea of a festival sparked something hopeful inside me. Maybe stepping into the town's rhythm wasn't such a bad idea. "I'll consider it," I said.

The sun was sinking now. A warm breeze rustled the vines, carrying the faint, earthy smell of wet leaves and stone.

"I just need to figure out what I'm doing," I expressed, more to myself than to them.

Mikayla squeezed my shoulder. "And you will."

"One step at a time, Nyla. Poco a poco." Mariana added. *Little by little*, it was a simple phrase I'd grown to love.

22

BLUEPRINT DREAMS

Dreams change shape when you let go of other people's expectations. Mine had transformed from a boutique hotel into a vision taking form in a modest property tucked away on a quiet street—the one Mariana had mentioned a while back.

"Come on, girl." I called Luna before grabbing my keys and documentation. "Time to check out our future home. Well, maybe."

The tuk-tuk ride to Don Manuel and Doña Teresa's property rattled my bones but not my resolve. My driver was chatty and overly fascinated with the United States. Dallas Cowboys and Las Vegas Raiders stickers were plastered in his red vehicle – poor thing. Those teams sucked.

I told him about the Miami Dolphins and Philly Eagles to navigate the small talk, and how I'd playfully nicknamed Miami "Latin America Lite" since there were so many immigrants there from Cuba, Venezuela, and yes, Guatemala. That it was a Guatemalan massage therapist who initially told me about Lake Atitlán.

"¡En serio?!"

"Yes, seriously."

He was enthralled! "¡Ahh...Bienvenido, señorita!"

Luna sat perfectly balanced despite the bumps as if she'd been born navigating Guatemala's streets instead of wandering them as a stray. Her little ears flapped in the wind as her mouth gaped open. Her presence beside me felt right, both of us finding our place in this unexpected life.

Mikayla waited at the entrance chatting with the elderly couple.

"Perfect timing," she called out. "Don Manuel and Doña Teresa were just telling me about the property's history."

I still couldn't believe I'd brought Luna along. "What do you think, girl?" I asked as we reached the entrance.

Her tail wagged, sending my heart into an unexpected flutter. The building wasn't grand like my original dream. Not even close. It was just two stories with twelve potential guest rooms and a small courtyard. But this time, it felt possible. I could make a hostel out of it. A nice one.

Luna darted ahead, sniffing corners and doorways while I took measurements. The rooms were small but bright, each with a view of either the lake or the garden. The kitchen needed updating but had good bones. No major structural issues jumped out at me.

This could work. I snapped a quick photo of Luna posed in front of an archway, sunlight catching her head just right. Without overthinking it, I posted it to my Instagram stories: "Meet Luna, my unexpected business advisor 🐾 #NewChapter #LakeAtitlan"

Within minutes, likes and comments started rolling in. Kendra: "OMG SIS YOU GOT A DOG! 😊" Mom: "She's precious! But are you sure...?" And there, among the notifications: "marianaartista liked your story."

I smiled, scratching Luna's ears. "Well, look who's becoming a social media star."

"Your dog has good instincts," Don Manuel said in Spanish, watching Luna explore. "She knows a happy home when she finds one."

Doña Teresa nodded, explaining how they'd run this as a small guesthouse for years until age made it too difficult. Their only daughter was physically unable to keep it going. The property had been waiting for the right person. Best of all, they already had all the old permits and licenses, such as they were, which could transfer with a simple lease agreement. No need for the mountains of paperwork and bureaucracy.

"Wait, really?" I turned to Mikayla. "It's that simple?"

She shrugged. "Yup. Sometimes the right handshake means more than the right paperwork. Especially when you're taking over an existing business rather than starting fresh." She gestured at Don Manuel and Doña Teresa. "They've been operating here for decades. Everyone knows them. That means something."

The elderly couple smiled warmly. It was clear they cared more about finding someone to continue their legacy than about rigid formalities. This was nothing like Miami's strict regulations and endless inspections.

That evening, I started documenting my journey properly. All of it, from the lukewarm showers that needed pressure boosters to feel comfortable to the random power outages and community dogs on roofs.

I posted a photo of my students practicing table settings, their faces bright with concentration. Another of Luna investigating the market's fruit stalls. A shot of my morning coffee view, complete with the neighbor's chickens wandering past. I could not believe how much my life had changed in less than a year and that I'd been surviving every hill and valley of it. Some nights were still full of questions, but the mornings of newness and possibilities made up for it. I'd even gone back up to Antigua and Guatemala City when I needed a break from rural life. The city had white tablecloth, fine dining options to soothe my homesickness and meet new people. I did some hikes in other areas too—one on horseback up an active volcano. The views were SPECTACULAR. Through it all, I solidified a few new friends in each area through BFF apps. I also happened upon some film students who promised to stay in touch for an opportunity to shoot at my hostel once it was done.

Back on the lake, I focused on sharing the small victories: successfully ordering lunch in Spanish, finding the perfect avocado, and

Luna making friends with the cafe owner's cat. Afternoon naps on wooden boats docked at the lake—God, I loved those—and my skin looked like it had been kissed by the heavens. Perfectly bronzed. Sunrise yoga and intermittent group meetups with other expats made my life much more about experience and savoring moments than rushing through them to make enough money to buy random material goods. Not to mention I'd been eating the best seafood of my life lately. Fried fish. Grilled fish. Steamed fish. Ceviche. Shrimp tacos. Shrimp cocktails. Oh, and the drinks. Margaritas and mojitos. Strawberry vodka lemonade. Piña colada. Rum punch. I didn't indulge in it all the time—I couldn't afford to—but when I did, it was mouthwatering bliss. This...*this* was life. I often thought, shocked at how polar opposite it was of what I used to think. But back to my plans...

I opened my notes app, starting a fresh list: "Property inspection. Loan research. Business plan tweaks." Each item felt like a step forward rather than a mountain to climb. The small guesthouse might not match my original grand vision, but maybe that was the point. I needed to thank Mariana for the tip.

Luna stirred, pressing closer as thunder rumbled in the distance. Another storm was approaching, but this time I didn't mind. We had shelter, purpose, and most importantly, we had each other. Outside, the lake shimmered under the rising moon, and somewhere in the distance, church bells began their evening song.

I picked up my phone, hesitating only briefly before tapping Mariana's Instagram handle. The video call connected surprisingly fast given the approaching storm.

"Nyla?" Her face filled my screen. A screwdriver was absentmindedly in her hand. "Everything okay?" For once, her long, dark hair framed her face instead of being pulled back and twisted in wires, pencils, or paintbrushes. She was even more beautiful.

"Yes, yes. Sorry. I just wanted to thank you," I announced. "For telling me about Don Manuel and Doña Teresa's place."

She smiled, moving through what looked like her home studio. "So, you like it?"

"It's perfect, actually! More perfect than my original plans," I paused.

She dropped the screwdriver and looked directly at me. Her energy was soft and undeniably intimate. I paused, watching her settle onto a window seat. Through the screen, I could see rain beginning to fall outside her window. It hadn't reached my area yet.

"Mariana, I really—" Thunder rolled and the power cut, plunging my room into darkness. Rain had arrived on my side. Damn it. My phone's screen illuminated my face as I waited for the WiFi connection to drop.

But it held. And in that moment, lit only by our screens and distant lightning, the space between us felt electric with possibility.

"You were saying?" she whispered.

23

UNCHARTED WATERS

My dreams were a tangle of black memories and maybes. Alex's firm hands on my waist during our first dance—I loved it before I hated it. Mariana's exquisite fingers brushing mine with lingering warmth. I enjoyed it even though I didn't know what it would trigger. The pull and danger of both moments were equally real. Equivalently true. I awoke breathless and to three missed calls from Mariana. Each was an hour apart, ending at 2 AM.

While I'd always noticed women and appreciated their looks, I'd never thought much of it beyond admiration. Until now. Until her. Looking back, I could see the build-up of all the moments I'd intentionally dismissed...the lingering gazes, the unexplained flutters, my nervous arrivals and embarrassed departures...all the connections that felt somehow different. Not better or worse than what I'd felt with men, just... different. Like another dimension of myself that had never been deeply triggered. Until. Her.

I thought about calling Mariana back, but what would I say? That I'd never dated a woman but was intrigued by her? That Alex was more than my ex-boss, and for a brief period, we were engaged? That I broke it off after I realized how flawed my "perfect" life was...and that I was excited about building my new life but still had daily struggles with adapting to a foreign world? Or...that when she looked at me, I felt seen in ways that had nothing to do with gender and everything to do with recognition?

A truck's horn blasted outside, followed by rapid Spanish curse words. Metal screeched against concrete. I popped up. Through my window, I saw men struggling with a massive sculpture. It was twisted steel with jagged edges precariously tilted on a dolly. It looked too wide for the doorway they were trying to squeeze through.

"¡Despacio! Te dije que lo inclines!" Mariana's voice ripped through the chaos. Full of fire and fury. She stood with her hands on her hips.

Diesel fumes mixed with the metallic tang of the sculpture, temporarily overwhelming my senses. I felt like the nosy neighbor character in sketch comedy shows – hand covering my mouth and all – still, I looked.

One of the workers cursed something under his breath.

"Si tienes una mejor idea, dímela." Their tone could have sliced steel.

I surveyed as the man shook his head and bent to adjust the base. Mariana turned, grumbling "Por el amor de Dios," before catching sight of me. Her hand shot up in a quick wave, breaking through her frustration with a smile that hit me like summer lightning.

I grabbed my keys and headed down. Luna was somewhere milling around the property, I was sure. It was sticky, thick, and dank with exhaust from the idling truck outside.

"Be careful with that edge, please" she said in Spanish to the workers, crouching to guide the base. Her jeans hugged her curves. And her Che Guevera T-shirt was damp with sweat against her back. When she stood, her eyes found mine again. "Well, look who came down to witness chaos up close."

"Just admiring your management style."

She tossed me work gloves from the truck bed. "Here. Since you're feeling brave."

"Who said anything about brave? And who told you I came here to work?"

"Your eyes did. Now, grab that corner and try not to lose any fingers."

"Umm...." I moved into position opposite her. "What's the actual plan here?" I asked, making note of how I fell right under her alpha spell.

"Plan A was that they listen. Plan B..." A smirk played at her lips. "You and I save this piece while they debate physics."

Two workers started arguing about angles in colliding Spanish. Mariana sighed. "¡Jóvenes! Lo levantan así o lo hacemos nosotras!"

I didn't know most of those words, but I got her energy.

They fell silent, exchanging glances heavy with grudging respect before adjusting their grip.

"Ever notice how a little well-placed authority works wonders?" she quizzed, eyes dancing.

"Is that what you call it?"

"That's what I call survival." Her gaze held mine. "Speaking of which, how are you holding up?" She dusted her hands on her jeans.

"Pretty good, actually. No more pop ups from my past. Getting things ready to finalize due diligence on the new place. Things are moving."

The sculpture groaned as the men made final adjustments inside. Neither of us moved to help.

"¡Perfecto, perfecto!" I didn't know if she was talking to them or me. Until she continued. "Have dinner with me this weekend, Nyla," she said suddenly. "Not at Café Loco. Some place nicer. More...of what might feel like home for you? You must still think about the States regardless of how much progress you've made here. Trust me, I know there's huge difference in standard of living."

The directness and thoughtfulness of her words knocked the breath from my lungs. "There is but...I'm adjusting, and...I do...and I would love to have dinner with you," I beamed.

"I know this place close to Zona 14," Mariana said. "Portal del

Angel. The view dares you to look away—and wins every time..." She paused, studying me. "It's a drive, but worth it."

"Guatemala *City*?" My pulse quickened. Three hours each way meant...

"Too far?"

"No. Not too far at all, and I love it there."

"I figured you would, Ms. Miami," she smirked.

Touché. The workers called out something about the sculpture's final placement. Mariana turned to respond, but her hand brushed mine first...deliberate, wanting.

"Saturday then," she said. "My driver and I will pick you up at three-thirty."

Her driver?

Luna appeared from wherever she'd been exploring, covered in mud and looking entirely pleased with herself. The moment shifted, but didn't break.

"Your dog has the best timing," Mariana giggled.

"She really does." I'd have to find someone to bathe her later. I wasn't in the mood.

Saturday came fast. I'd signed documents, made deposits, and had more meetings with the owners of my new project. The week was a rush of progress and excitement. All I could remember were flashes: the scratch of pen on paper, the blue ink of a notary's stamp, and the weight behind my eyes. But when I thought of Mariana, everything sharpened. Her voice, her presence, her touch...she woke up the most dormant parts of me, and I was so excited to see her!

The late afternoon sun slanted across the Pan-American Highway as we crawled out of the Lake Atitlán's nestle. Everything was golden. Mariana's driver, an older gentleman who'd introduced himself simply as Rodrigo, hummed along to vintage merengue while expertly navigating the dips and curves around the mountains.

Beside me, Mariana sat with me in the back seat. She'd traded her practical clothes for a deep blue dress that made her skin shimmer. A silver, circular pendant nestled in the hollow of her throat. The three-hour drive was only 20 minutes in when she said:

"You're quiet."

"I'm just wondering what other surprises you're hiding besides a personal driver."

Her laugh carried no apology. "A woman needs some mysteries, no?"

She winked at me and my legs clenched. *Breathe.* I reminded myself.

"Well?" Mariana continued, not noticing my fingers tightening on the seat edge, betraying my composure. "Though I suppose you have your own."

The upbeat music changed to something slower, more classical. Rodrigo sang the new melody without missing a beat. He was in his own world up front.

"Mysteries?" I chuckled. "Oh no...I'm an open book if you like to read."

"Even open books have chapters people skip." Mariana's fingers traced the edge of her pendant. What I originally thought was a circle was actually a sunburst. "Like how you watch the road when you're nervous instead looking at the person talking to you."

Gasp. I caught myself doing exactly that and turned to face her. "I do not—" Lies. I knew it, and she knew it. Mariana literally just called me out, and there was no way I could deny it. All I could do is smile.

The setting sun caught the silver at her neck. It drew my attention to the gentle rise and fall of her breathing...even the tiny hairs on her light brown skin. So beguiling. I finally met her gaze.

"See? Much better." Her smile was subtle but reached her eyes. "Though now I'm curious what made you stop mid-denial."

Ha! "The light," I confessed. "It does something to your necklace."

She glanced down. "Mmm. This was once my mother's." Mariana's hand went to it. "She wore it every day until..." She paused, then added softly, "I only wear it for special occasions now."

The car dipped around a curve, and I shifted closer to her to steady myself. Our shoulders touched but neither of us moved away. The warmth of her skin on mine...it felt too good.

"What makes this occasion special?" I queried. My voice tiptoed into the small space between our faces.

Rodrigo changed radio stations – not a streaming song or service – an actual radio station! Bachata suddenly filled the car with rhythm and passion.

Mariana's laugh broke our bubble. "Rodrigo! ¿En serio?"

"La música clásica me da sueño," he called back, grinning in the rearview mirror.

"He says classical music makes him sleepy," she translated, though I'd understood enough. "What's your vote, Nyla? Bachata or Bach?"

"Depends on the mood I'm chasing." I watched her reaction carefully. "Right now? I'm okay with either." I scooched back over to my side of the back seat.

"Diplomatic." Mariana paused to stretch, and her dress rode up just above her knee. "And you still didn't answer my earlier observation about your mysterious nature."

"Because you didn't answer mine about what makes tonight special."

"I asked first." Her eyes met mine. Locked in. "Maybe we're both waiting to see which mysteries are worth sharing."

The sun sank lower. Rodrigo's crooning merged with the bachata, creating an oddly intimate soundtrack to our verbal dance.

"I could start small," I offered. "Like how I actually hate Miami's humidity but miss it here anyway."

"That's not small at all." She rested her hand in the gap between us on the seat, her fingers less than an inch from my thighs. "That's about belonging. About what feels like home when home changes."

I watched her fingertips, remembering their texture and temperature. "Your turn."

"I hate driving," she said suddenly. "That's why I have Rodrigo. Everyone assumes it's about status, but really," she leaned closer. "I get terrible motion sickness if I'm behind the wheel. Ridiculous for someone who lives in the mountains, isn't it?"

The confession was so unexpected and human, it made me laugh. "Is that why you're always walking or taking tuk-tuks around town?"

She pressed a hand to her heart dramatically. "Now you know my shame!" But her eyes danced. "Your turn again. Something equally embarrassing."

The car whooshed out of the alps as we traded confessions, each one a small key unlocking something larger, while Rodrigo's music choices created an ever-shifting backdrop to our growing intimacy. As the vehicle wound round the final curve, the white bell tower of Portal del Angel emerged against the darkening sky. My breath caught as we pulled up to the entrance.

"This is beautiful." The colonial architecture was a glaring contrast to the modern city sprawling below.

"Wait until you see inside," she purred. Her hand found the small of my back as we entered. I could feel her thumb slowly swipe against my skin through my dress.

The hostess led us through the restaurant to a table by the giant window. Vines thick with vibrant leaves draped from wooden beams overhead. The city lights were beginning to twinkle below us like scattered stars. The table was set with snowy linens and flickering candles. I tried not to read too much into the intimacy of it all, but my racing pulse had other ideas. It was just so, so...romantic, but not in an over-the-top way. Just naturally. And it felt gooood.

"To combat you missing big city energy," Mariana said, settling into her chair. "I thought you might appreciate the view."

"Mariana..." I exhaled. "It's incredible." I meant both the vista and her thoughtfulness. The sprawl of Metropolitan Guatemala below reminded me of Miami nights yet felt entirely new. There were no palm trees. No Rodeo drives or neon-soaked nightlife, but endless hills and the teem of a city alive with its own tempo.

The waiter appeared with menus and wine recommendations. As Mariana conversed with him in Spanish, I found myself studying the way she gestured, how her eyes lit up when she smiled. And how she

so effortlessly slipped back into English with me to confirm I understood what I ordered. *Eight years in Vegas.* She'd told me about living
in the States a while back but never told me why. What had brought
her there? What had brought her back? There were so many questions I wanted to ask, yet I was almost afraid of the answers – afraid
they might make this feel too real too fast.

"You are thinking very loudly, Ms. Nyla," she teased after the
waiter left. Her animated eyes found mine across the candlelight.

"I'm trying to figure out if I should be..." I lost my words.

Her brow furrowed slightly. "What do you mean?"

I searched for courage. "This feels like... I mean, um...is this a...a
date?"

Mariana deliberately reached across the table and pulled my
fingers into hers. No accidental grazing like in the car. "Yes," she said
simply. "Unless you don't want it to be. Then it doesn't have to be."

My hand trembled under hers. "I—I—don't know what I want," I
whispered. "But I do like this."

"I understand. I bungled this and should have been straightfor-
ward. Truthfully, I didn't know what it was when I first asked you
either. I've never been the first to ask," she rambled. "But—"

"It's fine. I just don't know how to do this."

She smiled. "Neither do I. But I want to find out."

The waiter returned with wine and our appetizers, breaking the
delicate moment. Soon, however, Mariana and I fell into easier
conversation as we ate. We chatted about the sculpture delivery disaster, about Luna's muddy adventures, and about my plans for the
property. The tension didn't disappear, but it settled into something
like background music. Manageable. Neither of us tried too hard to
make it an official first date. Instead, we just got to know each other.
We laughed.

"So, is this your first time at this restaurant?"

Mariana swirled her wine. "No. I came here my first week back
from the US. Sat alone at that bar." She nodded toward the far corner.
"I was staying with family I have in the city. Was wondering if I'd
made a mistake coming home. But then the sun set, and the city lit

up, and..." She shrugged. "I knew I'd made the right choice. Some-times you need distance to see things clearly."

I thought about my own vantage point now – both literal and metaphorical. "And did you see things clearly right away or...?"

"Eventually." She caught my eye over her glass. "Though it took a while for some things are still coming into focus."

The main course arrived. There was perfectly grilled fish for me and a steak for her. We talked about so much. It was a normal dinner conversation. Well, except for the current beneath it all, but still. I was having a great time, and I did reveal more about my past and my old job—Alex, and all—and what I'd learned from the experience. True to my word, I was an open book.

"My sister would love this place," I found myself saying. "She's always telling me I need to send her more photos."

"The corporate lawyer?" Mariana asked, remembering my earlier mention of her.

"Yeah. Kendra. She thinks running a hostel is my midlife crisis." I smiled. "Maybe she's right."

"What do you think?"

I considered. "I think... maybe it's the first career move that isn't about proving something to someone else."

"This is more than a career move."

"True. It's a life change."

Mariana's expression shifted slightly. "Vegas was like that for me. Family expectations." She dabbed her napkin against her lips, leaving a red kiss mark on the white cloth. "Until I realized I was the one holding myself prisoner to them."

She didn't elaborate, and I didn't push. We both had our stories and our reasons for choosing distance to find clarity.

As we finished our meal, the sky became *entrancing*.

"It's getting late," Mariana said, checking her phone. "These mountain roads...ahh...I should have suggested lunch instead of dinner." She glanced at her wristwatch as if she hadn't just looked at the time. "I have a friend owns a boutique hotel near here. We should all stay tonight."

The suggestion made practical sense, even if it added another layer of complexity to an already complicated evening. I also made note that she had a friend in hospitality in the city.

"What about my contractors?" I asked, grateful for the tangible concern.

"I'll have Rodrigo drive us back at daybreak. Better than risking these roads at midnight. It gets really dark in some spots once we're out of the city."

"Umm..."

"Don't worry. Three rooms. You'll have privacy. And I'll take care of everything." She winked.

Well damn. This felt different coming from a woman. I *loved* it.

"Thank you."

"De nada, Nyla. De nada." She licked her lips and suppressed something.

SLEEP PLAYED HIDE-AND-SEEK with me that night. The antique ceiling fan clicked a lazy rhythm above me while my mind raced through dinner replays. I was hot! And I needed air. Or water. Or both. I slipped out of bed and into a light robe and pair of slippers they'd provided.

The hotel's narrow hallways were a maze of terracotta and shadow. I followed the sound of trickling water, expecting another courtyard, but instead found myself in what must have been the original library. Behind two large wooden doors, towering shelves of leather-bound books stretched into darkness. I noticed the intricate lettering on their spines catching hints of light from iron wall sconces. A stone fountain burbled in the corner. It was more sound than sight in the dim light.

I wasn't alone. Mariana stood at one of the tall windows. She was also wrapped in a white hotel robe. Her hair was loose now, freed from the elegant twist she'd worn at dinner. It dangled beautifully at the middle of her back. She didn't turn, but I knew she heard me. Or someone. Those old wooden floors had announced my arrival with a betraying creak.

The city lights painted her in silver and gold. "I couldn't sleep either," she said softly, still gazing out the window. "This room reminds me of my great-aunt's house in Antigua. She had a library just like this."

"Wow." It was old-world beautiful. I stepped closer to her.

The place felt like a secret. It smelled like clove oranges and ancient ink. And hints of tobacco lingered in the curtains' heavy folds. It felt like history.

A chess set sat mid-game on a side table. The pieces were arranged in silent warfare. I wondered what story lay behind the abandoned match. Which player had been winning when they walked away? Why did they walk away? What urgent whisper or stolen glance had made them forget their game, leaving the black queen poised for victory but frozen in her final advance? Or was it all staged?

My fingers moved over book spines, pausing on a water-stained collection of García Márquez. The volume fell open to a dry, pressed flower when I pulled it out. It was faded and as delicate as onion skin. Was it someone's bookmark? I carefully closed the book, not wanting to disturb whatever ghost had left their story behind.

"Found something interesting?" Mariana came over.

"Yeah," I whispered. "A pressed flower in this book."

She reached for the volume, and that's when I noticed a jagged scar across her thumb that stretched into the crease between her index finger.

"How did you get that?" I asked before I could stop myself.

A soft laugh escaped her. "This? Breaking up a fight between local kids and some tourist's son. The boy had a glass bottle." She traced the scar absently. "Everyone said I should've waited for the police, but... you know how that goes here. By then it would've been too late."

"Were you scared?"

"Terrified. But some things matter more than fear." She returned the book to its shelf. "The local boy's father repairs shoes in the market. Every Christmas since then, I find a pair of handmade boots outside my gallery door." Her voice carried no pride, just quiet certainty about choosing right over easy.

This woman had me under spell with each new revelation. "You did a wonderful thing." I inched closer to her but leaned against a shelf. "You always protect what matters...even when it costs you."

"Don't we all?" She stepped into my space.

"We should."

A rumble of thunder broke the moment. We both startled, then laughed, the tension easing into something warmer.

"We should try to sleep," she said, but didn't move toward the door.

"Probably." I didn't move either.

Instead, we stood there in borrowed robes, surrounded by other people's stories, writing our own story in the gaps between words. I could feel my heart beating in my throat, my skin prickled with awareness. The room crackled with possibility...even in the silence. I gulped. Then I stepped back. I needed distance to think clearly.

Mariana didn't chase the moment. She smiled with under-standing that made my chest ache. No pressure. No disappointment. Just acceptance that held more intimacy than any kiss could have offered. The contrast with Alex hit me right then. He would always push for what he wanted. He'd constantly turn every moment into a transaction or a step toward his vision. I don't know how I let that become my norm and not realize how much I did *not* have to bend to anyone's pace. Now here was Mariana, letting silence speak while holding space for meaning.

"You're unlike anyone I've ever known," I whispered, the truth of it contracting in my throat. "The way you make room... for your community, for art, for moments like this. It's so...deep. Beyond just strength."

She leaned against the window frame, moonlight silvering her profile. "Sometimes strength isn't about pushing forward. It's about standing still long enough to let things unfold naturally." Her eyes met mine. "Like you're doing now."

The wisdom in her words settled into my bones. Into the chambers of my soul. Here was someone who understood that new beginnings required courage *and* patience. Someone who could nurture growth without forcing it.

"Thank you," I offered.

"For letting me find my way." My voice wobbled. "For not making this feel like another thing I have to figure out right *now*."

"There's no rush. I think you should savor your discoveries."

Thunder rolled again, closer now. The library's shadows seemed to breathe with us. It was so intoxicating that I finally felt the need to lay down.

When I finally returned to my room, I carried with me not regret for what hadn't happened, but gratitude for what had. I was over the moon with the recognition of something rare and worth nurturing slowly.

24

BUILDING MATERIALS

Guatemala City yawned itself awake around us. Dawn painted everything in watercolors. I lowered my window to let warm air in. Noisy traffic hitched a ride in too. And the smell of wood smoke and fresh bread constantly slipped in as Rodrigo maneuvered the local streets to get us back home. He hummed quietly up front while Mariana dozed against her window.

"¡Tamales!" A woman's voice cut through my thoughts. Her cart blocked half the narrow street. Steam rose from covered baskets. Without asking, Rodrigo pulled over.

Mariana blinked to consciousness.

"El mejor desayuno de la ciudad," he proclaimed, already climbing out. The vendor's face lit up when she saw him. They chatted like old friends while she wrapped tamales in banana leaves, adding extra salsa on the side.

"Gracias," I thanked him. The package warmed my lap as we merged back into traffic. I peeled back the leaf, letting masa and chicken fill the car with spice and comfort. "Oh my God." This food was heaven.

"Your chin," Mariana giggled as she unwrapped hers. "A little salsa." She made a wiping gesture before laughing even louder.

I had no choice but to laugh at myself making a mess because I enjoyed the meal so much.

"Thanks for letting me know nicely."

"Of course," she chuckled. "You're too adorable to embarrass."

I blushed. Just then, a message from my boss, Martha, appeared on my screen – she wanted updates about next week's curriculum. Three contractors waited to hear about viewing the property.

Reality beckoned. I had decisions to make, a building to transform, and a life to build. But right now, the mountain roads stretched ahead through morning fog, and masa melted on my tongue. I settled back, savoring each mile with Mariana at my side.

Three hours later, my first contractor waited outside my building. It was Antonio. His dark hair blazed in the sun while a parrot perched on his shoulder, occasionally mimicking the sounds of hammering. Not what I expected. Not at all. The fowl was new.

"The bird is my apprentice," he announced before I could ask. "Better at finding weak spots in wood than any modern tool." He tapped the parrot's beak. Antonio's smile radiated across features carved by mountain sun – all angles and warmth, like a face that had never learned to frown. Laugh lines webbed from his eyes in a map of joy.

"You do have regular tools, too, correct?" I didn't believe him about the bird, but it was cute.

"¡Claro que siii, señorita! I double-check behind the bird for sure," he grinned.

"¡Excelente."

Mariana had gone off to her gallery, leaving me to navigate this alone until Mikeyla came. Antonio moved through the building like he was reading braille. His fingers found stories in every crack. The parrot fluttered ahead, landing on exposed beams and knocking its beak against suspicious spots. Quirky bird or not, I felt incredibly safe with Antonio around.

"Here." He pressed his palm against a wall. "Water damage from the pipes. But not terminal. Like a fever in a strong body...it can heal."

He spoke in metaphors, treating the building like a living thing. "Does your plan include preserving the tiles?"

"Yes."

"Smart. They have character."

The parrot squawked what sounded like "más café" and dive-bombed Antonio's thermos.

"Ignore him. He thinks renovation runs on caffeine. Though he's not wrong." He pulled out a worn notebook covered in sketches. They were more artistic renderings than a blueprint. The building as it was, and as it could be. "Most people want to gut everything, start fresh. But you're thinking differently, Nyla. Me gusta."

"The bones are good," I said. "They just need remembering."

"Mm hm." He smiled like I'd passed a test. "Then we understand each other. Now...about the electrical..." Antonio paused at an exposed junction box. "It is the original wiring from when they first brought power to the lake. Beautiful craftsmanship, but dangerous now. It's like poetry written in matches."

Mikayla's voice echoed from the doorway. "How bad?"

"Not impossible," he answered, his eyes still on the wiring. "But not cheap either."

I studied the ancient cables, remembering countless budget meetings at the Jeffrey where every decision required three levels of approval. Here, standing in my own building, the choice was mine alone. I snapped a pic for social media. A few videos for my stories, too.

"You're documenting all this?" Mikayla raised an eyebrow.

"Yup. People seem interested in the process. It's better than just showing perfect 'after' photos, I think." I panned my phone across exposed beams and crumbling plaster. "Besides, it holds me accountable."

"Have you considered offering cooking classes?" Mikayla asked while watching me record. "My friend's aunt makes the best pepián, and tourists are always asking where to learn traditional recipes."

I lowered my phone and jotted it down in my growing list of potential guest experiences. "Cultural immersion packages...that could work. Maybe partner with local artisans too? Weaving demonstrations, art workshops with established galleries..." I thought out loud.

"Like Mariana's?" Mikayla's smile was knowing.

I ignored her tone. "Yes, exactly. And sunrise hikes, lake tours, storytelling nights...things that give visitors a deeper Lake Atitlán experience."

Antonio knocked against a wall. His parrot mimicked the sound. This was becoming a fucking circus, and I was the ringleader. "This part tells stories. See these marks?" Antonio pointed at grooves in the wood. "Height measurements. Children growing up here when it was someone's home."

I zoomed in on the faded pencil lines, thinking of Don Manuel and Doña Teresa, who trusted me with the building. Decades of life measured in inches were preserved beneath layers of paint. Even as a child-free woman who never wanted kids, I could appreciate this. It was beautiful. My followers would appreciate this detail - not as Instagram bait, but as proof that buildings held memories worth saving. *Snap.*

"Nyla, the wiring needs to be completely redone," Mikayla brought us back to practicalities. "But if you're opening the walls anyway..."

"We can preserve these." I touched the height marks. "Work around them."

Antonio's eyes lit up. "Now you're thinking like a true builder."

His parrot landed on a window ledge, sending years of dust into sunlight while allowing me to see Mariana's gallery across the street. She stood in her doorway, watching. She lifted her coffee cup in a silent toast when our eyes met. My body warmed.

"I want to have something painted around these so they're interesting and not creepy," I said of the height marks.

Lake Atitlán commanded attention through east-facing windows, but I forced myself to focus on immediate decisions. "The common area here needs to feel discovered, not designed. Reading alcoves. A coffee station stocked with local beans. Real beds instead of bunks. I want budget travelers to wake up feeling like they stumbled into unexpected comfort."

Mikayla nodded slowly. "Hostel prices with boutique touches. Not bad."

Antonio's pencil raced across paper. "And the courtyard?"

"A garden that looks like it grew itself but knows its boundaries. Tables tucked into quiet corners where—"

Luna trotted in, dusty paws tracking across centuries-old tile. She tried to chase the bird, tail wagging as if she could actually catch it.

"Back ooffff," the fowl hissed.

"It's your perrito?" Antonio quizzed in Spanglish.

"Sí."

"She knows where home will be."

"I guess she does," I smiled.

The space vibrated with possibility. I knew I could build it into something that could welcome both sooty paws and travel-weary souls.

25

THE COST OF STARTING OVER

Luna's barking woke me at dawn. Antonio waited outside my building with two men I didn't recognize. All three wore cruddy work boots and toolbelts.

"My best team," Antonio said, introducing his brother Ruben who specialized in electrical work and Juan who'd spent twenty years repairing colonial structures. Antonio's parrot balanced on his shoulder, preening in the early light. They headed straight for the exposed pipes while his bird found its favorite spot near the ceiling.

"We start with the plumbing today," Antonio announced.

I hadn't slept well. My tourist visa expires in three weeks. The building needed more work than my initial budget allowed. And my carefully planned luxury touches kept hitting walls.

"The pressure's too low for rainfall showers." I pointed to the stack of boxes containing expensive fixtures. "We'll need boosters for every bathroom. Or, I'll need to return them and simplify. I'll decide soon."

Antonio nodded. "And the septic system?"

"Needs an upgrade. I refuse to ask guests to throw paper in baskets. I'll get bidets." Ugh. I myself could not adjust to using the trash can instead of flushing and had been using a handheld bidet ever since the beginning of my trip. It was much more hygienic.

"Bidets?" He had no idea what I was talking about.

I explained how they worked and that they were common in Asian countries but could work well here. "Without heated seats, though." I showed him the specifications. "That would cost too much even though I knew they'd be more comfortable. Well, I want the best for my room." Fuck it. I earned it.

"Rrrricoooo!" Antonio teased, exaggerating the roll of his R.

His parrot squawked in approval. The other contractors exchanged glances. I knew what they were thinking: another foreigner with big ideas. But I'd done my research this time.

Sofia arrived next. She'd been one of my brightest students at the vocational school, asking questions that showed Sofia thought beyond textbook answers. At twenty-five, she carried herself with quiet confidence, and her English was perfect. She'd learned from primary school and a few years of working in her uncle's tourism business in El Salvador. But Sofia had been in Guatemala for a year now, specifically for the lake, and I'd asked her if she wanted an apprenticeship.

"This interview is informal," I told her, remembering how she'd always stayed after class to discuss real-world applications. "I need someone who can help me navigate what will and won't work here."

She glanced at my planned keycard system. "Traditional keys might be better. You'll avoid inconveniencing guests when the voltage fluctuates or power cuts out. Unless...you have generators."

"Not yet. Noted." I appreciated her directness. It was why she'd stood out in class. "What about security?"

"Personal greetings work better anyway. Guests like the connection. But they can still be secure – just not so obvious but in the way everything always feels *right*."

Smart girl. I hired her on the spot. Mostly for experience but with a small weekly stipend. I didn't have full-time money. Having Sofia here felt like building a bridge between my teaching life and new venture. It felt correct.

A crash from upstairs interrupted our paperwork. Water gushed down the steps like a muddy waterfall. The pipe we'd planned to replace next week had made its own schedule.

"¡Mierda!" Antonio shouted. His parrot echoed the sentiment.

"¿Qué pasó?"

"Agua. ¡Mucho agua, señorita!"

"Fuck..." I lamented.

We spent the next hour mopping while contractors raced to contain the damage. The water had soaked into my sample of premium mattresses. The humidity here already made expensive bedding a constant battle. Now I watched hundreds of dollars begin the early stages of mold begin before my eyes.

"Fuuuccckkkk!" I was already approaching my limit. A little part of me thought of how stressed Alex would be when he came back from his Charlotte runs. I understood better now. He had made his job look easy just as much as I did mine.

"This is why local places use simpler materials," Sofia gently needled through my thoughts. "Things that can handle the climate."

"Entiendo...I understand." I gave in and slumped against a dry wall. "I just wanted to create something special."

"You can. Special doesn't have to mean imported." She helped me move sodden linen. "It means working with what's here in a more imaginative way."

The front door chimed. Dulce swept in wearing resort-casual clothing and a rehearsed smile. Luna growled softly. I hadn't seen much of her since I took a tour of her property then decided to stay somewhere else.

"Buenas tardes. I heard you were renovating." Her eyes took in the wet chaos. "Such an ambitious project."

"Just a few unexpected challenges." I kept my voice neutral.

Her gaze landed on one of Mariana's paintings, still wrapped and propped carefully against the wall. "I see you've been visiting the gallery."

"It spoke to me."

"Very nice." She drifted toward my plans laid out on a makeshift desk. "Though most successful properties around the lake aim for a certain established aesthetic."

Luna's growl deepened.

"Good thing I'm not mimicking most properties." I smiled. "Coffee?"

"No thank you. I should let you get back to your situation." She gestured at the water damage. "Do let me know if you need recommendations for more experienced contractors."

Luna barked sharply. Dulce startled then composed herself. "Such a protective dog." Her face was like glass. "Good day, Nyla."

After she left, Sofia released a breath. "She's just sizing up the competition."

Whatever. I surveyed the mess. "We've got bigger problems right now. This plumbing crisis needs solving before I leave for Tulum next weekend."

"Mexico?" Sofia asked.

"Yes. Mikayla explained about border runs last week. Said Tulum's the easiest option, even if it's not the cheapest. Or Cancun."

"I suppose. Just don't expect the paradise you see on Instagram."

She was right. Tulum's water glowed impossibly blue but dust coated everything else. Giant, jagged rocks were everywhere and even SUVs felt inadequate navigating some of the streets. Construction sites outnumbered finished buildings. The roads crumbled under too many tourist wheels. My meals cost as much as Miami prices and big ass lizards were everywhere. Blood-hungry mosquitos, too. When my taxi driver demanded double the quoted fare I didn't argue. I was warned that they wouldn't compromise, and Ubers weren't available. You either pay their fare or walk. I paid. The other rumor was that cartels controlled the taxis so they *couldn't* negotiate. I understood.

Standing on that perfect beach at one of the chic beach clubs, I knew I'd made the right choice staying in Guatemala. Tulum was beautiful but felt like it had been invaded by folks from Atlanta and... was trying too hard to be something it wasn't yet. The weekend couldn't end fast enough.

One evening, however, I scrolled through my phone. Mikayla had pinged me that all was well, and the contractors packed up for the day—she'd kept an eye on things while I was away. I noticed my renovation posts had gained traction in the Solo Sisters Travel Group. Women were commenting about wanting to visit, asking about opening dates. I'd been sharing the journey somewhat randomly, but maybe it was time to be more strategic.

"I should talk to her about this," I noted. Mikayla knew everyone in sustainable tourism, and it would be nice to chat about something other than construction chaos. Her network could be valuable now that I was getting closer to opening.

Just then, my phone chirped with a message from Jade: "Girl, when can I book? My followers keep asking about your place!"

Ha! I hadn't talked to Jade much since I first met the entire group of women that included Mikayla. Though she did say hi via Instagram direct message every now and then. This time, however, she offered to be an ambassador to recommend my place to Black women travelers once she came back for a visit herself. The casual social media presence I'd built was starting to feel like something bigger. It *was* time to take it seriously. I was over the moon!

Back at Lake Atitlán my building waited. The pipes were fixed. Sofia and Antonio had supervised the installation of pressure boosters. Progress happened in small steps, and I had a fresh 90 days to work with since my visa reset upon my return. Eventually, I'd get official residential status. Right now, this was the fastest and easiest way.

The next evening, I sat with Mariana at a lakeside restaurant reviewing my revised plans. Simple cotton sheets that breathed in the humidity. Local hardwoods that would age gracefully. Handwoven textiles that told stories.

"You're learning." She touched my knee as we gazed out at the water.

"The hard way."

"Is there another way?"

I thought about Dulce's perfect resort. About Tulum's forced glamour. About all the ways I used to define luxury.

"No." I leaned back, enjoying the night breeze. "There really isn't."

Luna dozed at my feet while sunset crept into the sky. It was time to go. This was the hour when mosquitos came out to feed—the witching hour, I called it. I'd gotten eaten alive enough times to know. Lather up in Off or go home if I didn't have any. I paid my check and hustled out.

THREE DAYS after my return from Tulum, new posters appeared around town promoting the annual Lake Atitlán Arts Festival. The whole community buzzed with final preparation. Market vendors hung colorful banners. Cafes updated their menus. Even Dulce's resort sprouted flamboyant streamers.

I found Mariana at her gallery, surrounded by canvases and packing materials. Luna followed me in.

"Need help?" I quizzed.

"Actually, yes." Mariana looked up from her inventory list. "These need to go to the exhibition space at Casa Cultural." She gestured at a stack of wrapped paintings. "Unless this rain drowns us first."

The afternoon downpour had caught everyone off guard. Water dripped from my curls as we loaded art into plastic-wrapped bundles. Luna darted between our legs, making the task harder but somehow more amusing.

"She's a mess," I said, watching her shake herself near a pile of empty frames. "Good thing she's more community dog than mine."

"If you say so. She definitely chose you." Mariana smiled. "I don't blame her..."

Thunder cracked overhead. Luna whined but I ignored her. Too enraptured by Mariana's last words.

"Anyway," Mariana picked up as if she hadn't let her last bit slip out, "the festival committee asked if your place will be ready to host any events next year."

"Next year?" I thought about my construction timeline. "Maybe. If Antonio's team stays on schedule and nothing else bursts." I chuckled. It was way too soon for me to know.

"No pressure. It's just..." She paused, arranging brushes in a carry case. "It would be nice to have a new venue. Somewhere between Dulce's corporate polish and the backpacker hostels."

"Maybe," I repeated. "But let's back up."

"To?"

I bit my bottom lip as if it would give me courage. "To not blaming Luna for choosing me.

"And..." She waited.

"That night at Portal del Angel. And after, in the library...you said some things matter more than fear."

Mariana's hands stilled on her brushes. "I did."

"I've been thinking about that. About fear, and choices, and..." I stepped closer, my heart hammering. "About how sometimes the scariest things are the ones most worth doing."

She turned to face me fully, her eyes searching mine. "Nyla..."

"You've been so patient. So helpful. So nurturing. So...everything with me, and *for* me."

"Nyla..." she breathed heavier.

"Giving me space to figure things out," I continued. "But I don't want space anymore." My voice shook slightly.

She stepped closer. "What do you want?" She spoke so quietly I had to lean more towards her to hear.

The deluge throbbed harder, creating a sanctuary of sound around us. My pulse strummed in harmony with it as I closed the final distance between us. "You," I breathed. "Just you." There. I finally admitted it.

Time stretched like honey as I reached for her face. My fingertips found the silk of her skin and it sent currents throughout my being. Her eyes held mine, dark with longing and something deeper that made my chest ache. When our lips finally met, the world tilted on its axis. Oh...my God. I liquified.

Everything I thought I knew about desire reconstructed itself in that moment. Her lips were soft. So...impossibly...soft. Yet they held certainty that made my knees weak. She tasted of coffee and promise, and her hands found my waist with delicate gentleness. I melted

into her, discovering new ways to hunger. Moaning. Groaning.
Sighing.

The kiss deepened slowly. Each breath between us carried years
of waiting, though I hadn't known I was waiting until now. Her
fingers traced fire up my spine, and I curved into her touch like that
sunflower seeking sun.

When we finally parted, the gallery had grown dark around us.
Or maybe I'd just forgotten to see anything else. Mariana's forehead
rested against mine, and our breathing synced.

"Dios mio...*my God.* I've wanted to do that since I first saw you in
this gallery," she murmured, her thumb tracing my bottom lip.

Heat built between my legs. Words failed me. I pulled her closer,
letting my body speak what my voice couldn't. This time when our
lips met, it was both recognition and revelation—as if my body had
always known hers in some forgotten dream.

Mariana's lips swept against my ear. With a warm and tantalizing
breath, she said, "Eres más valiente de lo que crees." The words made
my pulse stutter beneath my skin. Whatever she said made me feel
both seen and desired in ways I'd never experienced before.

26

FESTIVAL HEARTS

"Look at this view!" I rotated my phone slowly, letting my parents take in Lake Atitlán's splendor through my screen. Morning sunlight scattered VVS diamonds across the water. "This is what my guests will wake up to every morning." The volcanoes loomed like Mayan gods.

"It's beautiful, Nyla," My mom admitted. Worry still creased her forehead. "But you're still all alone in a foreign country."

"I'm not alone, Mama. I have a whole community here." I switched to the front camera, showing them the bustling street below where vendors were setting up for the art festival. "And the building's coming along great. Wait till you see—"

"What about security?" Dad cut in. "You mentioned power issues last time."

"All handled. I've got generators being installed next week, and—"

"Ooh, is that my future hotel-owning sister?" Kendra's face popped up as she joined the call. "Show me everything!"

"Everyone's on today?" I laughed, ignoring that she said hotel instead of hostel. It did sound better...something I was still working on accepting in my own mind. I huffed and switched my camera back to the view. "Well, it's perfect timing. The first furniture delivery just arrived."

I could see Antonio's truck pull up through the window. It was loaded with locally-made beds. Their wooden frames gleamed with fresh varnish, making me instantly less self-conscious and more proud. Each headboard was carved with subtle patterns that mirrored the lake's waves.

"Those are gorgeous," Kendra gasped. "Way better than standard hostel bunks. When do you open again?"

"In a few weeks, and that's the idea." I allowed my pride to swell. "It's comfort without pretension. The photos I've been posting are already getting attention from sustainable travel bloggers." I headed downstairs to direct the delivery, keeping my family on video. "Plus, with the art festival starting tomorrow, I can get some content that shows the cultural side of staying here."

"Festival?" Mom perked up. "Like with music and dancing?"

No, mom, like with tax audits and yawning competitions, I wanted to say. *Why did parents sometimes ask the most obvious questions?* But I caught myself. "Yes. And paintings, sculptures, traditional crafts. The whole town transforms." I steadied my phone as Antonio's team carried the first bed frame past. "It's actually a big deal here. Galleries come from Guatemala City, collectors fly in."

"Sounds like the perfect excuse for a visit," Kendra interrupted. "I could use a break from depositions, and you might need help decorating."

"Ken—"

"Already looked at flights. Two weeks from Thursday?"

Dad chuckled. "She said it's tomorrow. Slow down."

But I found myself nodding. "That might still work though.... The festival will be over, but the beds will be set up by then, and—"

"Done! Booking now." Kendra's grin filled my screen. "Time to see this lake life for myself."

I guess her finances had gotten better to book a spur-of-the-moment flight. I'd have to go up to the City to get her, though. There was no way I would let her try navigating the mountain trek alone.

Dad chimed in, half-joking. "I'll start the stopwatch for how long it takes you to turn it into a five-star resort."

I chuckled. "It's a *hostel*, not the Ritz. But if I ever do, you're paying for the spa, Daddy."

Mom jumped back in with questions about safe hotels, but Antonio called out for my input on bed placement. "Gotta go, family. Love you all!" *Click.*

After ending the call, I stood in what would become the main dormitory. Sunlight streamed through freshly cleaned windows. The clear glass caught dust mites dancing like tiny stars. The wooden furniture really transformed the space from empty potential to something tangible.

"¿Aquí?" Antonio gestured to a corner.

"No." I pointed to the window wall. "Let's arrange them so guests can see the lake when they wake up."

He nodded, understanding more than just furniture placement. "Como el amanecer," he said softly. Like the sunrise. "It sets the tone for everything that follows."

I thought of Mariana and our kiss, of how everything felt brighter now. More vivid and more possible now. "It really does." God, I wanted to taste her again.

I could see festival banners fluttering in the breeze outside, and I heard the heartbeat of Garifuna drums somewhere in the distance. My attention somersaulted back in time to Livingston, the amazing cultural stop on my journey to Atitlán flooded back to my mind. I remembered their distinct cadence —*boom-taka-taka-tak, boom-ba-da-boom*—like rolling waves. The rhythm regressed me to the night I first heard it by the fire-lit shores...when I'd learned about Afro-Latin and Caribbean history and resilience. About being able to thrive despite being pulled far away from everything you once were. *Boom, boom-ba-da, taka-tak-tak!* The essence permeated my soul.

I hadn't expected Afro-culture to be here, even though Mariana told me people would come from all over the country. The rise and fall of their drums interwoven with voices gave me chills. But two delivery men broke my spell as they carried in a queen mattress.

"Señorita?" Antonio called from the doorway. "The craftswoman who made the blankets is here."

A tiny lady with a single silver braid entered. She carried stacks of handwoven textiles in lovely shades of blue and gold. The dyes were made from local plants.

"Perfecto," I breathed, running my fingers over the nearest quilt. The wool was softer than I'd expected. Warmth and art woven into one – kind of like her. In a strange way, her braid reminded me of my mother. They had nothing else in common, but still, I held onto that miniscule moment of maternal presence.

"She says these are special," Antonio translated. "Made with sunset colors to match your windows."

I looked closer and saw how the golds caught the light just like the lake at dusk. She even made the blues progressively deepen like the sky between the volcanoes. I loved it!

Again, the sounds of festival preparation drifted in through the open spaces. Hammers tapping as vendors set up stalls. Children laughing as they helped string lights across the plaza. Voices calling greetings in Spanish, English, and Tz'utujil. Plus, the pleasant surprise of Caribbean-influenced accents from the Garifuna people. The streets would overflow with art, music and culture tomorrow. But today, watching my first room come together piece by piece, I built my own kind of masterpiece.

My phone buzzed with a message from Mariana: *I need a break from festival chaos. Granizada?* She mentioned a crushed ice drink often flavored with syrups like tamarind, lemon, or fruit punch.

I smiled, typing back: *On my way. Just making sure the beds have a good view of your gallery.*

Her response came quickly: *Lucky beds.*

That message went express to the gutter of my mind. The dark, moist corners where heat smoldered and restraint didn't exist. I almost grunted. Shit!

"I need to go," I told Antonio. "Will you be okay handling the rest?"

He shooed me toward the door. "Go, go. Art calls." Then he winked. "And some views are worth chasing."

"Stay out of my business, Antonio." I pushed him.

"¡Ayyeeee, que pasooo!?" He sucked his teeth. "I'm not in your business, Nyla!"

"You are!"

He grinned. Like a nosy brother...at least I thought so. Truthfully, I didn't know if I was being paranoid or obvious. It wasn't just physical attraction with Mariana. There was something grounding when I was in her presence. Something steadying. That's what she did to me with just a text. Even though I was afraid of the direction we were headed, I still couldn't wait to see her again and felt like everyone else could tell.

Mariana's gallery was relatively. Her hands were smudged with charcoal. That was different. I looked at them curiously. "New work?"

She nodded, opening her sketchbook. The images caught me off guard. They weren't her usual lake views, but coffee plants stretching into misty mountains, an old man's wrinkled hands sorting bright red cherries. And there, on the edge of a weathered barn, a teenage girl with a paintbrush.

"Is that you?" I asked, though I felt like I already knew.

"Yes. On the coffee finca where I grew up," she said quietly. Her usual confident energy was muted today, and her smile looked like a mask that didn't fit. "I haven't been back since I left for the States. Ten years of running, I guess." She traced the edge of one painting, her finger following the mountain's outline like she was trying to memorize it by touch.

Mariana had never shared much of her past. She usually pushed the conversation back to me when I tried to learn her history. The vulnerability in her voice made me want to reach for her, but something in her posture held me back. This was a side of her I'd never seen, a girl who had fled the coffee fields for neon lights?

"My father..." she huffed. "He never understood why I couldn't just be content with what we had. Said art wouldn't feed anyone. That I would be poorer than I already was if I thought painting would fill my belly." A bitter smile crossed her face. It looked so... wrong. And painful. "Turned out he was right about going to Vegas for school and work. All those casino murals I designed, and I still felt hungry. Not for food, but..."

"Family?" I guessed. I was eager to hear her story.

"Love." Her eyes finally met mine. Wide. Vulnerable. Wanting. They made my heart squeeze. "For everything. Home. Purpose. The smell of coffee plants after rain." She swallowed hard. "But you can't go home when home doesn't want you anymore."

Ouch. "Mariana..." I reached for her hand, and this time she let me take it. "So, you came back for family but—"

"Partly, but...yeah." She closed the sketchbook. "And I also needed to paint something meaningful to me again. Even if I couldn't go home. Even if no one wanted to buy it. I needed to do it because I loved it."

A burst of drums and trumpets from outside harpooned the moment. She pulled away gently, closing her art book. "I should check on the festival setup."

As I watched her go, I understood for the first time that we were both running from something, me, from a life I'd passively let someone else build and control. Her, from ghosts of low expectations that she ultimately met. Still, I wondered what incited this specific moment.

It suddenly felt like something else entirely was beginning – or maybe ending – and I wasn't sure which startled me more. The way my heart ached watching her walk away scared me. It was too familiar. I knew that pull toward someone else's pain and potential, that desire to fix and heal and protect – it was dangerous. Because loving someone meant loving all their pieces, even the broken ones. Especially the broken ones. But I'd learned the hard way with Alex that you can't fix other people's broken pieces. Not that I hadn't tried, but

I'd learned to leave before his sharp edges carved me into someone I didn't recognize.

This felt different though. Mariana wasn't asking me to fix anything. She was just showing me who she was. I wasn't sure if I was afraid of the unknown or afraid of finally learning something I couldn't unlearn. Maybe that was what frightened me most of all, not that she was broken, but that I wanted to stay anyway.

LOST in thought about Mariana's revelation, I almost missed the notification on my phone. Another booking inquiry through the hostel's new Instagram page. The message asked about availability for next month's full moon ceremony. The grand opening wasn't scheduled until Kendra's trip—we'd pushed her visit out so it could correlate. *Maybe I could do a soft launch to get even more photos and a few early reviews?* My finger hovered over the keyboard. My parents might even come down.

"Señorita, Nyla!" Antonio's voice cut through my indecision. He jogged over, phone in hand. "Look at these comments." He showed me the local community Facebook page where I'd taken a poll about an open house preview during the festival. The response was overwhelming.

"That's... a lot of people," I gasped, scrolling through the dozens of "interested" notifications. What had started as a casual request to showcase the local artisans' work had blossomed into something bigger.

"It's good, no?" Antonio grinned, but then his expression shifted. "Though we should probably tell Martha. If this many people come..."

I nodded, already mental math-ing the logistics. The furniture was only partially set up. One of the backup generators wasn't installed yet. And the bathroom renovations...

A notification from my booking software interrupted my spiral. Another inquiry. Then another. The algorithm was clearly favoring the posts, pushing them to more travelers. Usually, this would be great news, but now...

"Antonio," I said finally, "I need your honest opinion. Is it crazy to do an open house preview during the festival? With the property only half-ready?"

He considered, watching as more vendors set up their stalls. "Maybe not crazy. But risky." He paused. "Like jumping into the lake without checking the depth."

I laughed despite my anxiety. "When did you become so philosophical?"

"Since you started paying me to install beds instead of fixing real things." He grinned, then grew serious. "But Nyla, whatever you decide, the community will help. You know this, yes?"

I did know. That was the difference between here and Miami. Success wasn't a zero-sum game here. Even though I wanted independence. Wanted desperately to prove myself to myself—I wasn't alone. And I didn't have to act as if I were.

My phone buzzed again – another booking inquiry. I looked at Mariana, still absorbed in her work, carrying the weight of her own past while helping create something new. It seemed that's what we were all doing.

"Okay," I told Antonio. "Let's do it. But we'll need help with..." I stopped as I saw Dulce across the plaza, watching us with an unreadable expression. She'd been quieter lately, less openly hostile, but something in her gaze made me uneasy.

Antonio followed my line of sight. "Ah. Should we worry?"

"No," I said, more confidently than I felt. "But maybe we should be prepared."

I had to decide: was I ready to open my doors, even just a little? And was I ready for everything else that might come through them?

27

THE DAY WORE RIBBONS

Morning broke open like a ripe mango. Sweet. Sticky. And dripping with color—pure potential. Drummers had started before dawn and their rhythms rolled over the cobblestones into my hulk. The streets vibrated with life now. Women of all ages donned embroidered huipiles while spreading blankets heavy with beadwork into the sun. They glistened. Men hoisted wooden posts strung with paper lanterns that would glow like bottled flames come nightfall.

Luna, even bigger now, wove between my ankles as I watched Antonio's daughter deck their family's chicken bus out in wreaths of bougainvillea. She'd painted the windshield with delicate spirals. Even the stray dogs wore ribbons today—they weren't so stray after all. Someone, somewhere, still looked after them in some way.

"¡Atol caliente!" A woman's voice lifted above the crowd. Mist rose from sweet corn and cinnamon rushing out of her clay pot, penetrated the chattering voices. Damn, it smelled good. I ordered two and enjoyed the warmth seeping through my palms as I clutched the cup and searched for Mariana.

I found her arranging large canvases in the plaza. Her hair was twisted up with paintbrushes again, that one rebellious strand curling against her neck. Her more recent, more personal pieces were on display. Her heart. Wide open.

"The Garifuna dancers are setting up by the dock. It's a treat to have them here."

She was right. The sounds mixed with marimba notes trickled down from the church steps, where children spun in circles. Their mini-human shadows painted the stones with fleeting art.

"I know you said this would be a lot but taking it all in is almost overwhelming I admitted." *Vrooom!* A tuk-tuk rattled past, its entire frame wrapped in twinkling lights and trailing red streamers.

"I'm glad you're enjoying. It'll be a long day, but worth it. I promise."

Meanwhile, I watched my first batch of onlookers began to arrive to preview Resting Waters House. That's what I'd named my place.

"Ready?" Mariana's voice was soft beside me. She'd left a smudge of blue paint on her cheek, which I couldn't resist using my thumb to clear away.

I heard—and felt—her moan at my graze. She inched closer, reciprocating my touch...caressing my cheek and skimming my bottom lip with her thumb. My knees buckled, but I willed strength to not melt from the convergence of our energies. I wanted to kiss her so badly but was hyperaware of us being on display in public.

While most noticed our attraction, no one seemed to care...but I did. I felt I should be more conservative, especially since we didn't even have a title. Since I didn't know if we were a "thing" or not. Still, Mariana was a sacred experience to me. Her warmth. The texture of her skin. The rush of what was beneath both our shells...the increased blood flood and over-eager muscle twitches that came even without more touch was mesmerizing. We held hands and space below the table's line so no one could see.

"You okay?" she whispered.

"Yeah. Better than okay. I feel...safe," I confessed. "Thank you. For everything."

"De nada, Nyla. De nada."

The day unfurled like a banner in the wind. Mariana's gallery drew steady crowds. Her coffee farm series touched something deep in visitors' hearts. A variation of musicians from all over the country kept the festival's beat going. Even Luna made new friends, charming children who fed her bits of tortilla. It wasn't until late afternoon, when the light began to soften and the first evening visitors arrived to tour the hostel, that everything changed.

The first sign was subtle: lights dimming then brightening. A small voltage fluctuation. No big deal. It happened sometimes. But then the ceiling fans stuttered, and the new security system gave a harsh beep before going dark. Through the windows, I saw the same thing happening across the street, a ripple of darkness spreading through the festival's carefully strung lights.

"It's just a surge," I said to the crowd gathering in my entrance. "The backup system will—" The sentence fell apart before I could finish it as I remembered we hadn't fully installed it yet. Another corner cut, another temporary delay that shouldn't have been.

In the growing dusk, I could see Mariana moving toward me with concern. My phone pinged with messages from potential guests who'd planned to view the property tonight. Fuck. Fuck. Fuck. Fuck! These were the people whose interest I desperately needed to secure the hostel's future—to get some damn cash flowing.

"Todo bien?" She quizzed me.

As if responding to Mariana's words, a sudden burst of laughter and gasps came from the plaza below. I moved to the window to see what the fuss was about.

The lake flamed, not just with firelight or lanterns, but with surreal glimmers of bioluminescence that rippled out from the shoreline. Holy shit.

"Wow!" Mariana was just as shocked as me.

This wasn't a phenomenal common to Lake Atitlán. It was stunning. Incredibly bright blue over the darker waters. Magical!

Festival musicians drifted closer to the lake's edge, their rhythms coaxing swirls of eerie blue-green light to dance along the waves. Each drumbeat summoned a shimmer, and as the dancers twirled, their reflections in the glowing water mimicked the movement like phantom doubles. One daring performer leapt into the air and allowed her silhouette to be framed against the glowing lake. *Snap. Snap. Snap.* Everyone took photos and videos—even me—as ribbons trailing from her arms punctuated the air with streaks of liquid light before she landed gracefully. Thunderous applause and cheers from the crowd.

"How?" I asked, my voice barely above a whisper.

Mariana leaned beside me. Her face was lit by the strange illumination. "Not sure. Maybe the rains stirred the algae...I have no idea, actually." She shrugged.

The scene was otherworldly. Mariana repositioned behind me, gently draping her arms around me in a way that felt oh, so perfect. The cuddle heightened my angst around public displays of affection, but I let the moment stand. Trying to be fearless. We rocked and swayed a bit, and she kissed my neck while watching the spectacle below before another applause eventually erupted. I could feel her teeth gently scrape my skin. *Mmph...*

A group of festival-goers near the docks began leaning precariously over the edge, trying to capture the bioluminescent phenomenon with their phones. One brave—or stupid—soul took it further, clambering onto a fragile wooden pier that groaned beneath their weight.

"Idiots," Mariana muttered, her voice low.

I shook my head, but even I couldn't look away. But soon, a loud creak interrupted my thoughts. It was too loud. Too close. *What's that...?* The sound came from the back corner of the main room, where the balcony jutted out over the courtyard. I glanced over and froze. Eyes wide. Heart stopped. A small group of my guests had leaned against the railing, trying to get a better view of the festival lights.

"Wait!" I called out, but the words were drowned by the sound of splintering wood.

The railing gave way in slow motion. *No, no, no, no, nooo!* I panicked witnessing the wooden beam cracking under their weight and pulling free from the wall. *Oh my god. Oh my God!* A guest screamed as the group stumbled backward, just avoiding a fall into the courtyard below. The damaged beam dangled. Swaying precariously before hitting the wall with a sickening thud.

A hush fell over the room. Then, murmurs rippled through the crowd. One visitor checked their arm, brushing off a scrape, while another stared at me, dumbfounded.

"Is it safe here?" someone asked in a low voice that carried too far.

Heat rushed to my face. "I—yes, it's safe," I stuttered. My words were brittle and thin. Wholly inadequate. *Like me.* My thoughts taunted me.

Antonio arrived just then. His usual smile was replaced with concern. He glanced at the broken balcony and then back at me. "The wood is old," he said quietly. "The humidity must've weakened it faster than we thought. This needs a full replacement. It can be fixed, señorita."

I could barely hear him over the buzzing in my head. I saw the guests exchanging uneasy glances, heard someone whisper about safety inspections, and felt the load of their judgment pressing against my chest.

"This can't happen now," I begged the universe. The few emergency lights that were installed kicked, finally. "Everyone stay calm," I called out, proud of how steady my voice sounded. "We'll have this sorted soon."

"What do you need?" Mariana asked.

Everything. Nothing. You. "I can handle this," I lied. The words were full of pride and fear.

More phones lit up the semi-darkness as guests tried to document the chaos. Someone whispered about posting it online. Another mentioned Dulce's resort never having these problems. Each word felt like a nail in my dream's coffin.

Mariana translated my earlier statement for those who didn't speak English. I hadn't even thought about a language barrier in this kind of emergency.

When more help arrived with tools, Antonio admitted, "The electrical panel. It's more complicated than we thought. Could take days to fix."

"Days?" My voice cracked. "I have people booked. Reviews pending. I can't just—"

A crash from below, followed by Luna's startled bark. The sound of breaking glass. Everything I'd built, everything I'd risked, seemed to be crumbling in the dark.

And somewhere in the distance, festival beats kept trouncing, indifferent to my unraveling. Fuck, fuck, fuck, fuck, FUCK!! Why the fuck couldn't I just catch a break?

My hands wouldn't stop shaking. Not from the darkness though. I'd handled plenty of power outages in Miami. But this was different. This was me, alone, watching my second chance dissolve into gossipy whispers and worried faces. Every phone light felt like fault-finding and that twisted something deeper inside me.

"Let me help," Mariana tried again, reaching for my hand.

I jerked away. "I said, I've got this." The words came out sharp enough to cut. Because she was right—I did not have this. Not even close. And I did need help.

I was standing in a dark hallway surrounded by strangers documenting my failure, pretending I knew what the hell I was doing. Just like I'd pretended with Alex that I was fine with his version of my life – although I literally thought I was on the surface. But here I am now pretending that starting over at forty-four wasn't terrifying. The shit is difficult. It's nerve-wracking. And it's way too easy to wonder if the entire thing was a stupid idea, and that it would have been easier to deal with the demons I knew.

A sob caught in my throat. Fuck. Not here. Not now.

But it was too late. Everything I'd been holding back – the fear, the doubt, the desperate need to prove myself – hurtled through me like a wave hitting volcanic rock. It erupted in hot, uncontrollable tears that made me flee up the stairs, past confused guests, past Antonio's concerned face, past Mariana's outstretched hand. I ran. I hid. And I cried. Fuck. Did I do all of this just to...fail?

In my small office, I finally let go. "What was I thinking?" The words came out ragged. "Coming here, leasing a building older than my mother, thinking I could just... what? Wave some Miami hospitality magic and make everything perfect? Dumb ass idea."

Luna found me there. Her wet nose pressed into my palm. "Oh, girl...you don't understand." I stroked her fur. At least someone still believed in me. "I can't do this alone. I can't." The admission felt like surrender and revelation all at once. "And I don't want to do this alone anymore."

"You aren't." Mariana's voice came from the doorway.

I looked up at her, mascara probably streaking my face. "I'm so tired of pretending I know what I'm doing. Of being afraid to ask for help because it might mean I'm not strong enough or capable enough or—"

"Human enough?" She stepped closer. "Nyla." Mariana spoke softly.

I could feel the worry lines creasing my forehead. "I'm so freaking stressed out!" Unwanted memories of Alex telling me to consider Botox suddenly rushed back. "Maybe Alex was right." I cried. "Maybe I am nothing without him." The words broke my heart into a million pieces.

"No." She spoke definitively. "Look at me," she cupped my face. Her hands carried the faintest trace of citrus, like she'd been peeling an orange earlier. "Asking for help doesn't make you Alex's version of weak. It makes you brave enough to be real."

The truth of it cracked something loose in my chest. All this time, I'd been so focused on proving I could do everything myself that I'd forgotten why I came here in the first place – not to be perfect, but to be *free*. Free to succeed or fail on my own terms. Free to need people without losing myself.

"I don't know how to do this in another country," I gave in. "Everything is so different. So hard."

"Don't worry," Mariana comforted. "We'll figure it out together." She paused and looked me in my eyes before continuing with, "I want you to succeed, Nyla." She brought my hand to her mouth and kissed my knuckles. "You *will* succeed."

28

RESERVATION UNDER MY NAME

T he mirror caught me off guard as I checked the lobby one last time. I turned to the left and right, taking in all the details. My reflection had changed subtly over these months. Different. Very different. But I liked it. Now, my natural coils fell carefree about my shoulders rather than the updo I'd maintained in Miami. I still wore makeup daily, but not as much. And even though I had tons to worry about, cosmetic procedures involving needles and mildly burning my skin to make it clearer weren't any of them. My body glowed deeper from lake sun and mountain air, and my eyes held a spark that rivaled any on Independence Day. I was absolutely not the same Nyla that ran The Jeffrey.

"Three more days," I whispered to my reflection.

The fresh paint smell mingled with coffee and morning air drifting through open windows as I moved through the lobby ticking off final tasks.

"Nyla?" Mariana's voice carried from behind me. I turned to find her holding two cups of fresh Huehuetenango café. Her deep eyes took in every factor of my appearance as they always did. "You've been running on fumes. Take a minute."

I accepted the cup. "Thanks. You always seem to know what I need before I do."

"Es un regalo, mi querida." Her smile held the same quiet understanding that had anchored me through this rebuilding. Mariana wore ripped jeans and one of my old Miami skyline t-shirts she'd claimed weeks ago.

"How's the terrace?" I asked, taking a sip and feeling the caffeine hit my veins.

"Perfect. And Sofia's team just finished the string lights around the arches overlooking the lake. The vibe is magical." She paused, studying me with that gaze that always saw beneath surfaces. "You should see it before the opening. You'll want to add your touch."

I nodded, imagining guests'—and my family's—faces when they saw what we'd created. "Later. Let's get through today first."

A week had passed since we began rebuilding, and now, I couldn't shake the mix of exhaustion and exhilaration pumping through my body. I hadn't felt this much of a rush since I'd taken Alex's ADHD medication – that he didn't need but got a prescription for so we could both focus more. But this was a natural concentration. It was a deep and biological push to get this done properly my way. Resting Waters House had risen from chaos to transformation. Mariana had been my anchor through this whirlwind. When I was drowning in decisions, she'd quietly step in, whether it was coordinating deliveries or insisting I eat when I forgot. Her presence grounded me in ways I could never repay.

By mid-afternoon, the small hostel sizzled with energy. Antonio directed workers hanging textiles while Mikayla arranged native flowers in hand-thrown pottery. The scent of Martha and Sofia's test run of breakfast pastries wafted up from the kitchen. Everything felt purposeful.

Luna supervised from her favorite spot near the entrance, her tail thumping against tile. She'd grown into her role as unofficial greeter, her once-matted fur was now glossy and well-groomed, fresh haircut and all – another transformation this place had witnessed.

I was reviewing the guest book setup when Kendra's voice cut through the buzz: "Well, look who finally learned to delegate!"

I turned to find my sister taking in the scene, her sharp eyes missing nothing. I'd been so busy, the time slipped by from when she texted, "We'll be there in 20 more minutes – girl, I like having a driver!" Behind her, our parents emerged from the archway. They'd all decided to come for my grand opening. I'd wanted to escort them from the airport, but with the dangerous disaster that happened during the festival, I could not pull away. Mariana let me borrow Rodrigo to shuttle them.

"Oh, Nyla..." Mom's hand flew to her mouth, tears already threatening. Her eyes tracked from the hand-carved reception desk to the giant art on the walls to the fabrics draped over rustic wooden chairs. Each detail I'd agonized over reflected in her widening gaze. Not to mention the subtle, but automatic air fresheners injecting aromatic delight into the air.

"This is... not what I expected," Kendra admitted. She set down her designer luggage. Her attention drifted across the room. "It's so... real and exotic and...alive."

Dad stood quietly by the entrance, where Luna had already claimed him as her newest friend. Through the arched windows behind them, Lake Atitlán stretched vast and blue. Trailing vines and potted palms framed the walkway to the water. I'd positioned everything to maximize that first glimpse of water and volcanos.

"Nyla," Mariana appeared from the terrace with a manila folder. "The hammocks are ready for—" She paused, taking in my family. "Oh, perdón. I didn't realize..."

"It's fine," I settled her before turning back to my family. "Everyone, this is Mariana," I announced with a smile that felt gigantic. Hopefully, it wasn't. I watched Kendra's expression shift from polite interest to careful observation. "She's been essential in making all this happen," I continued.

Something in my voice must have given me away because Kendra's eyebrow arched slightly before narrowing, her nosey sister instincts kicking in. But she simply grinned and extended her hand. "So, *you're* the artist my sister's been talking about."

Here in her hostel as if you're a worker or partner, I imagined her thinking but not saying. If my face could turn red, it would have.

"The very one," Mariana smiled confidently, then turned to my parents. "Welcome to Resting Waters House. Ms. Nyla has put her entire soul into this place. I think you will be proud." She beamed.

My body warmed listening to how she spoke of me. *Me*. And not once did she try to take credit for anything. Heat rose from the center of my belly and spread out like sunlight breaking through clouds. I fought the urge to shudder or inch closer to her, and I worked hard to slow my pulse and breathing.

"Let me show you to your rooms first," I offered, noticing the fatigue around Mom's eyes despite her excitement. "Then we can do a proper tour after you've rested."

"I'll finish up with the hammocks," Mariana said, already backing toward the terrace. She moved with that easy grace that made everything feel natural, unhurried. "Take your time with your family...it was nice meeting you all!" She waved and disappeared.

I led them up the stone stairs, past walls adorned with local art and photography. The rooms I'd reserved for them overlooked the lake, each with its own private balcony.

"This is gorgeous," Kendra whispered, running her hand along the ornate headboard in her room. "I have to admit it is charming. And the views are breathtaking. I can see why you traded Miami for this. It's literally paradise."

"Mm hm." I nodded with a proud grin. When I turned to leave, she caught my arm.

"We'll talk later," she said softly, that knowing look back in her eyes.

After getting my parents settled, I found Dad alone on *his* balcony, staring at the volcanoes. "You did good, baby girl," he said without turning. "Real good."

"Thanks, Daddy." I stood beside him, letting the familiar smell of his aftershave mix with the scent of local plants. "I know it's not what you expected...it's no..."

"It's better!" He finally looked at me, really looked at me, seeing all the changes these months had brought. "*You're* better."

I almost splintered into tears. Happy ones this time. But I kept it together. I *was* better. Stronger. More myself than I'd ever been. And tomorrow, I'd show the world what that meant during the official opening. I was stoked about it and had a small crew of student film-makers coming from the city to document it all for me.

I'd arranged dinner on the main terrace that evening. Lanterns swayed in the breeze, casting warm light across tables draped with textiles from the best local weavers. The chef I'd hired outdid herself with pescado en papillote—fresh lake fish steamed with herbs and citrus in banana leaves. The aroma alone made Mom's eyes widen.

"This isn't typical hotel food," she marveled, taking her first bite. "This is...it's like someone's grandmother made it."

"That's because someone's grandmother did," I smiled. "Martha's family has been cooking on this lake for generations." I had explained my relation to everyone as they passed through to help me finalize things.

A young guitarist played softly in the corner, his traditional melodies mixing with the sound of water lapping against stone. When he switched to "Bésame Mucho," Dad actually hummed along, something I hadn't heard him do in years.

"And this," Kendra pointed to her plate of jocón, a traditional green chicken stew that had become my personal favorite, "is *not* what I expected from a hostel kitchen."

"We're redefining expectations," I told her, catching Mariana's eye across the terrace where she chatted with Antonio. "That's kind of the point."

The evening wrapped us in its gentle magic. Volcano peaks silhouetted against stars, the lake reflecting pinpricks of light from villages across the water, and my family finally saw my dream come alive. There was nothing else I could ask for in that moment.

MORNING LIGHT SPILLED across Lake Atitlán like liquid gold. I stood on the terrace, watching early fishermen's boats cut silent paths through the water. In a few hours, this space would fill with guests, local dignitaries, and press, but right now it was just mine. Mine and Luna's...she sat beside me, bushy tail sweeping the stone floor contentedly.

"Ready?" Mariana's voice came soft behind me. She'd worn a flowing dress in light pink, but her feet were still bare – always the artist.

"Almost." I smoothed my white linen dress, chosen carefully to bridge my Miami past and Guatemala present. "Just taking it in."

By ten, the hostel throbbed with life. Sofia guided guests through the property while the kitchen staff produced endless plates of local delicacies. Antonio beamed as visitors admired his work, and even Mikayla looked proud as people photographed her flower arrangements.

"Señorita, Baines?" Don Manuel and Doña Teresa appeared, their faces bright with approval. "Honraste el espíritu de nuestro hogar." *You honored our home's spirit.*

I blinked back tears, remembering their trust in letting me transform their family property. "Gracias por creer en mi visión." *Thank you for believing in my vision,* I told them. My Spanish had greatly improved, especially when it came to moments like this, but I was still working on it.

The crowd gathered for my speech, which was in Spanglish. Antonio translated where I stumbled. There were familiar and new faces. My parents sat front row, my mother already dabbing her eyes. Kendra stood at the back, phone ready to record everything. And Mariana... Mariana watched from the doorway, that quiet understanding in her eyes that had become my compass.

"Bienvenido a Resting Waters House," I began, my voice steady and sure. "This place represents more than just a hostel. It's a bridge between worlds, between traditions and progress, between what was and what could be." I paused, letting my gaze sweep across the crowd. "Aqui, luxury isn't about marble floors or butler service. Se trata de experiencias auténticas, conexiones genuinas...and the kind of peace you can only find when you stop running and start being present."

Luna chose that moment to pad up beside me, drawing appreciative chuckles from the crowd. I scratched her ears, remembering how far we'd both come.

"To everyone who helped make this dream real, thank you. And to our future guests..." I smiled, feeling the rightness of this moment in my bones. "Welcome home!"

Applause erupted, but I barely heard it. Because in that moment, I knew I'd finally found my own reservation; one written under my name alone. I cut the bright red ribbon to officially open Resting Waters House, loving how easy it was to do that ceremonial snip. I did it! Yes, I did!

"Felicidades" and "congratulations" were all around! My heart was full.

LATER, when the crowds had thinned, I found myself back on the terrace. Music and laughter still drifted up from the courtyard where lingering guests indulged in digestifs and desserts. My family had retired to their rooms, even Kendra finally admitting travel fatigue had caught up with her.

"Tu café," Mariana appeared beside me, offering a cup of the region's finest brew.

"Gracias." I accepted it, breathing in the familiar aroma. "Stay and watch the sunset with me?"

She settled into the chair next to mine, both of us quiet as the sky performed its nightly miracle. She'd brought a can of Off, too, so we could enjoy the hour in peace.

Pssht. Psssht. She spritzed me. "I think your sister figured it out," Mariana said finally, a smile playing at her lips.

"Kendra figures everything out eventually." I laughed softly. "It's kind of her superpower."

"Does that bother you?"

I considered this, watching ripples spread across the lake's surface. "No," I realized. "Not anymore."

Luna appeared from wherever she'd been exploring, settling between our chairs with a contented sigh. Somewhere in the village, church bells began their evening song.

"What now?" Mariana asked, her voice carrying all the possibility of that question.

I smiled, understanding finally that not knowing was its own kind of freedom. "Now we see what tomorrow brings."

The lake reflected the day's last light, and in that gentle glow, I felt my world expand once again. This time, I was ready for it.

The End.

If you enjoyed this book and want to learn more about Mariana and Nyla, check out the companion novella "What the Mountains Remember," to see what happens next (and before, for Mariana)

Book two in this series, "Before I Am Erased," is now available (and can be read as a standalone as there is a new lead character in this story universe)!

ACKNOWLEDGMENTS

Leslie Lehr, thank you for coaching and encouraging me to find all the ways to make this novel my best one yet. It was truly exciting working with you and having your mentorship on this project. You've stretched me as a storyteller and that's priceless to me.

Chris Erickson and Natalie Castillo, thank you for offering real-world feedback on Nyla's role as a hotel general manager.

Milos Jevremovic, thank you for such gorgeous cover art! You perfectly captured my vision and the essence of this story.

Much appreciation to Brianna Mbog, Erin Comeaux, and every ARC reader who gave their time to offer valuable feedback with early versions of this book. I appreciate you!

And finally, to my wife, thank you for your never-ending support of my dreams. You continue to be my life's greatest decision. I love you.

ALSO BY CHERIL N. CLARKE

Deep Pleasure Vol I: Softer. Deeper. Wetter (an erotic sapphic romance trilogy) - also available as individual ebook novellas

Before I Am Erase: The Keyhole Chronicles Book 2

What the Mountains Remember (a companion story featuring Mariana and Nyla)

Rift: The Sensual Portal Book 2

Trip: The Sensual Portal Book 1

When the Road Softens: A Novella

Kinky Cabins: A Halloween Novella

Trick or Treat: A Halloween Quickie

Whiskey Dungeon

Corsets and Cognac

Sweet Dark Rum

The Edge of Bliss

The Beautiful People: New Orleans

The Beautiful People: Las Vegas

The Beautiful People: New York

Losing Control

Candle Wax

Bite the Pillow (Poetry)

Oxygen (Poetry)

Spoken Word albums by Cheril N. Clarke (as C. Nicole):

Honey

Drip

ABOUT THE AUTHOR

Raised in Miami and now living in Puebla, Mexico, Cheril N. Clarke is the author of nine novels, two stage plays, several short stories and poetry collections, and numerous children's books. She has been featured in *Curve* Magazine, *VoyageATL*, *The Princeton Packet*, *Philadelphia Gay News* (PGN), About.com, *Out IN Jersey*, *Burlington County Times*, as well as Phillyburbs.com, among others. Her creative writing website is CherilNClarke.com. Clarke is also an executive ghostwriter and the woman behind PhenomenalWriting.com. She has written for Fortune 500 executives and entrepreneurs worldwide.

www.ingramcontent.com/pod-product-compliance
Lightning Source LLC
Chambersburg PA
CBHW050503260626
47157CB00004B/1168